Also by Ruth Cardello

LONE STAR BURN

Taken, Not Spurred

THE LEGACY COLLECTION

Maid for the Billionaire
For Love or Legacy
Bedding the Billionaire
Saving the Sheikh
Rise of the Billionaire
Breaching the Billionaire: Alethea's Redemption
Come Away with Me

LONE STAR BURN

TYCOON TAKEDOWN

RUTH CARDELLO

Montlake
Romance

Published by Montlake Romance, Seattle

www.apub.com

Amazon, the Amazon logo, and Montlake Romance are trademarks of Amazon.com, Inc., or its affiliates.

ISBN-13: 9781477821022
ISBN-10: 1477821023

Cover design by Kerrie Robertson

Library of Congress Control Number: 2014913783

Printed in the United States of America

To my friend Deb, for years of friendship and support.
Oh, the places we will go.

Chapter One

Whoever said time heals was full of it.

Melanie sat on her bed next to her one bag of luggage and laid a shaky hand on it. She could admit that time dulled the pain. Concealed it. But it sure as hell didn't fix shit.

She looked at her reflection in the mirror. Her jeans and faded blue plaid shirt were as worn as her leather cowboy boots. Her straight brown hair was long and healthy, but hadn't been more than brushed and tied back in a ponytail for years. She regretted not borrowing concealer for the telltale shadows beneath her eyes.

Why am I even worried about how I look? Because of Charles? It's not like there is any chance our paths will cross. New York is a big city.

Melanie frowned into the mirror.

Forget him.

Focus on what's important.

Her inner reprimand went unheeded. Images of Charles—or Charlie, as his sister called him—flooded her mind and sent her heart racing. On paper, he wasn't her type. Fancy limos, expensive suits, beautiful blue eyes hidden behind dark glasses as if he worked for some top secret government agency. The two times she'd met him he'd looked as out of place in her world as she was about to look in his.

Who wears a suit on a horse ranch?

Wall Street multimillionaires, that's who. People who need to prove to everyone that they've made it. I don't need a man like that. Neither does Jace.

She raised her chin and studied her reflection again. *I used to be beautiful. At least, a younger me used to think I was.*

When she'd first come to work at the Double C horse ranch, she'd wanted to be left alone, so she'd downplayed her looks. *Apparently I'm very good at it since not one man here has ever so much as flirted with me.*

She was tanned, but not from a spray bottle. Her color came from hours of chasing Jace beneath the hot Texan sun. Almost as soon as he could walk, he'd wanted to ride horses—a by-product of being raised on a horse ranch.

Horses and ranch life were all her son had ever known. At five he'd spent more hours in a saddle than most people would in their lifetime. Everyone said he had a natural talent with them. Another reason she was glad this upcoming New York trip was just that—a trip.

For a while, she'd been sure she'd have to move. Over the past summer, her solitary boss had met and fallen in love with a true Yankee—as green as pastures in the spring. Melanie didn't believe in love, at least not the romantic kind, but she had to admit Tony Carlton was a better man for having met Sarah Dery.

Melanie had worked as a housekeeper and cook on the reclusive horse trainer's ranch ever since her son was an infant. Tony had purchased the Double C after a deadly accident involving one of his clients. He'd closed the ranch off from outsiders and trained his horses in seclusion until he met Sarah.

It'd been easy to dislike Sarah in the beginning. Nearly everything made her smile and she spoke fast enough to make a person's head spin. She was also a strikingly beautiful natural blonde, with a figure that made men trip all over themselves in her presence.

Which may have been why I threatened to poison her coffee the first time I met her. Who knew she'd stick around and get engaged to my boss?

Fortunately, Sarah forgave as easily as she smiled and they'd become close friends. Over the years of self-imposed isolation, Melanie had forgotten how good it felt to have a woman to talk to. Her friends from high school and college had tried to stay in touch in the beginning, but Melanie hadn't answered their phone calls. She'd been angry and ashamed.

And when she'd surfaced from that dark place—she'd pushed everyone so far away, she didn't know how to begin to piece the friendships back together. So she hadn't tried.

"Are you ready?" David, the ranch manager, asked softly from the doorway. He was only nine years older than Melanie, but she and Sarah joked that he was an old soul. He was a true Texan gentleman, soft-spoken around women but also stubborn and opinionated. He'd offered to drive her to the airport and, given how shaky she was feeling right then, she was glad he had. He wouldn't let her change her mind.

Which is good because I put this off too long already. I can't hide here anymore.

"I'm as ready as I'll ever be," she said. "Is Jace downstairs?"

"He said he'd meet you at the main house. He's making cookies with Sarah."

Melanie stood and buried her cold hands in her jeans pockets. "I've never left him before."

"He'll be fine—maybe a few pounds heavier the way Sarah keeps giving him treats, but none the worse for the time he'll spend at the main house with them. And I'll check in on him daily. Maybe take him out for a few rides. He won't even notice you're gone."

Wiping away an uncharacteristic tear, Melanie said, "Is that supposed to make me feel better?"

David slapped his hat against one thigh. "It sounded good in my head." He cleared his throat. "I know it's none of my business, but I'm glad you're going. It's time you faced whatever brought you here."

Melanie shook her head and looked down at her boots. "If I were braver, I would tell you."

"No need. You and Tony, you've both spent way too many years on this ranch. Life is meant for living, not for hiding."

Lifting her head and raising an eyebrow, she said, "I'm not too sure you weren't hiding along with us. Sarah said you went up to help her friend with her ranch, but you hightailed it right back here. That doesn't sound very brave to me. I saw a picture of Lucy. She sure is pretty."

David lowered his gaze. "She's all right. Tony sent me there because he thought she was having some financial troubles. She found a solution, though."

"I'm surprised you didn't stick around to make sure it worked out."

A flush spread across his cheeks. "It wasn't my area of expertise."

He looked so uncomfortable, Melanie kindly dropped the subject. Sarah had told her that her friend Lucy had taken a quick liking to David, but what he did about it was entirely his own concern. He, Tony, and Melanie had lived side by side for a long time without getting into each other's business. It was a mutual understanding that had kept peace on the ranch. "Well, I'm sure she was grateful for your help." Melanie turned and lifted her bag off the bed. When David moved to help her, she clutched it tighter. "No, thank you. This is something I need to do myself."

He nodded and silently led the way out the door and down the stairs of her home to the car. Once they were both settled, with her bag tucked into the backseat, they drove together in comfortable silence to the main house.

As soon as Jace saw the car approaching, her son ran down the stairs of the home she'd cleaned for years. It would be strange to work anywhere else.

Jace threw his arms around her waist. "Mama, we made cookies with raisins and M&M'S. Can you believe we put both in? Do you want to try one?"

She hugged him to her stomach and ruffled his dark brown hair. "Sure, Jace. Pack me a couple for the road. I'll take them with me."

He ran off to retrieve the cookies. Sarah met her on the stairs of the porch while David went to speak with someone in the barn. Sarah threw her arms around Melanie and gave her a tight hug. "I'm happy to take care of Jace for you, but I wish you'd let me go with you. I hate that you'll be alone."

It was impossible not to hug Sarah back. "I'll be fine."

"Are you sure he's in New York?"

Sarah was the only one in the world Melanie had ever told about Jace's father. Part of her regretted doing so. It made it all real.

It is real. That's what this trip is about, facing the past and doing the right thing.

With all the changes that were going on at the ranch and the talk of Tony and Sarah getting married, Jace had started asking the questions Melanie had feared he one day would: Do I have a Daddy? Where is he? Why doesn't he come see me?

Melanie didn't have the heart to tell him the truth. *Your daddy doesn't know about you because Mommy was too much of a coward to tell him you existed.*

She'd only been a junior in college when she'd gotten pregnant with Jace. His father, Todd, had been the classic college player—Mr. Love 'Em and Leave 'Em. Melanie had never thought she'd fall into the *leave 'em* category.

Melanie cleared her throat. "His family is. Last I heard he moved there to be closer to them. I'll find him."

Sarah hugged her again. "Call or text me when you land."

Melanie gently untangled herself from her friend's embrace. "I will."

"You're all set with your hotel? You know how to get there?"

Uncomfortable in the face of Sarah's gushing concern, Melanie shrugged awkwardly. "I'm sure the taxi will be able to find it."

"Do not shower in any strange places."

A reluctant smile tugged at Melanie's lips. Only Sarah would say that and mean it. "I'll be fine."

She watched Sarah bite her lip, struggling to keep her opinion to herself. But Melanie knew she wouldn't be able to. It only took a minute for Sarah to burst forth with, "Are you sure you don't want one of your sisters to go with you? Or your mother? Any of them?"

"I appreciate how you've tried to smooth things over with my family. I can even take Jace to see them now. But things are as good as they're going to get with them. We all said what we had to say a long time ago."

Sarah held out a hand, then let it drop to her side. "I just wish—"

Melanie cut her off. "I know. And I appreciate that you care."

"If you need anything, my brother lives in New York City."

"I'll keep that in mind," Melanie said. As if that small fact hadn't been tumbling through her head all day.

Jace rushed out of the house and down the stairs with a bag of treats in his hand. He threw his arms around his mother and said, "I put in seven. One for every day you'll be gone. Sarah says we can

Skype every night. If you eat one and I eat one, it'll be like we're eating them together."

Melanie hugged him to her and leaned down to kiss his forehead. "That sounds like a lot of sugar. Don't go driving Sarah crazy by running around her house. You be good for her, you hear?"

He straightened in her embrace. "Mama, I'm all grown up. I know how to behave."

"I'll be back in a week."

"I know," Jace said and stood as proudly as a man. He'd spent very little time around other children, and until recently it hadn't been something Melanie had worried about. If leaving the ranch was scary, leaving Jace at his school on the first day of kindergarten had been downright terrifying. He'd gone in bravely and come home smiling.

I can be brave for him.

She knelt down in front of him. "You understand why you can't come with me, right?"

Jace nodded and parroted. "This is about a job and you'll be working the whole time. It wouldn't be any fun."

It was a lie, but he never would have been okay staying behind if he'd known the truth. "That's right. And I'll be back before you know it."

"Maybe I can go with you next time, when I'm bigger," he said.

Melanie swallowed hard and stepped away from him. "Maybe, Jace. Maybe."

She waved to David, who met her at the car, then forced herself to smile as she waved good-bye to her son.

"He'll be fine," David assured her as they pulled out of the driveway.

"I know," Melanie answered thickly, hating that her eyes filled with tears. She blinked them away, refusing to let them spill down her cheeks.

I am strong enough to do the right thing this time.

Charles Dery leaned forward in his office chair, addressing the man on the speakerphone as aggressively as if he were right there before him. He laid his hands flat on the table. "Wilmington is your safer choice. I understand why you've been with them so long. They've kept your investments at a stable profit margin through some global financial upheavals. You feel like you owe them. I'd ask you if loyalty is worth what it's costing you every year."

John Rawlings, the sixty-six-year-old billionaire and CEO of a network of manufacturing companies spread around the world, was silent for a moment. "You're one cocky son of a bitch, Dery. Are you as good as you think you are?"

And now to close. "My track record speaks for itself. I don't seek out new clients because I don't have to. You came to me, John. A contract was sent over to you yesterday. Hold on to it if you're not ready to make the move now. I have a meeting in five minutes. We can talk about this next week if you'd prefer."

But Charles knew a man like Rawlings wouldn't wait for anything.

He'll cave in five, four, three . . .

"I'll have that contract over to you within the hour, but you'd better have a full portfolio plan on my desk by tomorrow morning."

Charles reached toward the phone and said, "Welcome to Dery Investments, Mr. Rawlings." He hung up on him before the man had a chance to say anything in response.

Charles turned his leather chair parallel to his desk. A heavy rain beat against the floor-to-ceiling windows of his Midtown Manhattan office, blurring a view that wordlessly announced his level of success to his clients.

The rush of euphoria he'd expected didn't come. At least not as it had in the past when he'd reached a goal he'd set for himself. Confirmation that Rawlings would sign a client contract meant Charles's personal income would soon breach ten digits—a ceiling he'd been hovering just below.

He should celebrate.

Or at least want to.

Instead, Charles was drawn to the darker corners of his mind. Ever since his sister, Sarah, had moved to Texas and decided that facing the past was her path to happiness, memories of his childhood in Rhode Island had surfaced and choked all pleasure out of his achievements. Ripping open old wounds and confronting the festering guilt had worked well for his sister, but it was slowly tearing down the life Charles had built for himself.

When he'd left his hometown to attend Stanford, he'd sworn he'd exceed everyone's expectations. As the son of a man who had built a marginally profitable construction company without the benefit of wealthy parents or higher education, Charles had never been afraid of hard work. He'd hit the ground running in New York City, taken an entry-level position at the prestigious Wilmington Investment Company, and quickly built up a reputation for impressing even their wealthiest clients. He was gifted at using statistics to predict financial trends, and his track record for increasing a company's or individual's net worth was becoming as legendary as his rise through the ranks at Wilmington had been.

He'd refused an offer to become a partner, something that had previously been unheard of for someone of his age and background, and had broken away instead to start his own company. Wilmington had tried to thwart him, of course. Tried to utilize noncompete clauses to stop their top clients from following Charles, but when the wealthy want something, nothing stands in their way. And they'd wanted him.

Ten years later, Dery Investments had amassed both domestic and international clout. And now he had Rawlings, arguably the richest man in the Northern Hemisphere, on his roster. In terms of his personal goals for his business, there was no bigger fish to catch. No higher mountain to climb.

I've made it.

The achievement rang empty and meaningless through him, which was surprising since the only life he'd allowed himself to have was at work. It consumed him, calmed him, kept the past where it belonged—distant and forgotten.

Successfully behind him until recently.

Fucking rain. It had rained the day his little brother drowned and the day of his funeral.

The door to his office flew open and his college friend, Mason Thorne, entered unannounced. Charles stood and crossed the room to meet him. It wasn't surprising that Mason had gotten by June, Charles's usually efficient secretary. A former teenage movie star turned California politician, Mason still captivated women. June was not, by far, the only woman he'd seen become a stuttering mess around Mason.

Mason had cultivated his own presence. Even in an Armani suit, he looked relaxed and tanned, like he'd come from the beach. He purposely wore his unruly blond hair longer than what would be considered appropriate for a senator. He *wanted* to be under-estimated. Only Mason could plow through his opposition ruthlessly, then flash his Hollywood charm and instantly be forgiven by everyone. Including the press.

Charles shook his hand warmly. "What brings you to New York, Mace?"

"You do," Mason answered easily, and walked over to the window to look out. "Had I known you'd ordered cold and wet weather, I would have declined."

Charles shook his head briefly. Their busy schedules meant they didn't speak as often as they once had. He couldn't remember their last conversation.

With his usual carefree smile, Mason clarified the reason for his presence. "You're getting the Astor Philanthropist Award and you invited me to watch you accept it."

"Oh shit. I forgot it's tomorrow night." Then Charles frowned. "I didn't invite you."

Mason shrugged. "You mentioned it. Same thing. Did you think I'd pass up an opportunity to heckle you?"

With a smile of concession, Charles didn't argue the point. On the surface, they were different, but Mason was a good friend and Charles was happy to see him. Ever since they'd both played football for Stanford, they'd had each other's backs. At the time, Mason had been trying to rise above his reputation as a big screen heartthrob and wasn't being taken seriously by professors or classmates. Charles, at least when compared to many of the other students, had been far removed from the old money clique that ran the school. However, on the football field, both of them had crushed their opponents and earned respect through brute force. By their senior year, they were a formidable force on and off the field. Now in their thirties, neither had time for sports, but they made time for their friendship.

"Is it good form for a senator to heckle someone?"

"Perhaps not good form, but good fun." Mason looked his friend over with a critical eye. "What's wrong?"

Charles returned to the seat behind his desk, sat back, and stretched. There were drawbacks to having friends who knew you well. "Nothing."

Mason shot him a look that clearly said he didn't believe him, and leaned against the marble-topped table beside the window. "Are you still moping about that housekeeper down in Texas? I don't understand why you won't call her."

Drumming his fingers on the desk, Charles said impatiently, "I'm not interested in her."

Mason rubbed his chin thoughtfully. "So you've told me. You work your lack of interest in her into almost every conversation we have."

Charles raised one eyebrow in concession to Mason's claim. "She surprised me, that's all. I'm not used to women who . . ."

"Throw lemonade in your face? I can see how that would be hard to forget."

Hard to forget? Try fucking impossible. Charles could recall every detail of the first time he'd met Melanie with a clarity that defied logic. He'd gone down to Texas to convince his sister to come home. He preferred not to remember what Tony had said about Sarah that earned him a punch to the jaw, especially since it now appeared that Tony would soon be his brother-in-law. No, all he really remembered about that day was the fire in Melanie's eyes while she'd reprimanded him for his behavior. The attraction had been instant and powerful. "I deserved the dousing."

"Wish I'd been there to see it." His friend grinned. "How is your sister, anyway?"

"She's good. Still engaged. I've never seen her happier."

"Are you going back down to see her?"

"Not anytime soon."

"Because you don't want to see the housekeeper again."

"She has a name. It's Melanie."

"I know. I just like to give you shit. I want to meet her. Any woman brazen enough to give you a smackdown and beautiful enough for you to accept it, must be amazing."

"She is," Charles said and sat up, more surprised by his agreement than Mason appeared to be. The truth irritated him. "But it doesn't matter. I'll never date her."

"Because she has a child?"

Charles stood defensively. "You know how I feel about children."

Mason's eyes shone with sympathy. "One accident shouldn't determine the rest of your life."

"Don't. Don't lecture me like your life is any less fucked up than mine is. You want to fix something? Fix yourself."

"Hey, hey, hey," Mason said in a conciliatory tone. "I didn't come here to piss you off. Forget I mentioned Texas at all. What are you doing tonight? I have to meet with some Washington cronies who flew in for tomorrow's award ceremony, but I'm free for dinner after that. We could get a bite somewhere, then go to the opening of *Crushed*. An old friend of mine is starring in it along with some women who are guaranteed to be hot enough to make you forget anyone."

Charles joined his friend by the window and stared out over the gray skyline. "Dinner sounds good, but I'll have to call it an early night. I got the Rawlings account. The investment portfolio is due first thing tomorrow morning."

"Rawlings? When did you find out? Were you going to call me?"

"I found out just now."

"Then you should definitely come out tonight. We'll celebrate."

Charles held his tongue. Mason still clung to a lifestyle that never held much interest for Charles. A night out with Mason meant excessive drinking, followed by a guaranteed hangover and a high likelihood of waking up next to a woman whose name he couldn't remember. Mason joked that he did his networking beneath the sheets, so to speak—winning his voters one fuck at a time.

And because the son of a bitch had that Hollywood smile, neither women nor the press judged him for his sexcapades.

Mason gave him a healthy smack on the back and turned to leave the office. Charles half turned and said, "Hey, Mason, thanks for coming. I'll meet you at Red Hill Stone. June will make the reservation for seven." It was a restaurant some people waited a year to get into, but Charles knew neither of them would have a problem scoring a table.

"Seven works for me." He paused at the door. "I'll tell my friends you may join us afterward, in case you change your mind."

"I won't."

"I've seen it happen."

"Not this time," Charles said as Mason closed the door behind him. *Maybe I should have said yes. A good fuck might clear my head.* It was going on months since he'd been with anyone. He'd had opportunities but no interest.

Not since he'd met Melanie.

She wasn't his type, but he was having a devil of a time remembering why. Each night he lay in bed imagining how he would peel those jeans off her and bury his face between her legs. Tasting her was all he could think about . . . that and how his name would sound when he drove himself into her and she cried it out in climax.

Opening his eyes, he cursed.

She was a weakness he refused to give in to. She didn't belong in his life any more than he belonged in hers. Entertaining the possibility of more, even for a moment, would be a monumental mistake.

Chapter Two

After knocking softly, Charles's secretary opened the door to his office. "Mr. Dery, your car is downstairs."

Charles rubbed a hand over his tired eyes. Mason had kept him out late last night. Now that Rawlings was officially a client, the challenge would be keeping him. So Charles had worked until the sun came up on a plan that included just enough low-risk investments to put Rawlings at ease as well as cutting-edge ventures that promised substantial payouts. *It's more aggressive than he's allowed his portfolio to be up until now, and if I'm right, the results will be enough to quickly impress him.*

And his ultrarich friends.

Some of whom would be at the event he was attending that night, which was part of the reason Charles had agreed to speak at it. He'd go and pretend to be moved by what people said about him, but he found these events tiresome. Philanthropy was a political game, even for the charities involved. Good press was good business, nothing less, nothing more.

"June, did you have my tuxedo delivered?"

"Yes," his secretary answered smoothly. "It's at your penthouse. You said you wanted to freshen up there. You probably won't have time to eat at the event, so your housekeeper prepared a salad and sandwich. It's wrapped and waiting for you in your fridge."

"Good thinking," Charles said as he shut down his computer, stood, and stretched. "I sent you an e-mail about Rawlings. If he calls tomorrow, put him through. No matter what I have going on."

"Absolutely, Mr. Dery." Instead of leaving, she hovered at the door.

"What is it?"

"You told me not to interrupt you this afternoon, so I didn't, but your sister called twice. She said it wasn't urgent. Should I have put her through?"

"Normally, yes, but I needed to concentrate on those numbers, so you chose well. Did she tell you what she wanted?" With his sister, the possibilities were endless. Although having her back in his life was important to him, the detailed retelling of each blissful day she spent with her fiancé on his horse ranch was best listened to while on a treadmill, not in the middle of a workday.

Was I ever that happy?

He thought back to the summers he and his family had spent at their lake house. His memories of those times were filled with laughter. Sarah used to beg him to take her canoeing, then only row for the first hundred feet or so. He may have teased her about it, but he never actually cared.

A sad smile twisted his lips as he remembered the tragic day. The same place that had brought his family so much joy had also torn them apart.

"A friend of hers is flying into LaGuardia tonight," his secretary said, bringing Charles abruptly back to the present.

"Who?"

"I asked, but she wouldn't say. She seemed to think you would know who she was talking about."

"That's all, June. Thank you," he said, dismissing her. Seconds after his secretary closed the door behind her, Charles dialed his sister's number on his cell phone. His heart was thudding heavily in his chest. She picked up almost instantly.

"Charlie, I've been calling you all day!"

"Sorry," he said brusquely. "I'm working on a new project. I gave June instructions to not interrupt me."

"I figured you were working on something important so I told her not to bother you, but I need to ask you for a favor. Remember my friend Melanie?"

"Yes," Charles answered vaguely. Sarah already suspected he was attracted to Melanie and the last thing he wanted to do was confirm it. She was under the misguided opinion that he needed someone permanent in his life.

"She's flying into New York at six. Can you meet her at the airport? She's never been there."

Charles looked down at his watch. *Shit.* "I have an engagement at seven thirty. I'd never be able to—"

"That's perfect, then," Sarah said in a rush. "Just zip over, pick her up, drop her off at her hotel, then go to your party."

"It's not that simple." He didn't want to see Melanie again. Well, that was a lie. Every cell in his body wanted to go to that airport, pick her up, take her to the nearest hotel, and spend the night discovering how she compared to his fantasies of her. But that wasn't going to happen. "I won't have enough time."

As his cock jerked in the crotch of his suit, he closed his eyes. *Do not do this while on the phone with Sarah.* He needed something disgusting to distract himself. He pictured the mushroom of hair that he'd witnessed springing out the ass crack of the electrician who had fixed a faulty wire in his office the week before.

When that proved to be less than effective, he asked himself if the man's wife was just as hairy and contemplated the likelihood that they might have produced fur-ball children.

Thankfully, his blood returned to his brain and he opened his eyes again.

"Charlie, this is really important to me. I can't tell you why Melanie is in New York, but I can say it wasn't easy for her to decide to go there. I should've gone with her. She needs somebody, but she's too proud to ask for help. Imagine if it was me. Would you be comfortable with me running around New York by myself? Or would you want someone to make sure I was okay?"

He wished the reason he was tempted to agree to meet Melanie was as altruistic as Sarah's reasons for wanting him to.

"Did she bring her son?" he asked, knowing how dickish he sounded.

"No, I'm watching Jace. This is the first time she's been away from him, and I know she's taking it hard. She could use a friend right now. Please, go pick her up. Just show her that someone there cares about her. That's all. Nothing major—just a few quick check-ins. Please."

"Fine. I'll meet her. I'll need her cell number and flight info."

Sarah gave it to him and thanked him profusely. He hung up with a quick good-bye.

On the way out of his office, Charles told June to have his tuxedo taken to a room at the hotel where the Astor event was being held that night. With any luck, he could pick Melanie up, drop her off, and not be late to his event.

He knew all the reasons why even considering meeting her was a bad idea.

None of them mattered in that moment.

Melanie. In New York. Alone.

Charles smiled for the first time that day.

∼

Melanie looked down at the rows of buildings and snarls of traffic as her plane circled the airport and felt none of the excitement she would have had she been there for any other reason. As an interior design major, she'd often dreamed of visiting New York. She'd even made scrapbooks of upscale furniture stores she wanted to visit for inspiration.

Dreams I put aside when I had Jace.

She opened her backpack, took out the brown paper bag of cookies her son had sent with her, and wiped away a tear. She used to think she was a brave person, but when life had thrown her first real challenge her way, she'd run from it. Before Sarah turned up, Tony Carlton's ranch had been a place where strangers were not welcome and a person could hide from the world.

The tires of the plane squealed as they met the tar of the runway. The cookies flew up, almost leaving the bag. Melanie held them protectively to her stomach.

No turning back now.

Melanie started to second-guess her decision not to call his parents from Texas and merely ask for his number. But she'd wanted to look into their eyes and know that finding Todd was the right thing to do.

What the hell am I going to say to them? "Hi, I'm looking for your son. He never mentioned me? Yeah, that's because I was one of the many he slept with in college. He probably doesn't even remember my name."

I'll just say I'm an old friend.

The plane rolled to a stop at the gate and the seat belt light went dark and dinged, announcing they could disembark. Melanie placed the bag of cookies on her seat and put her backpack next to it. She waited for the people around her to collect their bags, then pulled hers down from the overhead compartment. There'd been no need to bring much with her since she wasn't planning anything beyond meeting Todd's parents and, if all went well, connecting with him. She swung her backpack over her shoulder and followed the other passengers down the aisle and off the plane.

Her stomach growled in protest as she walked, reminding her that she hadn't eaten anything that day. Her chest tightened and her breathing became shallow. It wasn't until a rush of passengers passed her on either side that she realized she'd stopped. The people around her blurred as panic seized her.

She forced herself to start walking again. Jace deserved to know his father, and to have a mother who didn't let fear control her.

I can do this.

She blindly followed the crowd to what she hoped would be an exit, and sighed in relief to see the signs for ground transportation. When she neared the baggage claim area, she heard a male voice call out her name.

"Melanie!"

At first she glanced around in confusion, wondering if the voice was calling her or another Melanie. But then her eyes flew to the man she'd chastised herself for hoping she'd see again. "Charles. What are you doing here?"

He stopped in front of her and, for just a split second, Melanie thought he might pull her into his arms. They stared into each other's eyes for so long it became awkward. Melanie looked away first.

He took the luggage from her hand with such authority she released it instinctively. "Giving you a ride to your hotel."

Quick panic set in. She shook her head and made a grab for her bag. "That's not necessary."

He took her by the elbow with his free hand, guiding her toward the exit. "I have a car waiting."

His touch, however impersonal he may have meant it to be, set her skin afire. She hadn't dated anyone since she'd found out she was pregnant with Jace six years ago. She'd told herself she didn't need a man. She didn't need anyone. But being around Charles had made her realize how lonely she'd become and she didn't know what to do with those feelings.

"You don't have to do this," she said huskily. *You shouldn't do this. Just like I shouldn't be so happy to see you.* She glanced up at him and quickly looked away. It was still there. That undeniable, embarrassingly strong pull she felt whenever she saw him.

"Sarah asked me to."

His words were a slap of reality. *Of course that's why he's here. Did I think he'd met me because he couldn't stay away? A man like him can have any woman he wants. He's not pining for a woman like me. Get a grip.*

As they passed the baggage claim area, Charles asked, "Do you have everything or did you check a bag?"

A bag? The cookies. Melanie came to a sudden halt and realized she didn't have them in her hands. She frantically searched her backpack. *I left them on the plane. Oh my God. I'm not in New York fifteen minutes and I've already lost something I can't replace.*

What if it's a sign that I could lose Jace here, too?

I can't do this.

She turned on her heel to head back the way she'd come, but was blocked by a wall of suit that stepped into her way. "What's the matter?" Charles asked.

Everything. Shaking her head as she waved a frantic hand in the air, she blurted, "I left a bag of cookies on the plane."

He looked away and then back at her as if he wasn't sure he'd heard her correctly. "You're upset over a snack?"

"Jace made them for me," she said sadly. *How could I begin to explain to him why they matter?*

Without letting go of her arm, Charles placed the luggage beside his leg, took out his cell phone, and made a call. A moment later he nodded and returned the phone to his pocket. "The plane has already been cleaned. Anything they found went in the trash."

It's just cookies. I'll buy some that look just like them for when I video chat with Jace. He'll never know. This doesn't change anything. Hold it together. Melanie took a deep calming breath and said, "Of course." She pulled her arm free and squared her shoulders. "Thank you for checking for me."

"If there was anything that you need with the cookies, we can have them search for it."

"No," Melanie said, still trying to shake her panic off, "some mistakes can't be undone. You just have to face that you made them and go on. No matter what happens. You have to deal with the consequences."

In a move that took Melanie completely by surprise, Charles pulled her into his arms and simply hugged her. She had denied herself the luxury of physical contact with a man for so long that at first she stood rigid, unresponsive in his arms. With her face pressed against his shirt, she breathed in the scent of him and almost shuddered from the pleasure of it. In his strong arms, she felt protected from the past, safe from whatever the future held. She gave herself to the moment and wrapped both arms around his waist. Right or wrong, in that moment he was offering her comfort and she didn't have the strength to refuse it.

A slow growing embarrassment began to spread through Melanie. *Poor Charles, sent to the airport to pick up a woman he doesn't really know, only to have her become a basket case.*

Melanie pulled herself out of his arms. She kept her eyes glued to the lapel of his jacket and the white shirt beneath it that she'd wrinkled. When she reached to smooth it, she felt his heart beating rapidly in his chest and pulled quickly away.

Without breaking eye contact, he picked up her luggage again and began guiding her toward the exit. Just outside the door, a driver in a black suit met them. Charles handed off her bag to him. The man offered to take her backpack, too, but Melanie shook her head.

"He'll put it inside the trunk for you," Charles assured her.

Melanie held it tighter beneath her arm. "I don't mind carrying it." The driver opened the rear door to the town car and Melanie slid in, not stopping until she was sitting on the opposite end of the seat. Charles kindly made no mention of the large space her action left between them.

"Where are you staying?" Charles asked.

Information that Melanie had memorized earlier flew out of her head. She swung her backpack around and opened the front pocket. A ticket. Lip gloss. A napkin she thought she might need later. No itinerary. She unzipped the second pocket. A magazine. A phone. More napkins. Some wet wipes. *God, I'm such a mother. Shit.* "I know where I'm staying," she said angrily.

Charles watched her wordlessly.

"I have it all written out on an itinerary: the reservation number, the address. Everything." Her hands shook and fumbled with one of the fastenings. *How the hell am I going to find Jace's father if I can't even fucking find my hotel? Stop. Breathe.* "It's in this bag somewhere."

He placed a hand on her thigh and she nearly shot through the roof of the car. Her eyes whipped up from her backpack and riveted to his. "Take your time," he said smoothly. "No rush."

His voice was husky and deep. Melanie's breath caught in her throat. She felt her cheeks warm with a raging blush that was half embarrassment and half a heated response to his touch. She shifted away from him and turned her attention back to her search. A moment later, in the third section she opened, she found the piece of paper with the hotel address on it.

Charles took the paper from her hands. "Would you like to . . ."

"I can't stay with you," Melanie said in a rush. "I'm not staying with you."

Both of his gorgeous eyebrows rose, but his tone remained neutral. "I was going to ask if you wanted to stop anywhere for anything you might have forgotten."

Melanie sank into the leather seat and covered her face with one hand, wishing she were anywhere but there. "Thank you, no. I have everything I need."

Charles told the driver the name of her hotel and they pulled out into traffic. As they drove into the heart of the city, the streets were crowded with people. If she had been there for any other reason, Melanie would have appreciated the differences between the rural lifestyle she'd been raised in and the bustle of the city streets.

But New York didn't matter.

The man beside her didn't, either.

There was too much at stake to worry about what Charles thought of her. "Sarah said this is your first trip to New York City."

Melanie nodded but didn't turn away from the window.

"How long will you be here?" he asked.

"Maybe a day. Maybe a week."

"Is there anything you'd like to see while you're here? A play perhaps? I could have my secretary procure tickets to almost anywhere. It doesn't matter if the event says it's sold out. Everyone keeps some tickets on the side."

For just the briefest moment, she imagined he was offering to go with her, but quickly decided not to make a fool of herself yet again and simply shook her head no.

"Normally I would offer to take you to dinner this evening, but I didn't know you were coming. I have plans that are, unfortunately, impossible to change."

How polite. How utterly civilized and the polar opposite of the way he'd been in Texas. She thought back to the first time they met. He'd been furious with the idea that his sister was shacking up for the summer with the cowboy. He'd walked onto Tony Carlton's ranch like he'd owned it and gone head-to-head with a man most wouldn't have had the nerve to tangle with. He'd been cold and dismissive—and more than a little insulting even to her. At least until she had thrown a glass of lemonade in his face and told him what she thought of him and how he was treating his sister.

Sarah said that, despite how he appeared, Charles would do anything for his family. Well, he was certainly proving her right. For Sarah's sake, his attempts to make Melanie feel welcome were unwavering.

And I'm being rude by not even looking at him while he makes polite conversation with me. Why? Because despite how tough I look on the outside, I am not. I'm scared, and I don't want him to see it in my eyes.

The car pulled up in front of her hotel. The driver opened the door. Charles stepped out and offered a hand to Melanie, but she ignored it. The less she touched him, the better. Her body wasn't on the same page as her brain for this trip. It wanted to fling itself into his arms and beg him to come inside with her. Lust and loneliness were a powerful combination.

If I threw myself at him, would his rejection be as polite and awkward as our conversation has been?

I should be grateful he's not attracted to me. This trip is already complicated enough.

The bellman took her bag. Charles stepped aside for a moment to speak with someone in the lobby while Melanie checked in.

"I'll call you tomorrow," Charles said when he returned. His deep voice sent ripples of pleasure through her.

Melanie's breath caught in her throat. *Is there anything about him that isn't above average?* Her eyes dropped to his crotch instinctively and she blushed.

Stop. I don't even like men in suits.

Well, not most men. Charles had an air of power that made his clothing choice irrelevant. Men and women alike stopped to watch him, and not only because he was a classically handsome man with broad shoulders and a square chin. No, he had what her friends back home would call the "don't-fuck-with-me" attitude. It gave his polished exterior an edge. People sensed he was important even if they weren't sure who he was.

"You don't have to call me." Melanie looked down at her worn jeans and hugged her backpack tighter. "I may not even still be here."

He took out his card and wrote on the back of it before handing it to her. "If you need anything, this is my cell phone number."

Melanie stashed it in her backpack, then raised her eyes to meet his. Her heart beat double time in her chest. She had no intention of calling him.

He waited for her to say something. Melanie shifted her feet awkwardly and buried her hands in her front pockets. "Thank you for the ride."

He glanced at his watch and swore. "I hate to leave, but I'm late. Do you have everything you need?"

Melanie nodded even though nothing could've been further from the truth. She fought back the desire to call out his name when he turned and strode across the foyer and back out to his car.

As he walked away, Melanie sank into one of the chairs in the lobby and covered her face with her hands. In a moment she would head up to her room, put a huge smile on her face, and video chat with her son. She would thank Sarah for sending someone to meet her and tell her again how grateful she was for everything.

Yes, she would look brave, happy, and appreciative.

In a minute.

She took a deep breath and kept her hands over her face.

Or maybe two.

Charles navigated the award ceremony on autopilot. Despite this one being held in Manhattan, many of these events were reruns of prior ones. The same people. The same conversations. People came to them either because they cared about the cause or they wanted people to think they did. He didn't waste his time trying to sort out which category any of them fell into. He supported the causes the same way he supported his family—financially and from a distance.

He smiled graciously as he received the award and posed for the cameras. He shook hands with all the right people, inquired about their families, and walked away from them, instantly forgetting each interaction as soon as it ended.

He was debating how soon he could leave the event, even while the mayor was telling him about his last golfing trip and some mishap that was supposed to be amusing. Charles listened just enough to smile at the right times, but couldn't have been farther away in his head.

Just before he'd exited the hotel, he'd made the mistake of glancing back at Melanie. The sight of her with her hands over her face in despair haunted him. *I should have stayed with her.*

And then what?

She needed a friend, not a lover. And Charles didn't do friendships with women.

He didn't get involved.

His cock countered with an opinion of its own. It didn't care why she'd come to New York. Just the thought of having her in the same city was enough to keep it in a constant, throbbing state of arousal.

Stand down, nothing is going to happen. She's not my problem. She'll call Sarah if she needs a sympathetic ear.

Still, he couldn't shake the image of her in the hotel foyer. What had brought her to New York and why was she so sad?

If she wanted my help she would have asked for it.

I was right to leave.

I don't get involved with women who have children.

I don't date them.

I don't fuck them.

Children have always been and will always be a deal breaker.

Sarah often called Charles overprotective, but in reality, when it had counted, he had failed to protect the one who had most needed him.

And that was something he could never forgive himself for.

Something he'd never put himself in a position to do again.

"Charles, if I can have a moment?" Mason broke in to the conversation between Charles and the mayor and pulled his friend away. Together they walked to a small landing that looked out over the throngs gathered for the event.

Frowning, Charles asked, "What do you need?"

"Me? Nothing. You need to stop smiling while the mayor tells you about the issues he's having with getting funding for his latest project."

"Shit, I wasn't paying attention." Charles looked back at the mayor, who was talking to his wife and waving his hands around as if reenacting their conversation. "I thought he was still talking about his golf trip."

Mason's eyebrows snapped together in consternation. "Hey, I can cancel my plans for tonight. Let's go for a drink. You look like you need one."

Charles shook his head. "No. I have work waiting for me. And a long day tomorrow."

"Something is bothering you. I've never seen you like this."

"Like what?" Charles asked impatiently.

"Guilty?" Mason said slowly. "Like you're holding in a secret that's eating at you. You didn't embezzle money or anything, did you? Is that why your company has been doing so well lately?"

"Don't be a fucking idiot."

"We've been friends long enough you can be honest with me. I know some awesome lawyers."

"I didn't steal anything." When Mason looked like he was going to ask another question, Charles said, "I didn't kill anyone, either."

Mason took a flute of champagne from a passing server and downed it. He made a face and handed the glass to the next server who walked past them. "I'll never understand why they can't serve good beer at these events. Now, spill. What's going on?"

"It's been a long day. I rushed from work to pick up someone at the airport, then came straight here. I'm tired, not guilty."

Mason winked at a woman across the room and then continued, unconvinced. "Who flew in?"

"Melanie."

Mason choked, gasped for air, and asked, "*The* Melanie? She's in New York?"

Charles nodded, then looked away.

"No wonder you can't concentrate. What the fuck are you doing here?"

"I couldn't not show. I was the main speaker."

"But you could leave now."

"I told you, there is nothing between us. My sister asked me to meet her at the airport when she landed and I did. That's all that happened. That's all that is going to happen. There is no reason for me to see her again before she leaves."

Mason put a hand on his shoulder. "This is so pathetic it's adorable. I may have to hug you."

Charles shrugged his touch off. "You've spent way too much time in California with your touchy-feely friends. Keep your damn hands to yourself."

Mason laughed. "Hopefully, that's not what my date will tell me tonight."

Charles looked at his friend and gave him a reluctant smile. "She will if she has any sense."

With a shameless grin, Mason said, "I can't help it if women lust for me. It would be wrong for me to deny them what they crave. I'm not cruel like that."

"Are you ever going to grow up?" Charles asked.

"Not unless I find a good reason to." He covered his heart with one hand dramatically. "Maybe someday I'll meet my Melanie and reform my ways. But tonight it's Danielle and maybe Tina if they're interested in that possibility."

Charles rolled his eyes.

Mason laughed again. "You're such a prude. Is it the cold weather that does it? Makes you all uptight out here? You've got to learn to relax."

"You *relax* enough for both of us."

They stood shoulder to shoulder watching the crowd below. Suddenly serious, Mason said, "I can't believe the woman you have the hots for is in New York and you're going to piss away the opportunity."

Charles frowned. He saw her in his mind again as vividly as if she were sitting before him. "I suppose I should call to confirm that she settled in okay."

Clapping a hand on his friend's back, Mason said, "Whatever you need to tell yourself, Charlie."

Chapter Three

Tucked into her hotel bed, Melanie closed her eyes with relief when the local news station finally began to highlight the weather. She was used to sleeping to the quiet country sounds of nature and had been a light sleeper since the day she'd brought Jace home from the hospital. The walls of her hotel were thin enough that she heard the occasional conversation and one woman's repeated high-pitched laugh. She'd turned on the television hoping the noise would help her sleep better. *That didn't happen.*

She'd just finished watching clips of Charles receiving an award for his philanthropic donations to a long list of charities. Sound bites of his speech aired again and again along with images of him shaking hands with prominent members of government and visiting famous people.

In his tuxedo, he looked every bit who he was—a member of New York's wealthy elite. She cringed as she remembered how he'd held her in the airport. No doubt shuttling his sister's friend around was the last thing he wanted to be doing before his big event. A weepy hot mess of a friend at that.

She flipped off the television and rolled over onto her side. *Stop thinking about what doesn't matter. Tomorrow is going to be tough enough without losing sleep over someone who has probably already forgotten I'm here.*

She closed her eyes, but her mind raced in circles, preventing sleep. At least Jace was happy. When she'd called him earlier, he'd excitedly told her about his day. Between Sarah, Tony, and David, they'd kept him so busy he didn't have time to miss her. Thankfully, he'd forgotten about the cookies, so her plan to pass off store-bought ones as his had been unnecessary.

Which made her grateful and, selfishly, a little sad at the same time.

Although she wanted him to be happy, his acceptance of the situation fed into her greatest fear that he would one day leave her.

Jace was all she had.

What if Todd wanted to see him often? Would he sue for partial custody? Would they become a family of scheduled sharing?

Will he want Jace to stay with him in New York?

Just the idea of letting Jace go off with anyone, even a man who was biologically his father, was terrifying. He'd be a complete stranger to Jace. *To me, too.* No one stayed the same. Todd wouldn't be the young man she'd slept with. What kind of person had he become? He likely had a career by now, maybe a wife, and possibly children.

Would that woman welcome or resent Jace?

Once I do this, it can't be undone. Everything might change once Todd knows about Jace. Am I ready for that?

No matter how much I'd like to, I can't pretend Jace doesn't have a father.

And Todd deserves to know that he has a son.

The ring of her cell phone startled her. Anxious something might have happened with her son, she scrambled in the darkness for the phone and answered it in a breathless rush. "Yes?"

"Melanie, it's Charles. I hope it's not too late to call you."

"Oh," she said and sagged with relief into the bed. "No. I was still awake."

"I wanted to make sure you settled in okay."

"I did."

After a pause, Charles said, "Come to dinner with me tomorrow."

Because Sarah doesn't want me to be alone or because you want to see me? Melanie hated that she cared what his answer to that question would be, but she didn't let herself ask it. She wasn't sure she could handle either possibility. "I have plans, but thank you."

"Lunch, then?"

"That's not necessary. I'm sure you're busy."

"I'm beginning to think you don't like me," he said softly. The purr in his voice sent a shiver of need down her spine.

If you only knew. "I know Sarah asked you to check in with me while I'm here, and I really appreciate that you have. Especially considering the night you've had. I was just watching you on the news. I feel awful that you rushed off to meet me before something like that."

"I'm glad you saw the news clip. If I hadn't been the main speaker, I would have skipped the event and . . ." He didn't say what he would have done. "Why are you in New York, Melanie? Is it something I can help you with?"

Melanie wondered what Charles would say if she asked him to find the father of her child. *Could he ever understand why I kept the truth to myself for so long?* He didn't look like a man who feared anyone or anything. *How could I ever begin to explain to him the weight of regret and a shame that only grew the longer I denied it?*

Until I felt trapped by both.

I had so many opportunities to do the right thing.

I should have called Todd when I first found out I was carrying his child. I could have told him when Jace was born. I did this to myself.

"Thank you, Charles, but this is something I have to do on my own." She cleared her throat. "You've done more than enough for me already. Sarah's lucky to have a brother like you." When he didn't comment, she continued. "I'm sorry. It's late and I'm tired. Thanks again for calling."

She went to hang up, but he said, "Melanie . . ."

She put the phone back to her ear. "Yes?"

After a long pause, he said, "Good night."

She let out a shaky sigh. "Good night." She hung up and tucked the phone beneath her pillow. It would have been so easy to agree to meet Charles. And would it have been wrong? Since the moment Jace was born, Melanie had put aside what she wanted for what he needed.

She didn't regret a moment of it, but stepping outside of that life to go to New York made her realize how profoundly lonely she had become. It had been almost six years since she'd kissed a man. Todd hadn't been her first, but he'd been her last.

Did Charles want more than dinner?

Melanie allowed herself to imagine what it would be like if he did. Did he have a sense of humor beneath his serious exterior? How did he feel about children? What would a first kiss be like with a powerful man like Charles? Would he hold her as he did in the airport and gently explore her lips, or would he take her mouth with a boldness that would leave her shaking in her cowboy boots?

She closed her eyes and pulled the blankets up around her.

It doesn't matter because I'm never going to find out.

∾

Frustrated, Charles threw his tuxedo jacket on the back of a chair as he walked through his apartment. He wasn't a vain man, but he also wasn't used to being brushed off by a woman. Especially not by one he wanted.

And that was the heart of the problem—when he spoke to her, nothing mattered except his need to see her again. Distracted, he uncharacteristically dropped his clothing as he walked. He had someone who came during the day a couple of times each week to tidy his apartment, but there wasn't much for her to do. He was at work most of the day, returning home to sleep. Occasionally June would have his housekeeper leave him something to eat, but typically his refrigerator was as empty as his apartment. Like his living room furniture, his house staff was mostly an unused luxury.

Charles wasn't a man who fumbled over his words or wavered in the face of a decision. Or he hadn't been, before Melanie. She had him all tangled up and confused.

He wanted to save her.

Claim her.

He met beautiful women all the time, but they didn't send his thoughts scattering and his blood rushing wildly downward with just one soulful look.

Only one woman had the power to do that.

Melanie, with her hair wild and free, as natural as the skin she didn't hide beneath a mask of makeup. He wanted to discover how much of her was tan and taste all the places the sun hadn't kissed.

Walking naked into the bathroom, Charles turned on the shower. He told himself to forget her. He'd be better off calling any one of the women he'd been with over the past few years, but he couldn't remember why any of them had appealed to him.

Melanie was a fascinating mixture of grit and vulnerability. His first impression of her had been of a passionate, strong woman who feared nothing and needed no one. However, the woman he'd picked up at the airport earlier had looked lost and alone.

He should have pressed her to explain why she'd come to New York.

He didn't like not knowing what was upsetting her.

Liked even less that he couldn't put her out of his mind.

He got out of the shower and called his sister. "Sarah, it's Charles."

"Charlie," Sarah said with happy surprise. "I'm so glad you called. I spoke to Melanie earlier. Thank you so much for picking her up. I feel better knowing that she's not there alone."

"About that. Is she in some sort of trouble? What is she doing here?"

His sister was uncharacteristically quiet, and her hesitancy fueled unwelcome curiosity within Charles. He waited, knowing that Sarah wouldn't be able to hold her silence long. Eventually she said softly, "If she didn't tell you, I can't."

Irritation with himself filled Charles. Melanie was remaining in touch with his sister. She had resources she could call on if she needed someone. He didn't need to get involved.

He should end it then and there.

Yet he said, "My schedule is flexible this week if she needs something. She can call me if she does."

"She probably won't, Charlie," Sarah said gently, "Melanie is a very private person. She's built this protective shell around herself that makes her look tougher than she is. She doesn't like anyone to know when she's hurting or when she's scared, but I can tell you that she's both right now. It's why I feel better knowing that you're checking in on her. I should have gone with her."

His heart thudded heavily in his chest. "Is she ill?"

Sounding a little horrified by the idea, Sarah exclaimed, "Oh no, Charlie, nothing that extreme. I hate not being able to tell you, but I promised her I wouldn't tell anyone. She's not sick and she's not in danger. That's all I can say."

That's not a hell of a lot. Charles fought down an impulse to charge over to Melanie's hotel and demand to know everything. The surge of primal protectiveness in him was outside his civilized norm.

Control was his strength. He didn't debate his strategies with his clients. He wrote his plan for action and gave them a choice to stay or walk away. They stayed because no matter how rich they were, they wanted more and knew he could deliver.

He was the same way with women—in control and detached. *This is what I can offer you. Take it or leave it.*

Most stayed. A few walked away. Neither decision affected him for long.

He kept his relationships simple, uncomplicated—everything that Melanie wasn't. From what Sarah was saying, Melanie needed a friend more than she needed a lover, and that wasn't what he wanted from her. He'd call her to make sure she was okay, but he needed to stay the hell away from her physically.

He said good night to his sister and hung up before he gave in and asked another question that would betray how his fascination with Melanie was bordering on an obsession. He remembered how Melanie's voice had been husky, as if he'd woken her when he'd called, and fought the desire to call her to hear it one more time.

Was she sleeping?

Or was she awake and upset?

He reminded himself that either way it was none of his business.

Chapter Four

"Do you want me to wait?" the cab driver asked when he pulled up to the front of the Jones's home early the next evening.

Amazing how easy it is to find excuses to delay what you don't want to do.

Melanie told herself she couldn't go to Todd's parents' home first thing in the morning. She needed time to plan what she was going to say. She also told herself it didn't make sense to go in the afternoon since most people worked during the day. They probably wouldn't be there until around dinnertime, so why waste a taxi ride? An hour ago, with her stomach churning nervously, she'd confronted her lack of action. *No more excuses.*

"No," Melanie said, handing him his fare and a tip. If she had an escape route, she just might use it. Besides, the neighborhood looked safe. As safe as any street in a big city could.

New York wasn't actually any more chaotic than parts of Melanie's life in Texas had been. She'd done her share of rodeo roping while in high school. She'd handled crowds, thundering hooves of excited animals when she took a fall, and even rodeo clowns occasionally groping her while pretending to help her up, even after she was back on her feet. Melanie raised her chin with determination. *I've never let spooked horses or drunk cowboys intimidate me. I can do this.*

She looked up at the town house and searched for clues about the people who lived inside. It looked like an expensive home. Did that mean Todd's family had money? Would that be a good or bad thing? She'd dressed in simple jeans and a white cotton blouse. Part of her had been tempted to buy a new wardrobe for the trip, but she felt strong in her cowboy boots and denims.

This is who I am.

It was important to Melanie for Todd's parents to see her for who she was. She was born country and would stay country. If they couldn't accept her, they wouldn't accept Jace for who he was, either.

And I'll have my answer. I'll know I was right to keep Jace away from them.

With strong, purposeful strides, Melanie walked to the door, rang the doorbell, and held her breath. She checked the time on her phone. Six o'clock. Could they still be at work? She rang the doorbell again.

No answer. She leaned back and searched for movement in any of the windows. Nothing.

Melanie reached into the back pocket of her jeans and pulled out a small piece of paper with a phone number on it. She dialed it and closed her eyes as it rang once and then again.

Please answer.

"You've reached Deborah and Ryan Jones. Sorry we missed you. If you're listening to this recording, Ryan and I are still in Mykonos. You can reach us at . . ." The woman quickly said an international phone number.

Melanie sank to her knees on the welcome mat outside their door. *They're not here and they're not going to be.*

What the hell was I thinking? Oh my God, I wasted so much money coming here. So much time. I spent last night looking at the ceiling, trying to figure out what to say.

And they're not even fucking here.

A man stopped and asked her if she was okay. She automatically answered that she was, then took a deep gulp of air.

None of this is fucking okay. Not me. Not this.

What do I do now?

She pushed herself off the ground, dug a pen and paper out of her purse, and called the number again. Once she had their international number written down, she buried her phone back in her purse and gave herself a mental shake.

She could still find Todd. There were eighty-seven age-appropriate *Todd Jones* listings in New York City's online phone book, and if she had to call each one of them, she would.

Worst case, that was at most eighty-six times a guy wouldn't know what she was talking about when she reminded him that she had slept with him in college.

No, I guess all eighty-seven not remembering me would be worse. Seriously, one of you slept with me. I just don't know which one.

She sighed, wishing phone books had photos.

Melanie almost hailed a cab, but she was too wound up. A walk would do her good. Luckily, New York streets were numbered. That would make finding the way back to her hotel easy. She was only fifteen blocks away.

Despite her mood, she felt a faint rush of pride that she could already navigate the city. She'd spent so much time hiding from the world that she'd begun to fear it. Those insecurities were falling away as she pushed herself outside her comfort zone.

As she walked, she took a paper from her pocket listing all of the Todd Joneses in Manhattan and studied it like there were answers in that long string of numbers. *I haven't failed. This is a delay, that's all.* Calling Todd's parents in Greece would mean that the conversation wouldn't happen the way she'd hoped, but maybe she was being foolish to think she'd see something in their eyes. Gain further insight from their body language.

Greece was about six or seven hours ahead, which would make it past midnight there. If they even answered, it wasn't the best time to call. She'd waited this long to talk to them. She could wait until tomorrow morning.

She put the paper into her back pocket again. For some reason, she heard her father's voice in her head: "Nothing worth doing is ever easy." It was one of his favorite sayings and one that she'd rolled her eyes at every time he'd said it. Today she clung to it.

Just because this isn't easy doesn't mean it's not the right thing to do.

Hopefully, it means the exact opposite.

She hadn't told her parents she was going to New York, and this was the first moment she'd regretted not telling them where she was. Even though she was on speaking terms with them again, they weren't what she would call close. They talked around everything that mattered.

It took distance to allow Melanie to see the role she had played in that as well. When she'd discovered that she was pregnant, she'd been ashamed to admit it was from a man she barely knew. So when her parents had pushed her for the information about the baby's father, she'd pushed back and said things she'd regretted the moment she'd voiced them.

She'd taken out her anger with herself and Todd on her parents. She saw that now. In a movie, her parents would have understood that and loved her through it. *Well, life isn't a fucking movie. In reality, anger doesn't birth deeper understanding—it spawns more anger.* And that's exactly what had happened. Her father had gone nose to nose with her, met her anger with his own, and followed her threats with some of his own.

She missed her parents in a way she hadn't allowed herself to since she'd walked out of their home. She decided then and there to do something about it when she returned to Texas. *I've come this far to meet Todd's parents. I need to find a way back to my own.*

Her phone rang in her purse. Melanie paused in the middle of the street to dig it out. She looked at the caller ID before stepping to the sidewalk.

Charles.

She laughed and shook her head. Of course it would be him. What a perfectly fucked-up way to round off the day. She answered it. "Hello?"

"Where are you? Your hotel said you're still checked in but you're not there."

"You called my hotel?"

Charles was silent for a moment. "Tell me where you are. I'll come pick you up."

She looked around and read the sign. "I'm on East 23rd and Madison. I don't need a ride. I'm only six blocks from my hotel."

"I'm on my way."

A nervous shiver went up her back and she paused from walking again. There was something in his voice. "Did something happen?"

Before he had time to answer, Melanie felt herself being pulled nearly off her feet as a young man grabbed her purse off her shoulder and started to run away with it. All the emotions that had been building within her that day rose and fused in a fury she'd never before experienced. "I'll kill him," she growled.

"Who? What are you talking about?" Charles demanded.

"Some little bastard just robbed me. He is not getting away with it." Melanie hung up on him, stuffed her cell phone into her front pocket, and took off running after the man who had taken her purse. He was fast, but she was faster. She grabbed one of his thin arms and swung him around, causing him to fall as his momentum continued to pull him forward.

He scrambled to his feet. He was tall, but upon closer inspection looked like he was no older than his late teens.

Melanie advanced on him. "Give me back my damn purse."

He whipped out a small knife. "Don't be stupid, lady. I don't want to have to hurt you."

Melanie took another step toward him. "My son cuts his food with bigger knives than that. One of us is going to get hurt, but I can guarantee you it's not going to be me. Now, one last time before I kick your ass. Give me back my purse."

Charles barked Melanie's location to his driver and cursed his decision to request a limo for the day. He normally found them cumbersome in the heavy New York traffic, but they did allow for a certain amount a privacy that a town car didn't.

A privacy he'd decided the day would require at two o'clock that morning, when he'd changed his mind about pursuing Melanie. He had written off the possibility of anything happening between them while she was there based on two assumptions that weren't necessarily true. First, although Sarah wouldn't share why Melanie was in the city, that didn't mean it was a bad thing. Maybe she was there for a potential job or to have an old tattoo removed or any number of reasons she didn't want everyone back on the ranch to know about. So staying away from her because she was in a fragile state was unnecessary unless he found out differently. Second, he assumed that she would want a relationship with him that wouldn't be possible because of her child. Not every woman did. She might be looking for exactly what he was—a quick fling to demystify their attraction.

The driver stopped at a red light and Charles slammed an open hand against the stationary part of the divider. "Run it. We need to get to her."

"Who, sir?"

"Melanie. Someone mugged her. It sounds like she's going after him. Run every fucking light. Just get there."

"Yes, sir. Maybe you should call the police."

The police.

Of course. He wasn't a man who panicked, but the image of Melanie confronting her assailant alone ripped away his usual calm. He was supposed to watch over her while she was in the city. He'd already failed to keep her safe.

He should have told her how to hold her purse. He should have warned her to be careful. She didn't know what to do or not to do in a city like New York. Fuck, he should have hired a car for her for the week. He could have cleared his schedule for the day and made sure she made it to wherever she was going.

He hadn't wanted to get involved. But he was fucking involved now.

Something in her voice when she'd decided to go after the man who'd robbed her had sliced through years of emotional scarring and ripped open an old wound. *She doesn't know how quickly a life can be lost. How one moment of stupidity can provide a lifetime of regret.*

He rang the local emergency number.

"911, what is your emergency?"

"There is a woman being mugged on East 23rd and Madison."

"Can you see her? Are you near her?"

He wanted to scream, *I wouldn't need you if I were fucking there.* But he didn't. He wasn't there and although he was racing to her, he'd take any advantage he could get. Anything that would save Melanie.

"No, I was on the phone with her when it happened."

"What was the last thing she said to you?"

Cutting through what he considered nonsense, Charles snapped, "Do you have an officer on the street near her? Is there a car in the vicinity? If so, get them to her."

"Sir, I'll need more information to be able to help her. What is she wearing?"

"I don't know," he answered angrily. "Probably jeans and cowboy boots. She has long brown hair."

"I have an officer on that street. He hasn't seen anything unusual. I'm calling one of the cars we have in the area. If you have her number, call it. She may be fine. People are mugged every day, sir. It's an awful thing, but it happens. If you have access to another phone, I'll stay on while you try to reach her."

"Give me your phone," Charles ordered his driver. He called Melanie. It rang, but she didn't answer. His heart beat painfully in his chest and he spoke to the emergency operator in a tight voice. "She's not answering her phone."

"I have a car on that street, sir. Keep trying her."

After what seemed like an unsurvivable amount of time, Charles spotted Melanie on the side of the road. She was standing in the middle of a circle of people. "That's her. Pull over," he ground out, and began to open the back door before the limo stopped.

"Sir," the operator said, "is she all right?"

Charles didn't answer. He burst out of the back of the limo and sprinted across the street. In all of his life he couldn't remember being as ready to kill someone as he was in that moment. If the man who had mugged her were still there, he wouldn't be standing for long.

The crowd parted and Charles came to a sliding stop as he neared what looked like a scene from an action movie. Melanie had her boot firmly planted on the back of a man who had his hands tied behind his back with a belt.

She saw Charles and held up her purse triumphantly. "He mugged the wrong woman."

Charles shook his head in disbelief as his fear was replaced with anger. "Are you insane? You could have been killed." He took Melanie by the arm and searched her face for any sign that she'd been hurt. "Nothing in your purse is worth your life."

The man on the ground struggled to stand, but Melanie shoved him back down. "By this guy? Shoot, he's never seen a day of hard work in his life. I've wrestled newborn calves with more muscle than he has."

With no words that could express how he felt in that moment, Charles gave in and pulled Melanie to him. He claimed her mouth, holding her tightly to him as he unleashed his emotions through a feverish kiss. She opened her mouth wider to him, welcoming him inside even though he'd given her no opportunity to deny him.

Emotions he'd long repressed surfaced even as the pleasure of finally tasting her shook him. Their tongues met and he groaned aloud. Their connection was as hot as he'd imagined it would be and, as her hands gripped his shoulders for support, he didn't care where they were or who witnessed their kiss. He hadn't lost her. He hadn't failed to keep someone safe a second time.

Only the sound of applause brought him back to reality. He tore his mouth from hers and looked around. People were snapping pictures with their phones and cheering.

A police officer pushed his way through the crowd. By the time he reached them, he'd heard the story of what had happened several times as excited onlookers gushed about what they had seen.

"Are you okay, ma'am?" the officer asked.

Melanie stared at the cop wordlessly and swayed. She looked from him to Charles and back but still said nothing.

"Can you get this crazy bitch away from me?" the assailant, who was struggling to stand with his hands tied behind him, asked.

The officer hauled the man to his feet and turned him to inspect the knot around his hands. "I spent some time in the rodeo down in Abilene. Looks like I missed one hell of a takedown here."

Melanie nodded. "Don't mess with a Texan who's having a bad day."

The officer tipped his police hat to her as if it were a Stetson. "I've been in New York for a long time, but not long enough to forget that." He held the man by one arm and said, "You'll need to come down to the station and file a report."

Melanie studied the young man's face and said, "No. Everyone deserves a chance to turn their life around. Maybe this is his wake-up call. Can you drive him to someone who might be able to help him see that?"

"He needs to be off the streets," Charles snarled.

"He's only a boy," Melanie defended hotly.

"A boy who will go right back to mugging people the moment we release him." He turned to the officer and said, "If he's not eighteen, then I would think you have every right to deliver him home to whoever his guardians are."

The police officer agreed.

Melanie looked earnestly at her assailant again and implored, "People make mistakes every day. Don't repeat this one. You're better than this."

The young man spit in her direction in disgust.

Charles pulled her away from him, planting himself between them. "You little shit. You don't deserve her sympathy. You deserve—"

Melanie stopped him with a hand on his chest. "Don't, Charles. We don't know what he's been through."

The police officer removed the belt and returned it to Melanie. He looked around the crowd as if he wanted to say more, but held his words back. In the world where everything was being recorded, it was a wise decision. "Come on," he said to the young man and put him in the backseat of the police car. "Where is home?"

The boy said something scathing that Charles didn't hear and, honestly, didn't care to. "Let's go," Charles said after the police left. He put his hand on Melanie's lower back to guide her, but she didn't budge.

She touched her slightly swollen lips with one hand and shook her head. "I don't think that's a good idea."

Charles leaned down and growled into her ear. "I am this close," he measured an inch in the air with his other hand, "to throwing you over my shoulder and carrying you to my car . . . or you can walk there with me and not make today more of a YouTube spectacle. Your choice."

She looked around and blushed when she realized that people were still filming their exchange with their phones. She nodded and started walking with him. "Okay, but I want to go back to my hotel."

He didn't say anything.

He didn't have to.

They both knew that wasn't going to happen.

Chapter Five

Sitting a good six inches from her in the back of his limo and staring straight ahead, Charles didn't look like a man who had just given her the most passionate kiss of her lifetime. She *definitely* did not imagine that. She may have been confused about many other things, but that kiss made his feelings pretty clear.

So why did she feel like she'd been called to the principal's office for throwing a stone through a window?

Is he upset that the kiss was photographed? That's not my fault. I didn't ask to be mugged. And I damn well didn't ask him to come rushing to my rescue or kiss me.

He must have given the driver instructions at the door of the limo before he'd joined her, because everyone seemed to know where they were going except her. All she knew for sure was her hotel was the other way. As the awkward silence between them stretched painfully through several traffic lights, Melanie became impatient. She folded her arms across her chest and stormed, "If you're angry with me about something, just say it. But I won't sit here while you give me the silent treatment. If you have nothing to say, pull the car over and let me out. I've had a bad enough day without this."

He swung around to face her, and his expression robbed her of further speech. There was a confusing mix of anger and passion in his eyes. When he spoke, his voice was ragged. "You could have been killed today."

The depth of his response to that possibility rocked her. She relived the scenario from his perspective and instantly regretted how she'd handled it. *Oh my God, I told the man I was being robbed and then hung up on him. Here I am thinking he was overcome with lust for me, when really I just worried him into a grateful-but-I-would-like-to-shake-you-for-putting-me-through-this kiss.*

Of all the ways she'd dreamed she could make him feel, scared for her life was not one of them. She closed her eyes for a moment, gathered her strength, opened them, and said, "I wasn't thinking. I'm sorry. I was angry and I reacted. I shouldn't have hung up on you."

His jaw tightened. "You shouldn't have chased that man."

"Not man. Boy. I bet he's not even eighteen, Charles."

Charles made a disgusted sound in his chest. "He had a knife. You should have pressed charges."

Melanie met his angry gaze but could not agree, not even if she thought that doing so would improve his mood. "Don't you want to know what brought him to the dark place he's in?"

"I don't care. I don't need his backstory to know that he's a criminal who needs to be taken off the streets." When Melanie didn't waver, he continued, "You have a lot to learn about surviving in a city. Watch the news tonight. The streets are full of crime. Do you want me to pretend I care about each offender? I won't. And your concern is better saved for their victims."

An image of the young man spitting at her on the sidewalk was still vivid in Melanie's mind. She thought about the people who had watched her chase the boy and how they had taken pictures instead of coming to her aid, not exhibiting much compassion for victim or assailant. "First, I don't want to learn whatever lesson you think I need. Maybe it would be overwhelming to try to care about everyone in need in the city, but I didn't meet everyone. I met one angry kid. And you may not care if he has anyone to go home to, but I do. If you can't understand that, then you're not the man I thought you were."

An angry red flush spread up his cheeks. "You have no idea what kind of man I am."

Shaking her head, Melanie said, "Ask your driver to stop. I want to get out."

"No," Charles said firmly.

Still sitting with her arms crossed in front of her, Melanie said, "I wasn't asking."

A new light entered his eyes. Charles turned fully toward her and ran a thumb down her jaw, taking her chin in his hand to turn her face toward him. "I want you, Melanie."

Melanie swallowed hard. Desire burst through her at his declaration, but that didn't make it a wise choice. "I'm not going to sleep with you."

A small smile of challenge curled his lips. "No?"

She met his eyes bravely. "No. I didn't come to New York for this."

He slid a possessive hand behind her neck and buried it in her hair, pulling her closer to him. "From the first moment I saw you, this is all I've been able to think about." He bent and again claimed her mouth with his.

She wanted to resist him. She told herself that she'd learned her lesson with men. He wanted her now, but what would she mean to him tomorrow? Probably nothing. *I'm a convenient fuck. Here today, forgotten tomorrow.*

No different than Todd.

Unfortunately, even as her mind argued for sanity, her body hummed and surrendered to him. This wasn't just any man—this was the one she'd spent months imagining doing exactly this with and who being with was far exceeding her fantasies. She was writhing against him, eager. His mouth left hers and went to her neck. He kissed it hungrily. Expertly one of his hands undid the front of her blouse and he pushed the material aside. Melanie didn't have time to regret her practical cotton bra. He unclipped it from behind and closed his mouth on one of her exposed breasts.

Her hands gripped his shoulders as he lifted her and sat her in his lap. She closed her eyes and lost herself in the hot pleasure that shot through her each time his tongue lapped her nipple. She shuddered when his teeth playfully nipped her.

Nothing in her prior sexual experiences had prepared her for how Charles made her feel. This wasn't the sweet tentative sex of high school. It wasn't the quick, unsatisfying sex she'd experienced with Todd. She didn't ask herself if this was right or wrong. There wasn't room for thought between the waves of desire that rocked through her.

His hungry kisses brought her to tingling life until there were only two parts of her, the scorched trail of where his mouth had been and the quivering aching areas that craved his attention. He took her other breast into his mouth, and Melanie cried out his name and buried her hands in the back of his hair. He made large circles with his hot tongue, warming and building anticipation for when he'd reach her eager nipple. When he finally closed his teeth around it, chasing the tip of his tongue back and forth over it with quick, forceful strokes, Melanie fisted her hands and cried out again.

She couldn't breathe, couldn't think past holding him there desperately, willing to do anything to prolong the sensations washing over her. Charles knew how to please a woman, and his every caress pushed Melanie toward a flame that threatened to consume her.

He impatiently unsnapped the front of her jeans and slid a hand down her lower back, beneath the elastic of her panties to cup her ass. His touch was more about ownership than exploration. He rubbed his hand over both of her cheeks and between, building a warm friction that had Melanie rubbing herself against the pulsing mound of his still-contained erection.

His other hand slid down her stomach, beneath the front of her panties, and sought her wet slit. Melanie shifted her position to allow him better access. Without hesitation, he slid his middle finger between her wet folds and circled her clit. Melanie threw back her head with a moan, moving herself against his hand, begging him wordlessly to continue. He ran his finger over her clit once, then again, experimenting with his rhythm until she was gasping for breath. Then he lifted his head and demanded, "Open your eyes, Melanie. Look at me."

She did because she was incapable of not obeying him in that moment. He took her nub between his thumb and finger and began an expert gentle rub that had her biting her bottom lip. Behind her, his hand continued to knead her, gripping her more forcefully as his own breathing became more and more ragged.

She brought her mouth down on his and gripped both sides of his head as she welcomed his tongue with hers again. His thrusts were deep and relentless and she offered him more.

He slid a finger deeper inside her and she gasped into his mouth. His other hand held her slightly off him so he could thrust his finger in and out of her powerfully.

She reached for the front of his shirt, but he broke off the kiss long enough to growl into her ear. "No."

She didn't question his command. His touch was all that mattered. He took her mouth again and thrust a second finger inside her. His expert rhythm made all thought impossible.

When he broke off the kiss, she was spiraling toward an orgasm, and still his mouth relentlessly claimed her body. Each time she thought she could take no more, he discovered a new equally sensitive spot. She threw back her head and exposed her neck more fully to him, loving how he began alternating hot kisses with light nips. His warm breath teased her ear before he kissed his way to it. He growled, "You're so tight. So wet."

It felt wrong and so right at the same time.

Melanie clenched her muscles around his thrusting fingers with a rhythm that increased her own pleasure. She moaned, then cried out his name again when his mouth returned to her breasts. Sucking. Nipping. Tugging on her nipples in a way that shot waves of heat through her.

Once again her hands sought the front of his shirt, but his fingers stilled and he raised his head and said, "Let yourself enjoy it, Melanie."

She did and was rewarded by his thumb once again circling her clit slowly, forcefully. He brought his other hand around and licked his thumb before rubbing it back and forth across her puckered nipple. Her position left her arched and bare from the waist up before him. Melanie gasped and shifted against his other hand, welcoming his fingers deeper inside her. She held his eyes because he silently commanded her to.

Heat spread up her chest and through her stomach. She gave herself to the orgasm and to him in the same cry of submission. He increased the pace of his thrusting fingers as he pinched her nipple, sending a sting of pain that only increased the intensity of her pleasure. She cried out again, helplessly jerking against his hand as her orgasm consumed her.

He withdrew his hand from the front of her jeans and brought his fingers up to his mouth and licked her juices off, then said, "You taste better than I imagined. I am going to spread you open and feast on every part of you tonight." He took her hand and placed it on the bulge in his pants. "And then, and only then, I want that sweet mouth on my cock. I want that glorious hair on my thighs as I come."

Melanie shivered and brought her arms around to cover the front of her. He took her hands in his and brought them to her sides, exposing her again. "You're too beautiful to hide, Melanie." He looked out the window and groaned. "Although, you should cover up while we walk into my building." He released her and handed her shirt to her, but tucked her bra into his jacket pocket.

Melanie shrugged into her blouse and straightened her jeans, then went to move off his lap, but he held her there with a hand on either hip. Desire for her burned in those dark blue eyes, giving her courage to lay a hand on his chest. His heart was beating wildly. She moved a tentative hand down his stomach, but he took it in one of his and held it captive against the outside of his thigh. "Not here," he said and instead slid her off his lap and brought her beneath his arm, against his side.

A part of her wanted to protest, but being in his arms, especially in the aftermath of a climax, was heaven. Tucked against him as she was, she felt safe and treasured. Even if their connection was temporary, it was what her life lacked—and no amount of common sense could have pulled her away from him in that moment.

A short time later, in what felt like a dream sequence, he escorted her from the limo in the parking garage to the elevator. She would have been hard-pressed to describe either later. He used a key in the elevator to unlock the penthouse floor. The air sizzled as they rode toward it without speaking. He led her through a large foyer, a hallway she didn't spare a glance at, and into his bedroom.

They stood at the foot of his pristine gray king-size bed looking at each other without speaking, the only sound in the room their ragged breathing. Very softly, he said, "Strip for me."

She hesitated. He had given nothing of himself. Without her clothing, she would be exposed and vulnerable before him again. She wasn't ready for that.

He held her eyes. Instead of reaching for her as she expected, he waited, eyes burning with desire for her. "Take off your shirt."

There was something in his soft command she couldn't resist. She wasn't one who followed direction without question, but when he looked at her, she wanted to go wherever he would take her. Unlike how she'd felt for years, here she felt free. Not looking away from him, she unbuttoned her shirt and dropped it to the floor.

"Now the rest." She did as he ordered and as each article of clothing hit the floor, her confidence grew. Not needing further coaxing, she slid off her boots, pants, and underwear and stood naked and proud before him. He didn't touch her, but she felt his hot gaze on her breasts, and her nipples puckered in anticipation of his mouth returning to them.

He wants me as much I as I want him. The thought was empowering. He might have thought he was in control, but she arched one shoulder and reveled in how his nostrils flared and a flush darkened his cheeks.

He stepped toward her and ran the back of one hand across her collarbone, down the curve of one of her breasts, and along her flat stomach until he cupped her sex.

"So beautiful," he said softly. He took her face in his other hand and forced her to meet his gaze.

In that moment, beneath his gaze, Melanie felt beautiful.

"Where do you want my mouth first?" he whispered in her ear. "Show me." He took one of her hands in his and guided it to her wet slit, thrusting one of her own fingers inside herself, then bringing her finger to his lips to kiss it. "Would you like me to start there?" He took her finger deep inside his mouth and suckled it. "That's where I want to start, but I'll let you decide."

Melanie couldn't speak, she was so hypnotized by her need for him. He ran her hand across her own breast. "Touch where you want my mouth. Show me, Melanie. Show me what you want."

Melanie brought her hand up to her lips and boldly circled her finger with her own tongue, testing his response. He hauled her to him and claimed her mouth, thrusting between her lips and seeking out the tongue she'd teased him with. He drew her into his mouth and they met with a frenzy Melanie had never before experienced. She was outside herself, lost to the sensations he elicited in her, a slave to her own desire.

Then he stopped.

And looked down into her eyes.

She touched the spot just below her right ear and gasped when his mouth followed her command. Everything she'd experienced earlier was repeated, but this time with a sense that she'd requested it and he was delivering in spades. There was a heady power in knowing she was guiding their coupling.

And it made her bolder.

She brought his hand to her mouth, licked it, and placed it on her left breast. Once again she experienced the wet delight of him circling, then sucking. He laved one of her breasts so thoroughly she thought she'd come again, then moved on to the other and Melanie was reduced to whimpering.

He stopped again and raised his head. She swallowed hard and turned before him, moving her hair to the side and exposing her back to him. He groaned and ran his hand from her shoulder down the length of her and rubbed between her buttocks. He kissed the back of her neck, then down her spine, and nipped one of her ass cheeks. Melanie shook from the sensations coursing through her.

Right or wrong, it felt too good to stop.

He spun her unexpectedly and pushed her backward until her legs hit the side of the bed and she sank down into it. Then, without waiting for further instruction, he pulled her forward so she was sitting on the very edge and, still fully dressed, knelt before her. With a hand on either of her knees, he spread her wide for him and smiled in a predatory fashion that made Melanie's heart thud loudly in her chest.

He ran one finger over the outer edge of her half-closed lower lips. "I can't get enough of you." His hot breath warmed her inner thighs. With two strong fingers, he separated her outer folds and blew on her clit. Melanie's hands tightened on the bedcovers beneath her. His tongue, which had danced within her mouth, now ran the length of her bottom lovingly. Wetting. Tasting. Claiming.

Lost in the feel of him lapping her, circling her, thrusting his thick wet tongue inside of her again and again, Melanie dropped back on the bed and once again gave herself over to the experience. Her head rolled back and forth helplessly as she writhed against his mouth.

He blew on her exposed clit again and Melanie shuddered. His other hand ran up her stomach and roughly massaged her breast. His breathing became harsher. He thrust his tongue deeply into her as his hand on her waist tightened painfully, but it was a pain she welcomed.

He pulled back and the cold air of the room was its own brash caress. He alternated circling her clit with his tongue with deep, bold thrusts that left her breathless and begging for release.

When she was nearing orgasm for the second time that day, he stood and shed his clothing, pausing only to sheathe himself with a condom before lifting up her hips, holding her legs on either side of him, leaving her draped down against the bed before him.

His first thrust was deep and sure. Melanie's body strained to accept the size of him as he pounded into her. She moved back and forth with him, unable to reach him with her hands. He controlled their rhythm and their connection.

She gave herself completely over to his control with a level of passion she'd never dreamed possible. In that moment, she was his to do with as he wished. It didn't make sense to her, but it didn't have to. Not while her body quivered and clamored for him to drive himself deeper into her.

And he did. His powerful thrusts pounded her again and again until he came with an animallike cry. She joined him, coming with her own shuddering cry and collapsing in the aftermath of it.

He withdrew and walked across the room to clean himself off. When he didn't immediately join her on the bed, she moved farther onto the mattress and pulled her legs up, wrapping the sheet around her. *No. No. No.* The past circled like a vulture she was powerless to fend off. *He's not Todd and I'm not an insecure young girl who needs to know he'll call me tomorrow.*

Still, the passionate man from a moment before was gone and in his place was a composed stranger she couldn't read. His withdrawal after the intimacy was devastating.

He opened his mouth as if he was about to say something, then closed it again and frowned. She hugged the sheet closer to her. *All you have to do, Charles, is crawl back into this bed and hold me. Just let me lay in your arms and have a few hours of believing you care about me.*

A few hours of not feeling so utterly alone.

She hated the tears that clouded her vision and hated him for not giving her what she couldn't ask for. For making her feel even lonelier than she had when she'd landed in this godforsaken city. He just stood there frowning down at her, clearly regretting what they'd done and seeking the words to tell her.

Shame nipped at her.

If I don't die from the mortification of this, I swear I'm done with men.

And that starts with you, Charles Dery.

Charles stood frozen in the middle of the room, watching Melanie get more upset, and feeling like more and more of an ass with each passing minute. This was exactly what he'd wanted to avoid. Yes, he'd wanted her, but not like this.

She was waiting for him to speak, but he was running internal damage control. Everything he'd imagined saying no longer fit the situation now that he'd seen tears welling in her eyes. He'd rushed her and he hadn't intended to.

He'd planned a nice dinner, followed by a recommendation that they spend time together that week. He'd imagined all the delicious ways he could persuade her to give in to him, but he'd resolved to talk to her first. She needed to know he couldn't offer her anything long-term.

If she agreed to his terms, then and only then, would he have had her.

Now she was curled up defensively on his bed, and he was furious with himself. He stepped into his trousers and frowned as he sought what to say to her. "Melanie, I'm sorry . . ." He realized it was a poor choice of words when angry fire shot from her eyes.

She hopped up and, still holding a sheet protectively around herself, wordlessly gathered her clothing. He took a step toward her, then stopped when she glared up at him. In a heartbeat she was dressed and stomping her feet into her boots.

He reached for her but she evaded him. "Don't touch me."

The pain in her eyes tore at him. "Melanie . . ."

She didn't say anything else, just looked around the room for her purse impatiently. When she spotted it, she swung it over her shoulder and started heading for the door. Still bare-chested, he blocked her way. Somehow he had to make her see that he wasn't rejecting her. "Don't go. We need to talk. I want—"

She pushed at him angrily. "Do you know what I want?" she growled.

He shook his head.

"I want this goddamned day to be over. I want you to stay the hell away from me while I try to forget this ever happened. Can you do that for me?"

Guilt rushed in, the only force strong enough to stop him from grabbing her and forcing her to listen to him. The anguish in her eyes was real and so was the remorse he felt. When she looked up at him with her heart in her eyes, even his ability to articulate how he felt left him. He didn't want her to go, but he wasn't ready to ask her to stay.

The door of his apartment slammed behind her as she left.

Charles strode into the living room and punched the wall beside the door she'd walked through.

I'm as fucked up as Mason says I am.

She's better off without me.

Chapter Six

"Hello, is Todd Jones available?" Melanie asked into her phone as she sat at the small desk in her hotel room.

"This is Todd."

"Did you attend Baylor University?"

The line went dead. Melanie calmly checked off the correct column on her growing list. Originally there had been only two columns: "Yes" and "No." Ten men into her list of Todds to call, she'd added a new option: "Unable to determine."

Calling Todd's parents would have been the more efficient route, but last night with Charles had reminded her of the perils of being spontaneous. *I will do this the right way. I'll find him, watch him, then make an educated decision about how to move forward before I tell anyone anything.*

Memories from the night before still stung her pride.

I'll survive. I'm a big girl.

I'm not the first woman to have a one-night stand with a man I shouldn't have and I'm sure I won't be the last.

Melanie called the next Todd on her list. A man answered on the third ring. "Hello?"

"Hello, I'm looking for Todd Jones."

"You got him."

Taking a deep breath, Melanie asked, "Is there any chance that you attended Baylor in Waco, Texas?"

After a moment of consideration, the man answered, "Why do you want to know?"

Because I may have slept with you? Because you may have a son who wants to meet you? Because after last night I deserve to ask every Todd in New York if he's the man I had sex with in college. Maybe then I'll remember why I'm here and what's really important. "I'm hoping to connect with an old friend."

"And you think I'm him?"

Melanie closed her eyes and rubbed an eyebrow in frustration. "You could be."

"Piece of advice? Forget the guy. If you don't remember his voice, he didn't mean that much to you."

"I wish it were that simple," Melanie said sadly.

The man on the other side of the line sighed. "I'd love to help you, but I've never been to Texas. I hope you find him."

Emotion tightened Melanie's throat. "Thank you."

She opened her eyes, hung up the phone, and put a check in the "No" column.

Only sixty Todds to go.

Squaring her shoulders, she called the next number.

"Hello?" a woman answered.

"I'm looking for Todd Jones."

"Who is this?"

"A friend?" Melanie said awkwardly.

"I'm going to kill him! He said he was done cheating. I can put up with the drinking if he's faithful, but he can't keep it in his pants, can he? My friends told me to leave him, but did I take their advice? No. I believed him—"

"Wait, you don't understand."

"Oh trust me, I understand perfectly. He told you he was divorced right? Or dying? Or is he making up some new story for this round? Maybe this time I'm dead?"

"I'm so sorry. I shouldn't have called."

"You did me a favor. Believe me—"

"No, listen, even if your Todd is the one I'm looking for, I haven't seen him in years."

"Then you're the lucky one," the woman said and hung up.

Well, that went well.

Melanie studied her list and added a new column—"HELL NO, even if it is him"—and put a check beneath it. That was one Todd Jones who would never meet Jace.

With a tired stretch, Melanie stood and walked to the window of her hotel room. The way the trip was going, Todd probably lived in Alaska now . . . or Australia.

She should have taken the money Sarah offered and hired a private detective.

What am I going to do if I find him? Follow him around the city until I'm convinced he's not dangerous?

Melanie took two papers out of her back pocket. She threw Charles's card in the trash and looked at the other one. *Todd's parents.* A quick glance at the clock revealed she would once again be calling them in the middle of the night.

Another wasted day.

Glad I don't keep a journal. I don't need written proof to see a pattern.

Everyone is gifted in something. I'm an exceptional procrastinator when it comes to facing something I don't want to.

Melanie took out her cell phone and called Sarah for a video chat. A picture of Sarah became live feed of the smiling blonde woman.

"Melanie, you're early. Jace is in the barn with Tony. Looks like Midnight will foal tonight or tomorrow. Jace didn't want to miss it. Want me to call him in?"

Melanie sat heavily down in the chair in front of the small desk. "In a minute. I need to talk to you first."

Sarah's smile fell away and she brought the phone closer to her face. "Did something happen? Did you find Jace's father?"

"Not yet," Melanie said, not even sure what she wanted to say to Sarah, though just hearing the voice of her only close friend was a comfort. Melanie lived only a few towns over from where she'd grown up. She'd had friends she'd known from before she'd started kindergarten. She always thought they'd grow old while living close by one another, but then she'd attended a different college from the rest of the crowd. She'd wanted to see more of the world. When she found out she was pregnant, some had rallied to her side, but Melanie had been too angry to accept their support. She'd distanced herself from them just as she'd distanced herself from her family.

Funny thing about the world—it goes on with or without you. When she'd turned down one invitation after the next, they stopped coming. Her old friends had graduated, married, and started families. Some had stayed local and some had moved away.

All while Melanie had hidden on Tony Carlton's ranch and blamed everyone but herself for how her life had turned out. Hidden with her boss, who had been just as bitter as she was.

Until Sarah had come into their lives and made them both believe in second chances. She was the most openly loving and understanding person Melanie had ever met. One would think someone that optimistic had lived a charmed life, but she hadn't.

Sarah had come to Texas with more than luggage and her horse. She'd brought a whole lot of guilt and sadness with her, also. Her younger brother had drowned while she, still a child herself, had been watching him, and that loss had, according to Sarah, shattered her family.

People talk about how strong families are, but no one warns that they can also be as fragile as glass left out in the snow. One wrong tap and they shatter into hundreds of irreparable pieces.

Or so Melanie had thought before she met Sarah.

Sarah's family may have been ravaged by a tragedy, but she hadn't given up. She'd refused to be defined by her mistakes.

Melanie didn't consider Jace a mistake. She couldn't imagine her life without him. But she wasn't proud of how she'd handled herself since his birth. Until she'd met Sarah, she'd let that disappointment in herself shape how she saw herself and what she considered herself capable of.

Not anymore. For that transformation, Sarah would always own a special place in Melanie's heart. "Sarah, I came here because I thought I could make things better, but what if I make them worse? What if none of this was a good idea?"

Sarah gave her the encouragement Melanie knew she would. "There is no way to know until you do it. But you're a good mother, Melanie. Trust your instincts."

Melanie blinked back tears and looked away. "That's the point. I don't know if I have any. I thought I did. Now I'm so confused."

Case in point, sleeping with Charles.

"Do you want me to fly up there? David and Tony can watch Jace."

"No, I'm okay," Melanie said quickly. Having Sarah join her in New York was the same as admitting that she couldn't do this alone. And it was important to Melanie to prove to herself that she could.

"I'll call Charles. He's really good at giving advice. Trust me, really good. Most of the time you don't even have to ask for it."

"No," Melanie said emphatically.

A line of concern wrinkled Sarah's forehead. "Did he say something to offend you? He doesn't mean to. He's really a big softy once you get to know him."

A beep on Melanie's phone revealed an incoming call.

Charles.

It's like he knows we're talking about him.

She let his call ring through to voice mail.

"Please don't call your brother. He's done more than enough for me."

"If you're sure," Sarah said doubtfully.

"I couldn't be more so," Melanie said firmly. Changing the subject, Melanie asked, "Do you mind taking your phone out to Jace? I'd like to talk to him before I lie down, in case I fall asleep."

"Absolutely," Sarah said. As she walked to the barn, she continued to talk. "Don't think you have to go through this by yourself, Mel. If you need me, just call me. I don't care what time it is."

Love for her friend spread through Melanie, giving her the strength she'd been looking for. She put on a brave face in preparation for talking to her son. "I'm probably just tired today. Thank you, Sarah. For everything."

"Mama!" Jace exclaimed as soon as Sarah approached him with her phone. All of Melanie's concerns took a backseat to the joy she felt listening to her son tell her about his day.

An image of Charles hovered, but she beat it back.

This is what's important.

It was well past midnight when Charles sat up in his bed and flipped on the light. He threw back the bedcovers and, dressed only in boxers, went onto the large balcony of his apartment. He might have been trying to sleep, but New York never did. He found the sound of traffic below soothing.

Nothing has changed, he told himself. He was exactly where he belonged.

He didn't need a woman coming into his life and confusing him when he was so close to having everything he needed.

A woman who doesn't even answer my phone calls.

He rested his elbows on the railing, leaned forward with a sigh, and ran his eyes wearily over the surrounding buildings. Even this late at night, some offices were illuminated, most likely by people eager to achieve even a slice of what he had.

Should he tell them the ugly truth that he was just now starting to realize?

Offer rare personal advice?

Go home—if you still have someone to go home to. Being at the top feels empty if you have no one to share it with.

He slammed a hand down on the railing in frustration. He'd always considered himself one of those men who'd been born to be a bachelor. He'd never wanted the complicated mess marriage and kids brought. He'd never understood why any man would.

If the twisting in his gut were merely loneliness, calling any of the single women in his social circle would have sufficed. This was more than that.

Fight it as he tried, something about Melanie called to a part of him he'd denied for years. She was real in a way few people in his circle were. He barely knew her. But he wanted to.

He wanted that more than he had wanted anything in a very long time.

Calling her again wasn't an option he liked considering, but he needed to hear her voice—to make sure she was okay. In business, Charles was known for being decisive and dogged. He didn't back down. He set a goal and destroyed whatever and whoever stood between him and achieving it. He was a man who was used to winning.

By some men's definitions, he'd won when it came to Melanie. He'd wanted her and he'd had her. But the price had been higher than he could have guessed.

Every time he closed his eyes, he saw her face and the hurt she'd tried to conceal beneath her anger as she'd left him.

Anyone else would have hauled her back into bed and put her fears to rest. She thought he didn't care about her—he could tell. But he did. His initial instincts about her had been correct. She wasn't the type to have sex casually. He'd seen it in her eyes when she'd looked up at him, naked and vulnerable—waiting for him to proclaim something or callously walk away.

He wasn't the type to do either, but that didn't mean he didn't care. Which was what he would have explained to her if she'd been ready to hear him. The idea that she was hurting because of him was unbearable. He walked into his apartment and found his cell phone.

Melanie answered in a voice husky and groggy from sleep. "Hello?"

"It's me."

He heard a rustle of bedcovers, the click of a light, and then an audible groan. "It's one o'clock in the morning."

"We need to talk."

"No, we don't. I'm hanging up now."

He refused to let this conversation end as their last one had. "You'd rather discuss this in person?"

"I'd rather you take the hint and go away."

He took a deep breath and pushed forward honestly. Somehow, he would make her understand. "I never meant to hurt you. I shouldn't have slept with you. We should have taken it slower. That was my fault. I'm—"

"If you say you're sorry, I will scream. I used to think that not being called after sex was the worst thing that could happen, but I was wrong. I don't want to hear all the reasons why what we did was a bad idea. You think I don't know them? I do. I feel bad enough without you listing them for me. I don't need this. Don't call me again."

The line went dead.

Charles threw his phone onto the bed.

Fuck.

He paced back and forth, angry with himself for calling her, angry with her for making him feel even more like a heel.

He wasn't a man who stumbled over his words, but with her he found himself saying the most idiotic things. *Who the hell apologizes for sex? No wonder she hung up on me. What did I think she was going to do? Absolve me?*

Especially when they both knew he wasn't sorry.

Coming to a decision, Charles went to his closet and, merely out of habit, donned a suit. He gathered his phone and wallet, then called down to have his car brought around.

On the drive over to the hotel, he called his assistant. After giving her the moment she needed to wake up, he told her to clear his schedule for the next morning.

"Is everything okay?" she asked, her voice tight with concern.

"Not yet," he answered vaguely, "but I intend to remedy that." He hung up and called Mason's cell number.

"Hey," Mason answered easily. "What do you need?"

"Some advice," Charles growled and shifted the gears of his car forcefully.

"You have some nerve calling me at this time of night to discuss supporting your bill." Mason covered the phone partially and said to whoever was with him, "I have to take this call, darlin'. It's important. Call me next time you're in town, though."

Charles stopped for a red light, grunted with disgust, and raised a hand to press the disconnect button on his car phone. "You're busy."

"No, hang on."

Charles rolled his eyes through the sound of Mason saying good-bye again to a woman. A moment later, Mason let out a relieved sigh. "Perfect timing. I did not think I could get her to leave tonight. This is why I don't usually bring them home." It sounded like he flopped down on his couch. "Now, let's start over. What do you need?"

"I slept with Melanie, but I screwed it up."

Mason said with some amusement, "Most of the process should come naturally. If you're looking for pointers, though, I do have a few techniques I'm proud of."

With a groan, Charles said, "Why do I call you?"

In a much more serious tone, Mason said, "Sorry. I'm just not used to you like this."

"Like what?" Charles asked harshly.

"Unsure of yourself."

"Every time I talk to her I say something worse."

"Come on, it can't be all that bad."

"I apologized to her for sleeping with her."

"No fucking way."

"Twice."

Mason laughed. "You do need my help."

"She told me to stop calling her."

"I can't imagine why."

"I'm driving over to her hotel now."

"Because you've put the past behind you and it doesn't bother you anymore that she has a child?" When Charles didn't answer, Mason continued. "Or because you want to fuck her again?"

This was why he'd called Mason. He might be able to lie to himself, but he couldn't lie to someone who knew him so well. "I don't know," Charles said angrily, then repeated more quietly, "I don't know."

"I'm going to throw this out there and you do with it as you want. Most women don't appreciate a two a.m. apology."

"I have to see her. It's all I can think about. You've known me a long time, Mason. What the hell am I doing?"

Mason didn't answer at first, then he said, "I felt the same way about my first Ferrari. I had to have it. That first ride was sweet. I mean *amazing*. But after a while, any car is just that—another car. Date her. Get her out of your system. She's exciting because you put her on the forbidden list, but once you spend more time with her, I guarantee you the fascination will fade."

"I don't want to hurt her."

"So don't lie to her. Lay it out for her and let her decide what she wants to do. You may be surprised by her answer."

Charles nodded. "You're right. I'm making this into a bigger deal than it is."

"Exactly."

"I'll just tell her how it has to be."

"And then it's on her to stay or go."

Chapter Seven

Melanie had given up trying to sleep and was absently flipping between channels on the television as she ran through her last conversation with Charles for the hundredth time.

Why keep calling to apologize? Is he afraid I'll run back to Sarah with a sob story? That's not my style. I knew what I was doing when I went to his apartment with him.

He wanted me.

I wanted him.

There was nothing wrong with what happened.

The problem was in my head. I wanted him to tell me it meant something to him . . . that I meant something to him. Unfortunately, that doesn't happen when you sleep with men you barely know.

A loud knock on the door startled her out of her thoughts, and her hand stilled on the remote. Her head snapped to the clock to check the time. Half past two in the morning.

Her hotel was in a decent area, or so the travel sites had claimed, but it was cheaper than many she'd priced and sometimes that meant a wilder crowd.

Melanie looked around the room for something she could use as a weapon if it came to that. She picked up one of her boots and held it next to her on the bed. If swung just right, the heel of it could knock someone back long enough to buy her some time.

There was another knock, this time louder. "Melanie. It's Charles. Open the door."

An entirely different kind of fear filled Melanie. She clutched the boot to her, went up on her knees so she could see herself in the mirror, and groaned. There was nothing sexy about the disheveled woman in the knee-length T-shirt who stared back at her.

She sat back on her heels and shook her head.

No way in hell am I answering the door like this. Wait him out. He'll give up and go away.

"Melanie," he said her name as if he were issuing an order.

So much for plan A. "Go away. I don't want to see you."

"No."

Melanie stepped off the bed, still clutching the boot to her stomach, and approached the door. "I won't tell anyone what happened between us, Charles. You don't have to worry about that."

"Open the door."

Melanie peered through the peephole in the door. He was dressed in a business suit. Nothing in his hands. *What did I expect? Flowers? When am I going to learn?* She looked down at her unpainted toenails and shook her head.

Might as well get this over with.

Boot still in hand, she opened the door impatiently, placed a hand on her hip, and glared at him. "What do you want?"

He stepped forward, cupped her face between both of his hands, and pulled her into a kiss. She had been hurt by this man mere hours ago. She should throw him out. Tell him to go to hell.

Anything but give in to the kiss. But the second his lips were on hers, common sense and caution shook hands and left the room. Passion swept through Melanie and she came alive beneath his touch. He kissed her with the passion of a man returning to his woman. No excuses. No hesitation. And she couldn't help herself. She gave herself over to it. In that kiss she was his and they both knew it.

At the sound of her boot hitting the floor, he broke off the kiss and lowered his hands. "I want you, Melanie—like I've never wanted anyone in my life." He stepped past her into the room and closed the door behind him. He picked up the boot she'd dropped and tossed it across the room. When he looked up at her, she saw desire churning in his eyes.

It would have been ridiculous to claim she didn't feel the same. Whatever was between them was mutual.

But that didn't mean giving in to him again was a good idea. "Please. Just go."

He pulled her into the solid comfort of his embrace and buried his face in her hair. "I can't," he said simply.

She pushed against his chest angrily. "Why?"

His eyes burned. "Because I don't want to be anywhere else."

This time when he kissed her, it was a gentle request and one she didn't try to deny. She met his lips hungrily. *I don't know how to fix yesterday and I don't know what tomorrow holds—but I need this.*

"I don't, either," she said baldly.

With that, he swung her up into his arms and carried her to the bed. He lowered her to her feet just before it. With one sure move, he whisked her long T-shirt up over her head.

Melanie gasped and sputtered at his almost overwhelming forwardness, but all protest died on her lips when she saw the expression in his eyes. Never before had she felt adored by a man, but his gentle touch followed his gaze in an act of worship. He ran a hand down her exposed neck, the side of one breast, and settled on her still panty-clad hip. She shuddered in response.

"How long are you in New York?" he asked softly.

"I planned to leave Monday." Her voice sounded husky to her own ears.

He buried a hand deep in the curls of her hair at the nape of her neck. "That gives us four nights." He arched her, exposing more of her to his hot lips. Wherever his mouth went, fire followed.

She fought for sanity. Charles was a guilty pleasure, a luxury she shouldn't allow herself. Hadn't she learned the price of being impulsive? Of giving in to desire?

Stop. This doesn't have to be as dramatic as I've made it. I need to stop overthinking it and let myself have some joy for a change.

Don't romanticize it and you won't get hurt.

She dug her fingers into the strong muscles of his back. "I may not stay that long."

He picked her up and tossed her onto the bed. She righted herself into a seated position quickly as he shrugged off his suit jacket and tossed it onto the chair beside the bed. He flashed a wicked smile at her—one filled with dark promise. "Oh, you will, and I'll enjoy every moment I spend persuading you to."

Melanie swallowed hard as he slowly unbuttoned his dress shirt and threw it on top of his jacket, then reached for his belt, never taking his gaze from hers. "Tell me to go and I will. Or give me four nights."

"All or nothing? You set the terms and I'm supposed to agree to them?"

"Yes."

Bold. Unyielding. And sexier because of it. "Four nights. Then what?"

His hand stilled on his belt. "I can't offer you more than that."

There was a vulnerable and tormented undertone to his declaration that took Melanie by surprise. He wasn't married. As far as

Sarah had said, he wasn't even dating anyone seriously. What was it that prevented him from being able to consider anything beyond their short time together?

Was the pain in his eyes linked to the loss of his little brother? Sarah had spoken in length about how that tragedy had affected her life, but Melanie hadn't looked at Charles in terms of how it may have affected his.

Underneath his expensive clothing and arrogant persona, could he be as lonely as she was?

She took in the powerful muscles of his chest, his broad shoulders, the lean waist and flat stomach. Her gaze dipped lower, long enough for her to blush as she remembered the satisfying size of him thrusting into her.

He's not promising me forever. Hell, he's not even promising next week, but what if that's okay? What if we can find something in our short time together that we couldn't have found on our own?

I've spent years locking everything away—this may be exactly what I need to put the past behind me.

"Melanie," he said, his voice thick with desire.

She lifted her hips and slid her panties down her legs, crushing them into a ball in one hand before she threw them at him. He caught them midair. She said, "I swear on all that is holy that if you apologize for this tomorrow . . ."

He was naked and beside her before she could finish her threat. Between kisses, he promised, "I don't intend to do much talking tonight or tomorrow." His hand slid down her stomach and cupped her sex possessively while he kissed his way across her collarbone and down to one breast.

Thank God.

Melanie arched her back with pleasure when his teeth closed on one of her nipples and tugged gently. His hand rubbed her mound, then moved down to stroke the outside of her thigh. His touch explored and warmed every inch of her. His mouth teased and worshipped. He laved her breasts with his hot tongue until she was writhing beneath him.

He sat back on his heels and pulled her up into his arms, kissing the last of her reservations—as if there were any left—away. He moved onto his knees and took her hair in one of his hands, gently guiding her mouth toward his hard cock.

Melanie struggled to accept the size of him. He waited, then pushed the limits of what she would accept and groaned when she started to suck him deeper still. He closed his eyes and moaned again when she cupped his balls and rubbed the sensitive area behind them. The power of being in control of such a man was such a turn-on, and Melanie whimpered and moved closer to him.

Sucking. Licking. Loving the feel of him inside her mouth, jerking uncontrollably. His breathing became ragged, and he stopped her by holding her head on both sides. "I'm going to come," he warned, giving her time to withdraw if she chose.

Melanie didn't stop laving her tongue around him. She felt him tense, heard him make an animallike grunt as he climaxed, then welcomed his release and swallowed, licking at him with the same feverish hunger he'd tasted her with earlier.

He rolled onto his side and pulled her down with him, and there was a giddiness to their embrace. She kissed his chest spontaneously.

He rolled on top of her, settling himself between her legs and holding both of her hands above her head in one of his. His cock was already coming back to life and nudging against her wet lower lips.

"You make me feel like a teenager again," he said and kissed her deeply.

Melanie laughed. "Teenage sex was *never* this good."

He grinned down at her, so damn handsome. She felt her chest tighten. *This* Charles was even more dangerous than guarded and demanding Charles. He looked younger, more playful, more *open*.

Not checking the impulse, she reached up and brushed her hand through his hair. Frowning when he pulled away, he reached into the pocket of his slacks and retrieved a strip of several condoms.

"How many of those are you packing?" Melanie asked with a laugh. "Are you sure you brought enough?"

"Only one way to find out," he said while expertly sheathing himself and bending to kiss her neck.

Sweet Jesus, I'm in.

He took one of her legs and put it over his shoulder, then rammed his cock in her readied pussy. He withdrew, then thrust powerfully inside again. Melanie cried out in pleasure as he drove into her again and again with increasing speed. He filled her, positioned her so his intimate caress found her G-spot, and took his time bringing her to the most exquisite orgasm she'd ever experienced. It came in waves, one heated tingle after the next, until she was sobbing from the intensity of it, grabbing at him to pull him deeper. He took her to the edge of what she could handle, paused long enough for both of them to suffer, then took her to the edge again.

When he finally increased his rhythm and came within her, she joined him in a vocal and convulsive release. This time, he didn't immediately withdraw from her. He lowered her leg, released her hands, but stayed on top of her, intimately connected.

After a few minutes, his breathing returned to normal. He got up and disposed of the condom, then returned to the bed.

Melanie's heart beat painfully in her chest as he did everything she'd hoped for the last time they'd been together. He slid in beside her, flipped off the light, and pulled her into his naked embrace.

For a long time, breathing was the only sound in the room. Eventually he said, "I took the morning off, but I have a charity dinner I committed to before I knew you'd be here. Attend it with me."

"Like a date?"

He hugged her to his side. "Whatever you want to call it."

Melanie stiffened against him. "I'd rather not. I didn't bring anything suitable to wear to something like that." She wasn't sure she wanted to attend a public function with him.

In the dim light of the room, he looked down at her, his expression unreadable. "It's a formal event, but I don't care what you wear."

He wouldn't. His arrogance was part of what she found attractive about him. He didn't give a damn what others thought of him. Still, she couldn't help but test his limits. "Really? You're okay if I go in jeans and my boots?"

He took her chin in his hand and turned her face so she'd have to meet his eyes. She couldn't read them in the shadows. "Why are you angry?"

She tried to pull back from him, but he held her to his side. She didn't want to admit it, but the idea of attending something with him intimidated her. She told herself she didn't care what others thought of her, but that wasn't true. And this was his world. She didn't need to be reminded that she didn't belong in it. "I'm not one of your fancy New York girlfriends. I don't wear makeup. My nails are chipped from hard work. What will your friends think of me?"

"These people aren't my friends. I can't promise you that no one will wonder why you chose jeans over a gown, but I can guarantee that none will have the nerve to say anything."

"Because they're too polite?"

A hard expression darkened his face. "Because you're mine."

His words ricocheted through her in the most wonderful way. Her pride whispered that she should throw his words back at him.

But the fact was, she didn't want to.

Yours? Since when does belonging to someone have an expiration date shorter than most lunch meats?

I shouldn't let him talk to me that way.

Yep, I should stomp on out of here.
And I would.
Except for two things.
It's my hotel room.
And I love it when he talks that way.

When she didn't respond, he nuzzled her ear. "We don't have to go if you'd rather stay here."

Hadn't caring what others thought of her cost her enough? She wondered what her relationship with her parents would have been if she'd celebrated Jace's birth instead of hiding it away. Her old friends had said they supported her, but she hadn't allowed herself to believe they could. She'd judged herself and she saw now that her friendships had crumbled beneath the weight of her insecurities.

Who cares if his friends accept me or don't. I have to do this. I have to stop hiding. "I really don't have a dress."

"I'll have one delivered."

Melanie pulled back. "No. I'll have time to find something. You don't know my taste."

He ran his hand down her back, settling on her bare ass. "But I know mine. Tomorrow you dress for my pleasure."

"That is so wrong." Melanie shivered as he lowered his head and kissed the curve of her shoulder. "And so hot."

In all her life, she'd never felt more beautiful or wanted.

Having an end date to this may be a good thing.
I could get lost in this feeling.

That afternoon Charles leaned back in the chair at his desk and stared up at the ceiling of his office. *Four nights will never be enough.*
Not with Melanie.

Just the thought of her had his cock swelling with anticipation. And he'd only been away from her a couple of hours. He closed his eyes and tortured himself with how she'd looked beside him in the shower that morning. He groaned aloud as he remembered how deeply she'd taken him into her mouth.

Sex should have taken the edge off his need for her, but it had done the opposite. He wanted her more now than before. Although he'd managed to talk his way through a couple of conference calls so far that day, his thoughts kept returning to Melanie.

He walked over to the window and unhappily stared at the skyline.

There was a knock on the door behind him. He turned, realized his state of arousal, and returned to sit behind his desk before answering, "Enter."

June came in with her tablet. "I contacted Irene McKinney and she's assembling a team."

Charles rubbed his forehead with one hand. "Who?"

"The personal stylist I told you I knew? She's on her way over to the Best Western to meet with your friend."

"Good." Melanie hadn't looked sure of herself last night when he'd invited her to come out with him. He didn't like to see her that way. He loved the cocky smile she'd had on her face after hog-tying the purse snatcher. That's how he always wanted her to look—confident and thoroughly pleased with herself. "What do you mean *team*?"

The woman's eyes widened apprehensively. "Her dress is being delivered within an hour, but you said she'd probably like her hair done. I asked Irene if she does packages and she said she does everything."

Charles frowned again. "What's everything?"

June chewed her lip. "I should have asked. I'm not used to doing anything personal for you, sir. I didn't know if you wanted me to know. I agreed to the whole package. I can call her back and tell her no if it's not what you want."

"No, it'll be fine," Charles said dismissively. "Thank you, June."

After his secretary left, Charles smiled wryly and shook his head.

The whole package?

I wonder what Melanie will think of that.

Chapter Eight

"What are you, a sadist? No." Clutching a thick terrycloth bathrobe around her, Melanie did something completely uncharacteristic of her—she retreated a step. One of the large curlers bounced against her temple as she did. "Absolutely not."

"Let me just see it," the petite woman in a white cosmetologist's coat who had introduced herself as Irene said as she advanced.

Melanie clutched the robe tighter. "It's time for you to leave."

Shaking her head, the petite woman said, "My reputation depends on the quality of the work. Aren't you happy with your eyebrows?"

Melanie instinctively raised a hand to one perfectly shaped arch. "Yes."

"Then trust me."

"I am not showing my hoochie-coochie to everyone."

Irene looked around impatiently and clapped. "Go. Everyone take a thirty-minute lunch break. But do not come back without my grande, quad, nonfat, one-pump, no-whip mocha." She turned to Melanie. "Do you want anything?"

Feeling like she was caught in a strange dream she couldn't wake herself from, Melanie merely shook her head. The three women Irene had brought with her had spent the past two hours adding highlights and trimming her long hair, adding gel to her nails, and applying all sorts of lotions to Melanie for reasons she'd lost track of.

The same woman who had done her nails had also waxed her legs and eyebrows, and had suggested something called a Brazilian.

"Never heard of it," Melanie had said.

When the woman explained what it was, Melanie had sprung from the chair and drawn the line. Yes to the dress. The hair had needed a trim and the highlights were beautiful. But Melanie was not budging on this final point.

What kind of stylist doesn't take no for an answer?

One that Charles hired, apparently.

Irene folded her hands over her chest and said, "We're alone now. Drop the granny panties."

A red flush of outrage went up Melanie's neck and face. "Excuse me?"

Running her eyes over Melanie critically, Irene said, "You're a beautiful woman, but those are a dime a dozen in the city, honey. You want to keep a man like Charles Dery, you have to step up your game. Now drop them."

Maybe it was the authority with which the woman spoke, but Melanie opened her bathrobe and stepped out of her underwear. It was a little like being at a doctor's office, but a whole lot more embarrassing. "Happy?" Melanie snarled.

"Oh, Lord. Did you trim that in the dark? You do need my help."

Melanie whipped the robe closed. "You are the rudest, most insulting woman I've ever met."

"It's called honesty and I get paid for it," the woman said confidently. "If you're a complete wimp, choose a partial wax, but I'd go for the full if I were you. Men love it."

"They do?" Melanie asked, suddenly uncertain.

Both of Irene's eyebrows rose. "He sent me, didn't he?"

Not giving Melanie time to change her mind, Irene took her by the arm and led her toward a table they had set up in one corner of the room. Melanie stood beside it, her eyes wide. "So women do this all the time, right? It can't hurt that much, then. It's like having my eyebrows done, right?"

"Sure," Irene said and instructed her to lie back on the table.

An hour later, alone again, Melanie stood in the bathroom of her hotel room. Draped in a floor-length, form-hugging black dress, she eyed her reflection in the full-length mirror. From the sophisticated updo to her freshly manicured toenails, the woman who stared back at her was a complete stranger. Her brown eyes stood out, expertly accentuated. The red lipstick made her lips look fuller, pouty. Any imperfection in her complexion had been artfully concealed.

She winced as she remembered how intimate some of the makeover was. The soothing lotion had taken away the sting, but Melanie still winced whenever she remembered the pain—as well as the names she'd called Irene from the first strip to the last. Irene hadn't so much as blinked, so Melanie figured she wasn't the only one to express her feelings about having a Brazilian vocally.

They don't make fairy godmothers like they used to. Whatever happened to the painless wave of a wand? Or did they simply leave these details out? Did Cinderella get a Brazilian? No one ever talks about what was going on under that dress.

Melanie turned and studied the low-cut back of the dress, admitting to herself that the tiny black thong fit beneath it better than her white, flowered cotton panties would have. She felt like a gift that had been carefully wrapped with one purpose in mind: pleasing the man who had paid for the makeover.

That thought sent a shot of excitement through her stomach. *He told me that today was about dressing to please him. Is that what tonight will be about, too?*

Teetering on strappy shoes with ridiculously high heels, Melanie walked out of the bathroom and over to a small pile of papers near the TV. She picked up the one with the phone number of Todd's parents and closed it in one fist.

She should have called them . . . Instead she'd been distracted by her unexpected makeover. *Is Charles the ultimate act of procrastination?*

She reached for her cell phone and video conferenced Sarah.

"Melanie, are you wearing makeup?"

"Yes."

"Hold the phone back from you. I need to see what you're wearing."

Melanie smiled self-consciously and did as she was asked. "It's just a black dress."

"Just a dress? Have you looked in the mirror? You could be a model. I always knew you were pretty, but oh my God, you're gorgeous."

Although Sarah's words warmed Melanie, she'd never been comfortable accepting a compliment. "Is Jace there?"

Sarah put the phone close to her face again and said confidentially. "Oh no. You're not getting off that easily. Where are you going? Did you find Todd?"

Melanie looked guiltily down at the paper in her other hand and threw it onto the counter. "No. His parents aren't here. They're in Greece." Then she looked down at her dress again. "I should have flown back when I found out. I'm sorry."

"Don't be. You never take a vacation. You need this."

"Maybe." She took a deep breath. "I don't know what I'm doing."

With an encouraging tone, Sarah said, "It looks like you're going on a date."

Melanie shrugged, still not looking at the phone. "Charles asked me to attend a charity event with him."

Sarah made a happy whoop. "He is so into you. Wait until he sees you in that dress."

As if sensing Melanie was holding back, Sarah quieted and asked, "What's the matter?"

"I know you think Charles and I would be good together, but we have nothing in common. That is even more painfully clear now that I'm here with him."

"What did he do?" Sarah asked with a sigh.

Melanie met her eyes and lied. "Nothing."

"You don't have to lie to me. I love both of you. My brother can be a royal, bossy pain in the ass. I know that. But beneath that, he has a good heart. And he needs someone like you to help him remember that."

"Someone like me?"

"You didn't judge me when I told you about Phil. And you didn't tell me the guilt I felt was wrong. You accepted me the way I was and Charles needs that. He needs someone he can be himself around."

Melanie shook her head. "Your brother doesn't care what others think of him."

Sarah smiled sadly. "There is something I didn't tell you about the day my brother drowned. Charles was there. He was supposed to be watching Phil. Charles was twelve. I was eight. We were playing by the lake the way we always did. He wanted to ask my parents something, so he asked me to watch Phil."

"Oh my God."

"It was only a few minutes. Phil was playing beside me and I was daydreaming about something. It happened so fast. I would give anything to be able to go back and not have let Charles down that day. He blames himself."

"It was clearly an accident."

"He calls it that. And he's never blamed me. Ever. Not even that day. He just pulled away from us."

Melanie understood that reaction all too well. "I'm so sorry."

"I didn't tell you about how it affected Charles because I felt it wasn't my story to tell, but it's still holding him captive. He won't let anyone close to him anymore. It's like he's worried he'll let us down again. He sends my parents money, but he rarely visits them. I've only started talking to him again because I've made it my mission to. I'm sure the fact that you have Jace terrifies him. He has avoided children since Phil's death."

"I had no idea." So much of what Sarah was saying made sense. It explained why Charles looked unhappy about his own declaration that they couldn't have anything beyond that week.

Her heart broke for him.

Part of her regretted speaking to Sarah about Charles. The more she learned about him, the more she cared about him. And that wasn't a good idea.

Regardless of the reason, Charles wasn't looking for a long-term relationship. Nor was she. At least, not with a man who wouldn't want to be around her son.

"I hear Jace in the background. Can I speak to him?"

"Sure," Sarah said. After a hesitation, she added, "Don't tell Charles what I said. He doesn't like to talk about the past and I don't want to lose him again."

"I won't say a word," Melanie promised.

Jace spent the next fifteen minutes telling her all about how Tony had taken him to a local rodeo and introduced him to everyone. "He got me a rodeo buckle. A real one," Jace gushed. "And we sat right in the front. It was awesome."

In his enthusiasm, Jace didn't ask why his mother was wearing makeup, but just before they hung up he did say, "I love you, Mama, and you sure look pretty today."

Melanie would have cried happy tears, but she was afraid to mess up what had taken hours to achieve. Her son was fine. Her week away wasn't hurting him at all.

After telling him she loved him and reminding him to be good, Melanie hung up. She caught her reflection in the mirror again.

Charles would be back soon. What Sarah had revealed about him had changed everything and nothing. Melanie's instincts had been right. Charles was as trapped by the past as she was.

She just wasn't sure either one of them had what it took to free the other.

Dressed in a tuxedo, Charles stepped out of his limo and onto the sidewalk in front of Melanie's hotel. The street was full of paparazzi. He scanned the area. No celebrity he knew would stay in the hotel Melanie had chosen. He assumed they weren't there for him. He was wealthy, but that didn't normally make him photoworthy.

Photographers swarmed and took photos of him. Something had happened and he didn't like that he was unprepared for it.

He looked down at his phone. Six calls from June. Two from Mason. He'd turned his ringer off that morning while he was with Melanie and had forgotten to turn it back on. Instead of going to his office, he'd gone online at home and read reports he'd been putting off. *Shit.*

"Are you here to pick up your cowgirl?" one reporter called out from back in the crowd.

"Where are you taking her?"

Some would have walked away, but Charles had never been one to back down. He walked up to one of the reporters and demanded, "Why is everyone so interested?"

The young man was clearly surprised to be asked a question directly. He pulled out his own phone and after typing something in, held it up to show a video clip of Charles and Melanie right after she'd chased her assailant down. Her face glowed with that triumphant smile he remembered, then the footage showed him dashing through the crowd and kissing her. Music started and the scene replayed and looped in a video montage. The young photographer said enthusiastically, "It went viral, man. 'Cowgirl ropes a criminal and a billionaire.' Unleashed, Unchained put music to it, and you got four million hits since yesterday. You're trending on Twitter and YouTube. You didn't know? That's wild."

Fuck.

Charles looked around at the flashing cameras, put on a diplomatic smile, and walked through them into the hotel foyer. He knew better than to take on the paparazzi unprepared. Like rats or cockroaches, they weren't foes one confronted alone. Dealing with them required hiring professionals and, luckily, Charles knew the best.

As soon as he was inside the foyer, he was on the phone with his head of security. He wanted men on the street pronto and a decoy vehicle. No one would get close to Melanie.

Satisfied that the immediate issue would be dealt with effectively, Charles called Mason next to address the root of the problem. Not wasting time with a greeting, Charles demanded, "What the hell can I do about this?"

Mason laughed. "So you finally saw the news? Some would plan a whirlwind tour of all the national morning stations followed by some late-night talk shows. You could contact the person who posted because you're likely due some of the profits, although that one doesn't have nearly as many hits as the Unleashed, Unchained video. You should call them. Maybe you could do appearances on their next tour."

Charles rubbed one throbbing temple. "I mean how do I make it go away?"

"Oh," Mason said slowly, clearly not having considered that option. "Yeah, that's probably not going to happen. People are eating it up. You're officially more popular than that angry cat video. How does it feel to be a star?"

"This is not fucking funny. How do I get it taken down?"

"I'd say you can't. It's everywhere now."

"What are my legal options?"

"I'm sure you can have your lawyers call their lawyers—but it's out there already. It's not going away. Want my personal advice?"

"Strangely, that's why I called." *A sure sign that things have gotten out of control is seeking advice from Mason.*

"Put your own spin on this. Grab that bull by the horns. Name a charity, demand half the profits go toward it, and ride it out. A week from now, no one will remember anything but who you helped. Plus you look like an asshole in the video. Melanie wants to save the kid and you're practically suggesting the death penalty. You could use the good PR."

"You saw what he did . . ."

"I did."

Charles searched online on his phone until he found the version of the video that had been put to music. It was a remix of the other clip with parts of it looping. He groaned at the number of downloads listed below. Mason was right. There was no undoing this one.

Charles thought he looked ridiculous in the video, and he couldn't see the allure. "Why does anyone care about this? I don't usually get this kind of press."

"It's not for you. Well, not really. Everyone is talking about Melanie. She is fucking amazing. When she puts her foot on the mugger's back and slams him into the cement, you can't help but cheer her on. She did what every one of us would like to think we would do if we were mugged. She kicked some ass. Then you sweep in and talk like you're reading lines from some B-rated chick flick and lay a kiss on her. Hell, even I couldn't wait to share the video when I saw it. It left me all pumped up."

A second later Mason laughed again. "I'm looking at the newest photos of you getting out of your limo at her hotel. You look pissed."

"I don't like surprises."

"You wouldn't have had one if you'd answered my phone calls. I imagine you've been occupied, though. That was some street mauling you gave your cowgirl. I didn't know you had that in you."

Charles hung up on Mason, which likely didn't faze his friend in the least. He pulled the video up on his phone again and groaned. The evening he had looked forward to all day had taken an unexpected and unwelcome turn. It was one thing to take Melanie to a charity event and let people speculate about their relationship. It was another to take her to one while weathering a scandal.

He stood outside the door of her room and gritted his teeth angrily. *I was supposed to keep her safe.*

I couldn't have done a worse job had I set out to.

She was no longer anonymous and, in the city, that could be a dangerous thing. He called his head of security again. He'd never needed or wanted a bodyguard, but Melanie was going to have one.

Two if that's what it took to keep her safe.

"I'll send someone right over. Is this for a night, sir? The week? What should I tell them?"

"It's a temporary job," Charles snarled.

Temporary.

I said it.

I meant it.

Nothing has changed.

After hanging up, he texted his lawyer, instructing him to contact any person who posted the video and inform them that half of the profit would be procured for . . . He thought of the various charities he donated to. He told his lawyer to pick one and get back to him. Giving in to a sudden impulse, he asked him to also check what had happened to the kid in the video. Where did he end up? *Keep that final request between us*, he wrote.

The door to Melanie's room opened. Dressed in a black gown that looked like it had been painted on her curves, she smiled up at him and Charles forgot everything else.

"I thought I heard you out here. What are you doing?"

Charles held out his phone wordlessly and shook his head, trying to remember what had been important enough to keep him from her. He stepped inside, pulled her into his arms, and gave in to his hunger for her.

They'd be late to—

Where the hell are we going?

Chapter Nine

"There is something we need to discuss before we go anywhere tonight," Charles said later as he shrugged on the jacket of his tuxedo.

Melanie was already back in her black dress and fixing her makeup in the bathroom mirror. He was tempted to tell her that he preferred her naked—bare of clothes and makeup. Her smooth as silk pussy had been an unexpected treat. Women spent hours covering and concealing their real beauty. The more she put on, the more he wanted to carry her back to his bed and strip it all off.

He was smart enough to keep that thought to himself, though.

"What is it?" she asked, her eyes round with concern.

He considered not showing her their trending video. He already resented its intrusion on how he'd thought the evening would go. How would she react? Would she be too embarrassed to attend the event?

He prepped his phone, then held it up facing her. She stepped closer and her eyebrows rose as she realized what she was watching. "We're on YouTube?"

He nodded and watched her expression closely.

An embarrassed smile spread across her face. "Oh my God. I look crazy. I can't believe I did that. I wasn't thinking about anything except how angry I was. Oh, look, they have the part where you showed up." A blush spread across her face as she watched their kiss. She took his phone and scrolled down. "Is this right? Have that many people seen the video?"

"It looks that way. I'm trying to have it taken down."

"Can you do that?"

"Probably not. We were in a public place. I don't know, but I'm having my lawyer look into it."

"Did you see how many comments there are? Thousands." She scanned them. "They think I'm a hero." She smiled, then made a circle of surprise with her lips. "And they think you're an ass." She chuckled and met his eyes. "Sorry."

A reluctant smile pulled at Charles's lips. "An ass, huh?"

Melanie's eyes lit with mischief, and she turned the phone and pointed to the comments below the video. "I didn't say it. They did."

He pulled her to him, holding her by her hips against him, and kissed her smiling lips. "You just find it funny."

She wrapped her arms around his neck and gave him a quick kiss back. "I wouldn't have last week. I probably would have been mortified. But being here with you . . . I can't explain it. I'm realizing that I wasted way too much time worrying what other people think of me."

She looked up at him with two of the darkest brown eyes he'd ever seen and asked softly, "Are you okay with it?"

"As long as it doesn't make you regret your time here."

She touched just above his heart. "I don't. I won't."

Charles cleared his throat. "Celebrity status doesn't come without a price. The paparazzi are downstairs. The way out to the car has been cleared, but anything could happen. You have two bodyguards. If we do encounter the press, let the bodyguards do their jobs. They'll keep everyone away from you. Keep walking. The paparazzi will say anything to try to get a response out of you. Ignore them."

Melanie's eyes darkened with emotion. She lowered her hand and turned away. "Are you afraid I'll embarrass you?"

Charles grabbed her hand and swung her back to him, pulling her flush against him and arching her backward over his arm. She struggled, but he held her immobile as he fought back a wave of emotion. Couldn't she see that he was trying to protect her? "The public can be nasty. The same people who called you a hero today might call you my whore tomorrow . . ."

Her chin rose defiantly. "Is that what I am?"

"No. You're . . ."

He didn't finish the sentence because he didn't know what she was to him. This was all new. The civilized lover he'd always been slid away when he was with her. He wanted to do more than fuck her; he wanted to own her. An image of her, tied to his bed, completely under his control, filled his imagination and sent blood rushing down into his already half-erect cock. Desire thwarted his ability to engage in any verbal sparring match with her. He bent his head and claimed her mouth with his.

Her gasp of surprise was all the invitation he needed. He thrust his tongue past her slightly parted lips and kissed her with all the emotions swirling within him. *Mine.*

Melanie wrapped her arms around his neck, arching even more intimately against him. She opened her mouth wider to him, pulling him deeper into her until he couldn't think past his need to sink into her again and again. The more he tried to claim her, the more of himself he gave to her and it shook him.

He broke free of the kiss and unwrapped her arms from around his neck as he fought to regain control of the situation again. "Tonight you stay at my apartment," he growled.

Breathing as heavily as he was, she raised a hand to her kiss-swollen lips but didn't protest. Confusion and desire warred in her eyes as strongly as they did within him.

Charles grabbed her purse from the bed and handed it to her, then took her arm and guided her out of the hotel room. A security team met them in the hallway and escorted them out a back door to the car that awaited them. Charles gave them instructions to have her things brought over to his place while they were at the party. A party that would only get a cameo appearance from him.

Once seated in the back of his limo a foot away from Melanie, Charles turned to her and said, "Stay one more week. I'll fly you back next weekend."

She looked him in the eye and shook her head. "No. Don't start changing the rules now. I'm flying home on Monday. That's it. That's all I agreed to."

Arms folded across her chest, Melanie kept her eyes focused on the limo's dividing panel. For a long time she and Charles didn't speak, even as the car left the packed buildings of Manhattan behind and entered the more upscale suburb of Westchester.

"Why did you come to New York, Melanie?" Charles finally asked as if the question were wrung from him.

Maybe because she wanted to ensure their time together would have a clean ending or maybe because she was still angry with herself, Melanie threw the truth at him. "To find Jace's father."

His head snapped toward her. "And did you?" he demanded.

"Not yet."

Face tight, Charles asked, "Do you still love him?"

"And if I said I do?" she challenged.

He let out a slow breath. "It wouldn't matter."

Melanie looked out the limo window. *Because this is just about the sex. Don't forget that.*

Charles possessively caressed one of her thighs. "I don't like the idea of you and another man."

It wasn't at all what she'd expected Charles to say. She glanced over her shoulder at him in surprise. His eyes were dark with emotion and a history of pain he tried to deny. "Really?" she prompted softly. She couldn't help but push him further. "You don't have the right to feel one way or another about anything I do."

His hand tightened on her thigh. "I don't?"

The air in the limo was charged with emotion, which had to be momentarily put aside when the vehicle pulled into a private courtyard in front of a mansion and came to a halt. As expected, the driver opened the rear door a moment later.

Charles helped Melanie out of the limo and held on to her hand. He pulled her closer to him as they walked toward the entrance of the home. "This conversation is not over."

He's jealous.

The idea was both inconceivable and exciting for Melanie.

A butler in a dark suit opened the door of the private residence and welcomed them.

"Good evening, Mr. Dery."

"Good evening."

"Mr. Reed is in the main salon and asking about you."

"Thank you."

As soon as Melanie and Charles stepped into the foyer, moving farther inside proved difficult. Everywhere she looked there were elegantly dressed couples sipping glasses of champagne from crystal flutes. The main entry of the home was the size of Melanie's house back in Texas, and the chandelier that hung above them wouldn't have fit in the bed of her truck.

Melanie's head spun with the number of people who approached them. She was pretty sure she could have sold tickets to meet with Charles, the way people lined up, waiting for their turn to speak to him. He introduced her to each of them and guided her slowly through the crowd.

Charles bent his head to her ear and said, "Neil Reed hosts this fund-raiser party every year. There's always a theme to the silent auction."

Melanie nodded. "Our local church has those. Everyone donates a basket, and the person who writes the largest amount on the sheet next to it before the end of the auction wins it. One year it raised over a thousand dollars for our food bank. Is this the same?"

With a small smile, Charles said, "Essentially."

"Which charity does tonight's auction support?"

Charles frowned. "I don't remember."

"Isn't that the point of this?" Melanie looked around at the outrageously expensive jewelry on the women around her. Diamonds everywhere. She didn't know clothing designers, but if she had to guess, there wasn't a gown in the room that had been bought off the rack.

Charles looked uncomfortable with the question, but Melanie didn't back down from it. Finally, he said, "Yes, for everyone here—well, except for the McMillans, who are notoriously cheap."

"And you'll all be lauded for your donations even though you don't care about the actual charity."

"It'll be a worthwhile cause or Reed wouldn't have chosen it. Rather than get upset, when I introduce you to Reed just ask him where the money goes."

"You're missing the point," Melanie said and pursed her lips angrily. *I want you to care—care about tonight, care about me—about Jace.* His indifference to the charity of the evening fit what Sarah had said about her brother. He didn't let himself get involved.

The crowd parted as they approached the host.

A man who appeared to be in his late fifties broke away from the circle of men he was talking to when he saw Charles. "I didn't think you were going to make it, Charles. You're not one to be late."

Charles shook the man's hand. "Neil, good to see you. I'd like you to meet Melanie Hanna."

There was a light of recognition in the older man's eyes, and for a moment he looked like he was tempted to say something. But then he offered his hand to Melanie with a polite smile. "A pleasure, Miss Hanna."

He turned and gestured toward the white linen–covered table in an adjacent room that displayed photos of the auction items. "This year it's all vehicles. We need someone like you to start the bidding on the Viper. It'd be a shame to return a prize like that."

Charles nodded. "I'll check it out. Where is the money going this year, Neil?" Charles asked as if inquiring about the weather.

The older man looked behind him and squinted as he read a small poster across the room. "I need my glasses to read that far away. My wife picked it. Literacy for . . . Damn, it's over on the wall. She told me. If she asks, say I knew. I can't keep up."

As if the conversation had made his point, Charles swept Melanie to the table with the auction items. Melanie wasn't a car connoisseur, but even she knew how expensive the donated vehicles were. Bentleys, Porches, even a Rolls Royce. They stopped in front of a photo of a red SRT Viper and Melanie bent to read the details. She stood straight up with a gasp and her eyes flew to Charles. "Does that say that the starting bid is a hundred and fifty?"

Charles bent beside her and answered blandly. "It does."

"Thousand?"

Charles nodded.

Melanie looked at the photo of the car again and then back at Charles. She waved a hand above one shoulder in the direction of the host she'd just met. "That man . . ."

"Neil Reed," Charles supplied the man's name as Melanie struggled for it.

"He thinks you're the one who will bid on this? You'd drop that on a charity you don't even know?"

Face tight, Charles once again looked uncomfortable with the direction of the conversation. "Some women would be impressed by the mere fact that I could do it."

Melanie looked around the room again. Women were eyeing Charles as a hungry crowd would an hors d'oeuvre tray. Would he be with one of them next week?

Charles guided her to the far corner of the room. "That was tactless of me. You're entitled to your opinion."

Melanie looked up at him through her lashes. "I wasn't trying to make you feel badly, Charles. Donating to charities is a good thing."

"But?"

She couldn't hold her questions in any longer. "But don't you want to know who you help? Don't you care?"

There it was again, that sad look in his eyes. The one that made her want to hug him and never let him go. "No. No, I don't."

In that moment she saw past his denial, past his surface indifference, and glimpsed a pain she understood. He'd been hurt and didn't want to be hurt again, so he kept his distance. She'd done the same. She took one of his hands in hers and gave it a gentle squeeze. They stood staring into each other's eyes, their connection going beyond the sexual attraction that had brought them together. She understood and accepted him. "I get that."

He nodded and let out a long, slow breath as if her words had relieved a long-held tension. "I asked my lawyer to find out what happened to the kid who tried to steal your purse."

"You did?" Mixed emotions filled Melanie. She didn't want to find another reason to like Charles. He was already going to be impossible to forget.

"When I saw myself in the video, I wasn't proud of my reaction to the kid. You said I wasn't the man you thought I was—I wasn't the man I thought I was, either."

A lump of emotion clogged Melanie's throat. "I shouldn't have said that. You're a good man, Charles. Don't listen to me. I'm all talk. I told you to care about him, but what have I done for him? Nothing. I'm not exactly living up to who I thought I was, either."

"We're a sorry pair," Charles said drolly, lightening the mood with a dash of humor.

"The worst." Melanie smiled and then Charles did.

He raised her hand to his lips and kissed the inside of her wrist. Suddenly serious, he asked, "What do I do when I find him?"

Melanie wiped away a stray tear his question elicited. "You see if he has a place to sleep, food to eat. You take some of that money you would have donated tonight and you make sure he has shoes that fit him."

"I don't in—" He cut off what he was about to say and started again. "He might expect much more than I'm willing to give."

"Maybe," Melanie said. "Or maybe you will change the course of his life."

Charles pulled her closer and kissed her forehead. "We should go back to mingling unless we want to end up in another online video."

With a chuckle, Melanie agreed. After meeting another wave of people, she excused herself to find a bathroom, seeking a moment to clear her head. She was alone in one of the long hallways when a man, maybe in his late thirties, who looked like he'd had a few too many drinks, stepped into her path. Melanie veered to the side, but he stepped with her.

"You're too beautiful to be with a man like Dery."

The lust in the slick man's eyes made Melanie's skin crawl. She'd spent the past five years living on a ranch with all men. She wasn't easily intimidated, but there was something dark about the man. Something vile. She was about to turn and head back to the party when he grabbed her arm.

"Are you as rough in bed as you are on the street?"

Melanie tried unsuccessfully to pull her arm free of the man's grasp, but he was stronger than she'd anticipated. "Get your hands off of me. Charles . . ."

He tugged her a step closer, the side of his hand brushing over the curve of her breast while the stench of his alcohol-laced breath assaulted her senses. "You think he'd do anything if he saw me with you? My father would crush him if I told him to."

Anger filled Melanie as the man's hold bit down into her arm. She snarled, "I don't need Charles to defend me. You think you scare me? I've castrated bulls without blinking an eye. I'm trying to be on my best behavior, but I will seriously kick your ass if you don't remove your hand right now."

The man released her and raised a hand, whether to strike her or emphasize his next words, Melanie didn't know—and she wasn't going to wait around to find out. She turned and walked into a wall of muscle.

Charles.

He touched her arm where there was still a mark from the other man. He put Melanie behind him and said, "Ethan, you know better than to mistreat a woman." He advanced on the other man. He looked about to wring the smaller man's neck. "Especially one who belongs to someone else."

Ethan took a step back. "Careful, Charles. My father would ruin you if you ever touched me."

"Your father won't do me in. The law will, because if I get my hands on you, I will kill you." Charles took another step forward and the other man made a hasty and cowardly retreat.

When Charles didn't immediately turn back to face Melanie, she walked over to him and lightly touched his tense back. His muscles flexed with aggression beneath her hand. "Forget it, Charles. I'm fine."

Charles swung around, his eyes burning with fury. "He needs to learn to keep his hands to himself. I don't mind teaching him that lesson . . ."

"His father . . ."

"Will transfer him to his branch office in Asia," Charles said, taking a deep breath.

"Why would he do that?" Melanie asked, her eyes rounding.

"Because when it comes to business, information is power, and I know enough about the trouble Neil's company is having to send his stocks plummeting to zero. And he knows it." Composing himself, Charles forced a smile. "Come on, let's say our good-byes and go home."

The way he said "home" sent a shiver down Melanie's spine. Guiding her back through the party, she smiled politely as he explained to a few key people why they had to leave early. Honestly, she wasn't paying attention to what he was saying.

That one word stuck in her head.

Home.

He'd said it so easily—as if they had the same one.

Chapter Ten

"That was actually fun," Melanie said as she snuggled up to Charles on the ride back to his apartment.

Charles nuzzled her hair. "You sound surprised."

Melanie took a moment to enjoy the beat of his heart beneath her ear before answering. "I don't consider myself a city girl, but when we spoke to that couple from upstate New York . . ."

"The Brenners."

"Yes, I loved when the husband told the story about how his wife convinced him to create a company softball team and then was mortified when they lost every game. My side still hurts from laughing so hard. Didn't he say they were in their third season of techie-ball—softball the way only computer nerds could play it? He was hilarious."

Charles nodded with a chuckle. "A man in love will do some crazy things."

They both froze as his words hung in the air. Eventually, Melanie was the one who broke the uncomfortable silence. "Well, both he and his wife were very nice."

Charles cleared his throat and absently rubbed a hand down Melanie's arm as if he was deep in his own thoughts. "They were."

Resting her cheek on his shoulder, Melanie said, "I don't love Todd. I never did. I was young and stupid at the end of my junior year in college. I knew his reputation, but I thought I was different. It only took one time to create Jace."

"I don't have much respect for a man who doesn't support his children—no matter how they were created."

Melanie closed her eyes and confessed. "He doesn't know Jace exists. I never told him."

Charles tensed beneath her but remained silent.

Shrugging in the face of her shame, Melanie said, "I told you I'm no saint."

Charles cupped her chin and raised her face to his. "So why tell him now?"

Melanie searched his face for a hint of how he felt, but his expression was carefully neutral. "Jace wants to know about his father. My son is growing up fast. He needs a mother who isn't ashamed of how he came to be. And who isn't too much of a coward to at least tell his father the truth."

The limo pulled up to the apartment building and Charles helped Melanie out. Without speaking, they walked inside and rode the elevator up to his penthouse.

"We've all done things we're ashamed of, Melanie," Charles said once they were inside his apartment.

Melanie wanted to tell him that she knew what he was referring to, but she held her silence just as Sarah had asked her to. "I was surprised you wanted to leave before they announced the auction winners. Did you bid on anything?"

"No," Charles said gruffly. "I consider not strangling Ethan Reed my charitable act for the evening."

"I've seen your temper. I agree."

"You have?"

"The first time I met you was right after you'd punched Tony. I thought the two of you were set to kill each other."

"So you threw lemonade in our faces."

Melanie hid a smile. "It worked, didn't it?"

Charles made a noncommittal grunt deep in his chest. "It did. I haven't had a good night's sleep since."

Melanie held his eyes and her breath. "No?"

"No. I couldn't get you out of my head. You were full of fire and spunk. The women here aren't pushovers by any definition, but you were different. I can't explain it."

"I thought you were unbearably arrogant."

"Really?" he growled as he kissed her neck. "And now?"

She laughed and pulled his head down for a kiss. "I kind of like it."

"Is there anything else you like?" he asked as their bantering turned sexual.

"Oh yes."

Charles woke up early and made phone calls that would allow him uninterrupted time with Melanie. *Three fucking days left.*

He dragged her out of his apartment and to tourist sites because he had to get himself under control. By then his interest in her should have been waning. He should have been sick of her laugh, annoyed by something she said, or simply bored.

I shouldn't be angry, but I am. Angry with myself for wanting her to stay longer.

They were standing at the foot of the Statue of Liberty when he looked down into her eyes and suddenly wanted to know more about her. "What did you study in college?"

She shrugged, seeming embarrassed by the question. "Does it matter? I didn't finish and it feels like another lifetime." He waited and she finally answered, "Interior design. I had a sketchbook that I used to take everywhere with me. The strangest things could inspire me and I wanted to capture it all. I wouldn't know how I'd use every item, but then I'd come across the perfect place for it . . . and it fit as if it had been meant for that space." She looked down, then back up again shyly. "I considered myself an artist of sorts, but one who made a picture you could live in."

He tucked a wayward curl behind her ear. "You should finish your degree."

She turned away from him and closed her eyes, letting the wind carry her hair off her shoulders. "Maybe someday."

He pulled her back so she rested against his chest, and wrapped his arms around her waist. "I could pay for your classes."

She stiffened. "I don't want your money."

"It'd be nothing to me."

"Exactly," she said and stepped out of his embrace, the distance between them stretching farther than just the step she took. "What about you? What do you want to do when you grow up?"

"I'm doing it," he said somewhat defensively.

"So you have everything you want?" she asked without looking at him.

He felt her putting up walls to protect herself from him and growled, "Not everything."

"Sarah told me you don't visit your parents very often."

"I do when I have time."

"Do you?" she turned and looked up at him.

He couldn't sustain the lie. "No."

Melanie hugged her arms around herself and said, "It sucks, doesn't it? I used to watch those after-school television specials and love how everyone made up after a fight. Always a happy ending. That's not life, though. My parents and I had a huge falling-out when Jace was born and we've never gotten past it. I visit my parents, but it's not the way it was before. Amazing how you can be in the same room with someone and still feel so far away from them."

"Is that why you moved to Carlton's ranch?"

Melanie nodded. "I'd left my parents' home without a good plan of what to do next. David was actually the one who hired me. He'd heard about my situation and sought me out. He's like that. He can't walk away from a person in need. It's how he ended up working with Tony. Tony was losing a battle with alcohol after one of his clients died. David pulled him back from the edge, so to speak. Saved his life, really. And saved mine in a way."

At first Charles wasn't sure how to respond to that. He was grateful to the man even though Melanie's admiration for him ignited a twinge of jealousy. "David is the ranch manager I met? The beefy one?"

Melanie smiled. "He *is* a pretty big guy. Cowboys come to that naturally. It's a tough life. A lot of manual labor, but I don't think David would want it any other way."

The only thing Charles liked less than imagining Melanie living on that ranch with a bunch of single men was the idea of her returning to it. "The two of you are close?"

"Yes. He helps me with Jace. And I've never met a kinder man."

"He sounds perfect for you," he said, hating the jealousy he could hear in his own voice.

"He would be," Melanie said, and Charles's heart froze in his chest. "But I don't love him. I'm holding out for someone I can't live without."

He let out a slow breath.

"What about you?" Melanie asked. "What are you waiting for?"

Her question shot right through him, leaving him feeling raw and exposed. He checked the time on his phone. "Let's head back. The island is about to close."

She studied his expression. "I bet you could keep it open if you wanted to."

She wasn't talking about the island and they both knew it. He didn't know what to say, so he said nothing. He wasn't ready to commit to more, but he also wasn't ready to let her go.

Later they walked around Central Park and out onto the streets, hand in hand. Charles couldn't remember the last time he'd felt—dare he admit it to himself?—happy. He looked down at her and caught her smiling. "How does New York compare to the way you'd imagined it?"

"Better, except for the smell," she joked.

"Says the woman who lives on a horse ranch," he countered with easy humor.

"It's all what you're used to, I guess. People aren't very friendly here, but they aren't overly friendly where I'm from, either. Not anymore. The town I grew up in has changed a lot since I was in grade school. Businesses moved out. The economy took a dive. A lot of people had to leave to support their families." She shrugged. "No, New York hasn't surprised me too much. Except the hotel's bellman. He loves me. Can't stop asking me if I need anything. I gave him a five-dollar tip when he brought up my bags. Maybe not many people remember to do that?"

Charles hid a smile. He'd handed the man a hundred-dollar bill that night and told him to keep an eye on her for him, promising to leave him more if she was satisfied with the hotel when she checked out. Melanie's innocence when it came to how the city worked was a delight to watch. "That must be it."

The evening was cooling off nicely. Charles told his driver they wanted to walk for a while and that he'd call when they needed him. He had two plainclothes security men scouting ahead, blending into the crowd, but the initial fervor over their video seemed to be dying down. Nothing stayed in the headlines long in a city that moved as fast as New York did.

As they walked by a mostly vacant sandwich shop, Melanie paused to read the menu. She said, "They have chili. You think anyone up here knows how to make it?"

"What are you saying about my city?"

She smiled cheekily. "I'm saying y'all think you're badass, but I could bring the heat."

You already do, Charles thought, and shook his head to clear the images of what he would do with her later. He guided her inside the small shop and to the counter. "One chili and two waters," he ordered.

Melanie smiled again. "I doubt I'll need the chaser."

Charles couldn't help smiling right along with her. When he was with Melanie, his mind wasn't racing with everything he needed to do when he returned to his office. He was in the moment and loving every second of it. "We'll see."

Seated at a small round table in the corner of the shop, Melanie closed her eyes while tasting the chili. She took her time evaluating it, then opened her eyes and, with painstaking slowness, licked the spoon clean. "Not half bad, but I'm not sweating."

I am.

"Do you want to try it?" she asked.

"What?" He was lost to the image of her tongue circling the tip of his cock the way it had circled the spoon.

"The chili." Melanie laughed and scooped a spoonful out of the cardboard bowl.

Charles obediently opened his mouth, holding her eyes, and not letting go of the scenario running through his mind. There was a mild burn from the spices in the chili, but nothing that could compete with the sensations that throbbed through him every time she smiled.

A heavyset woman in an apron, who looked to be in her late forties, approached their table. She noted Melanie's Western clothing and said, "I have to ask, what do you think?"

You should go away, is what Charles thought, but he didn't say it. He didn't want anything to interrupt their day together, but Melanie had already turned and was smiling at the woman.

Melanie took another bite of the chili and answered in a kind tone, "You have all the right ingredients, but it lacks fire. My mother always said if you're going to make chili, you make it so that people have no choice but to remember it."

The woman took a notepad out of her apron. "What would you change?"

"It's not a recipe," Melanie said vaguely, "but you know when you've achieved it. Would you like me to show you? I could tweak what you've already made." Then she stopped and looked at Charles, suddenly self-conscious. "If we have time."

Watching Melanie light up while talking to the other woman was mesmerizing and something that Charles didn't want to miss, even though it meant temporarily postponing his plans for the rest of the evening.

"My husband does the cooking here," the other woman said. She walked away to talk to the man behind the counter, then returned with a funny expression. She studied the two of them, looked back at her husband, and nodded. "Danny says you can change anything on the menu as long as we can have a picture of you two."

Melanie sat up straight with surprise. "Why would anyone want—"

Charles stood, preparing to escort Melanie out of the shop. "That's not going to—"

The woman put her hand up to stop them. "Please. We would only put the picture on the wall." She clasped her hands in front of her. "I can't believe I didn't recognize you two when you came in. You're all over the Internet. No one will believe you were here without a photo." After a pause the woman offered, "We could name the chili after you."

Melanie stood beside Charles and asked, "How could I refuse that offer?" She wasn't asking his permission, but he nodded and gave it anyway. She followed the woman behind the counter, pulled her hair back in a ponytail, and donned an apron.

Bemused, Charles watched Melanie laugh with two complete strangers while she added spices and Tabasco sauce to their chili. She tasted it, then added more spices, and tasted it again. When she was finally satisfied, she scooped some out for each of them to sample.

The owners snapped a picture of Melanie leaning across the counter to spoon-feed a taste to Charles. He was about to tell them to delete it and use another shot, but the chili scorched all thought out of him. Sweat instantly beaded on his forehead and he shamelessly reached for the water bottle behind him.

Melanie clapped happily when the owners of the restaurant had a similar reaction. "Now that is a chili you won't forget." She was grinning from ear to ear as she took off her apron.

She was back at his side still laughing when Charles was rocked by a realization: He didn't want her to leave. Like one of the objects she would have drawn in her sketchbook, she had a place where she was meant to be.

Here with me.

It would mean bringing her son to New York, but people had nannies. He could provide for her and for her child, without having to actually raise him.

"Are you okay?" Melanie asked, and he realized that she'd been saying something to him that he hadn't heard. He took another sip of water. "Do you hate it?"

He shook his head.

No, I like it too much.

Too much to let you go.

Chapter Eleven

Melanie awoke with a start and realized Charles was sitting straight up in bed beside her. She rolled over onto her side and strained to see more than his outline in the darkness. "What's wrong?"

"I've been thinking," he said and flipped on the light beside the bed, temporarily blinding Melanie.

Covering her eyes with one arm, Melanie groaned. "What time is it?"

"A little past three."

"Any chance I can convince you to turn that light off?"

"You should stay."

Melanie sat up abruptly. "What did you just say?"

"You don't have to go back. Stay in New York."

"And do what?" *You? Daily? Because that is great for a vacation fantasy fling, but not so good as a life plan.*

Charles frowned. "Live with me. You won't have to work."

"Just sleep with you."

He studied her expression for a moment. "Of course."

Maybe it was the serious consideration he seemed to give his answer, but Melanie wasn't offended—in fact, she bit back a smile and decided to have a little fun with him. "How often?"

"As often as you want."

"Will I have to sign a written agreement?" she asked, fighting to appear sincere.

"I could have my lawyer draw up some paperwork if you'd like, but I don't feel it's necessary."

"Oh, I think it is. I want to read that agreement and, if possible, I'd like a video of you asking your lawyer to write it." No longer able to conceal her amusement, Melanie rolled her eyes dramatically.

Charles frowned, then a half smile tugged at his lips. "You're mocking me."

Raising one hand, Melanie used her thumb and forefinger to measure an inch in the air. "Maybe a little."

He pulled her close and rolled her beneath him, kissing her deeply until she forgot everything but the feel of him. He nipped her lower lip gently and said, "I'm not used to women laughing at me."

"Well, after this weekend you can replace me with one who is appropriately respectful."

Charles frowned down at her. "You're not leaving."

He wants me to stay. Although his words sent a warm rush through Melanie's chest, they didn't change their situation. "What about Jace?"

"Of course he'd come, too."

There was no of course *about it. Oh my God, he wants us to move in with him. He's serious.* Putting a shaky hand to her mouth, Melanie said, "It's not that easy. Jace is happy where he is. I can't take him away from the only home he has known."

"He'll like the city. Children adapt," Charles said dismissively.

"You don't know that." She shook her head doubtfully. "If you saw him with his horses . . ."

"He can ride in Central Park if he likes horses so much."

His tone was a cool splash of reality.

He leaned down and kissed her neck. "We are so good together. Why pretend you don't want to stay?"

His words flamed her doubts. Fighting the licks of desire that shot through her at his caress, she pushed at his chest. "It's not just about us." When he didn't move off her, she glared up at him. She was a jumble of emotions that tangled and folded over each other in a bundle of desire, frustration, fear, and sadness. *Of course I want to stay with you, you big oaf, but not like this. I won't settle for less than I deserve—than my son deserves.* "Get off of me."

"You're mine."

She shook her head. "No, I'm not." *And I can't let myself forget that.*

"You may lie, but your body doesn't." She'd gone to bed in only his nightshirt. He sat back and with one forceful move tore the front of her covering open, sending buttons from it scattering around them. He laved one of her nipples, and desire shot through Melanie. She couldn't stop herself from arching backward and offering herself more fully to him.

Their time together had a fantasy element to it, one that would end when she flew home in a couple of days. She'd be back in her normal, solitary existence. Back to a life that held few if any surprises and revolved mostly around what others wanted.

He thinks this is about him, but it's really about me.

I want to go where only this man can take me.

Melanie ran her hands over his bare muscular shoulders. She dug her fingers into them when his teeth grazed her neck.

"Tell me you don't want this." Charles ran a possessive hand down her stomach and slid a finger between her folds. "You're already wet for me." His finger circled her clit slowly, teasing her until she was squirming, wantonly rubbing herself against his hand. "Say it. Tell me to stop and I will."

He took her breast deeply in his mouth and mirrored his lower tease, circling her nipple with his tongue but not giving her the direct contact she craved. Melanie grabbed his head with both hands and held him, willing him to repeat what he'd given so freely before. Instead, he raised his head and growled, "You can't because you want this as much as I do. You know you belong to me, Melanie. Don't fight it."

He reached down and took the belt from the bathrobe she'd worn earlier and tied it around one of her wrists, then quickly looped it around the other and pulled the knot tight. He took the other end of it and tied it to part of the headboard.

If asked, Melanie would have said she wasn't the type of person who could enjoy being restrained, but her heart was thudding with excitement and her skin was on fire in anticipation of his touch. He wanted to dominate her and that knowledge was excruciatingly hot.

She twisted and tested her restraint. He pulled the knot tighter.

"I could get out of this," she claimed, even though she had no desire to.

"But you'd have to want to. And you don't." He shed his lounge pants and opened a drawer of a table beside his bed.

Although Melanie didn't know what Charles was reaching for, her breathing became ragged as her excitement grew. He held up a blindfold.

"Do you trust me?" he asked.

"Yes," she answered honestly.

He gently placed the blindfold over her eyes and settled himself beside her, running a hand slowly down her neck, down the middle of her chest, and farther down to cup the inside of one of her thighs. "When you can't see, all you can do is feel." He loosed one of her hands and wrapped it around his jutting cock. "Feel what you do to me?" He retied her, then kissed his way down the path his hand had traveled. The warmth of his breath tickled her thighs as he continued to speak. "Feel what I do to you."

He started his passionate assault on her legs. Claiming every inch of them first with his hands and then with his mouth. He took his time exploring her. Each touch shot through Melanie so intensely she shuddered beneath it.

He spread her legs and thrust his tongue deeply inside her while rubbing her clit with one hand and gripping her ass from beneath with his other. He withdrew and used the slight stubble on his chin against her sensitive nub, and Melanie groaned with pleasure. Had her hands been free, she would have buried them in his hair and held him there, but he was in control.

When she felt the heat of an orgasm beginning to build within her, he lifted his head. "Are you close?"

"Yes," she practically sobbed. "Don't stop."

"Say you belong to me. Tell me you're mine."

She shook her head and his kisses moved to her stomach. "No," she said, hearing the frustration in her husky voice.

Just when she thought he'd cheated her of her pleasure, he began to tease and suckle her breasts, and the wondrous heat from before returned tenfold. She thrashed back and forth, unable to think past the need that was building within her. His mouth continued its assault while his hands kneaded and caressed, warming her skin until there wasn't an inch of her that didn't crave him.

She heard him open a condom wrapper and whimpered at the momentary lack of his touch. Unashamed, she spread her legs, eager to feel him inside her.

He untied her hands from the headboard, but left them bound together. She felt him lie down beside her. "Sit up," he ordered.

She did. She could easily have moved the blindfold now so she could see, but he'd been right—she'd have to want to. And, God, she didn't want to. Every touch, every breath she felt on her skin shot through her more intensely than she'd known it could.

And from the way he was breathing, she knew he was enjoying their game as much as she was. In that moment she was both vulnerable and powerful.

"Ride me," he commanded.

With her hands tied in front of her, Melanie stood and placed one foot on either side of his waist, then lowered herself down until she felt his rigid tip graze her sex. He gripped her hips and guided her onto her knees and moved his hips so his sheathed cock moved back and forth against her wet clit.

He dipped his tip inside her, withdrew it, then thrust powerfully upward and into her. Melanie cried out and threw her head back with pleasure as he guided her to meet his thrusts, taking him deeper each time. An orgasm rocked through her, clenching her inner muscles around him and she bent over to kiss him as she came.

His lips clung to hers, but his thrusts were relentless. They took her through the lull after her climax and toward another, even stronger one. With an animallike cry, she untangled her hands and freed herself, grasping at his shoulders, clawing at his back while she ground down against him.

He nipped at her breast and finally gave himself to his own release. She joined him, then collapsed down on top of him.

"Mine," he whispered in her ear.

Melanie awoke again at the first light of dawn. She was naked and tucked against Charles. Careful not to wake him, she rested her head on his chest and let the steady beat of his heart soothe her.

At what point will I wake up and realize I'm still at home and this was one wild erotic dream? She smiled. *My dreams were never this good.*

Who would have thought he'd be the one asking her to stay and she'd be the one sprinting away?

But it didn't matter. Jace deserved a father who wanted him. And she deserved a partner. A real partner.

Not just someone who gave her mind-blowing orgasms.

And right now she needed, more than anything, to remember Jace was why she was in New York. Not Charles.

She carefully inched away from him, pausing when he stirred.

Melanie gathered her clothing off the floor and dressed silently in her jeans and blouse. She tied her hair back in a simple ponytail and took one last look at Charles, then closed the bedroom door softly behind her. She saw the time on a clock on the wall: seven o'clock.

The perfect time to call Greece.

Time to stop letting fear hold her back. No more excuses.

She dug through her purse for the paper with Todd's parents' number. *I'm not perfect, but I love my son and that will guide me through this.* She stepped out onto the balcony.

It rang once.

It rang twice.

"Hello?" an older woman's voice answered cheerfully.

Melanie's first attempt to speak came out as a nervous croak. She shook her head and started over with determination. "Hello, I'm looking for Todd Jones."

The line went dead silent. Then the woman asked cautiously, "Who is this?"

Looking down at the already busy streets below, Melanie cleared her throat and plowed forward. "My name is Melanie. I'm a friend of his from college. I'm in New York for a few days, and I was hoping to see Todd while I'm here. Could you help me find him?"

The receiver was muffled for a moment and then a man's voice asked, "Who am I speaking to?"

Don't hang up.

"My name is Melanie Hanna. I knew Todd in college. I heard he moved to New York, but no one had an address after yours. Please. It's important. I need to speak with him."

There was another long pause, then the man said, "I'm sorry. My son passed away last year."

It took a moment for his words to sink in, then Melanie dropped to her knees on the balcony as bile rose in her stomach. "He's dead?" she whispered in shock.

"Yes." The man's tone softened as he heard the emotion in hers. "He was running in a marathon and had a sudden aneurysm. Were you close?"

The balcony began to spin around Melanie and she couldn't catch her breath. *Todd's dead. I waited too long. I can't make this better.* Tears clogged her throat and blurred her vision, and she dropped the phone into her lap.

"She's crying," Todd's father said to his wife. "Maybe you should talk to her."

"Melanie, are you alone? Can we call anyone for you?" Even at the distance the phone was from her ear, Melanie heard the concern in the woman's voice and it tore through her. She didn't deserve their concern.

"No, I'm . . . I'm . . . I need to go."

Overwhelmed by the guilt washing over her, Melanie hung up and stood. Still breathing shallowly, and feeling like she was on autopilot, she gathered her luggage and paused at the door.

She needed to leave. She had to get back to Jace.

Through the years since she'd found out she was going to have Jace and through all the excuses she'd given herself to put off contacting Todd, she'd held on to the belief that there would be time to make it right later. It was that loss that sent her spiraling into a panic.

I can't fix this.

I waited too long.

She paused and considered writing a note for Charles.

But what would I say? I've found out what I came for. Both Charles and I knew this wasn't forever. I'm just ending it early.

Besides, Charles is probably as interested in messy good-byes as I am.

She closed the door behind her quietly and took the elevator down to the lobby. Once outside, she hailed a taxi. "LaGuardia Airport please."

Her mind was blank except for one clear thought: *I need to see Jace.*

By the time she arrived at the airport, she was outwardly composed, even if inwardly she felt as if the world had crashed down around her. People in line were smiling and laughing and she wanted to scream, "Don't you know that nothing will ever be okay again?" She went straight to the ticket counter.

"You're lucky," the ticket agent said, "we have seats available on our next flight out in thirty minutes."

Yeah, that's me.

Lucky.

Melanie bought a ticket and headed to security. After clearing the security line, she walked blindly to the designated gate just in time to board. She buckled herself in with cold hands and stared out the window.

"I should sit in coach more often," a deep male voice commented appreciatively as he sat down beside her.

She turned to look into the friendly face of a man who appeared to be in his midtwenties. He was conservatively dressed in a casual suit and his hair was expertly cut, which made her imagine that many women would have found him attractive. *You picked the wrong woman to try to hit on, buddy.* Melanie turned away from him coldly.

Undeterred, the man continued to address her. "Are you headed home?"

Home? The word seared through her.

I don't know where that is anymore.

With Charles in New York?

Hiding out on a horse ranch in Texas? Is that any kind of home?

I was so busy worrying about me and how people might judge me, I didn't think of Jace. I just hid him away.

Until it was too late.

Tears streaming down her face, she turned back to the man beside her and shook her head wordlessly. He froze at her display of emotion and almost comically scrambled to stand and move to another seat.

Melanie turned back toward the window. She heard the rustle of another passenger behind her but didn't turn to see who it was. She tightened her seatbelt and closed her eyes, crying softly against the cool side of the plane.

A hand touched her shoulder and Melanie looked up into the concerned eyes of a stewardess. "Are you okay, ma'am? A few of the passengers are worried about you."

Melanie accepted a tissue from the woman and blew her nose loudly. *I'm very far from being okay, but I have to get myself under control. I can't be like this when I see Jace.* "Sorry," Melanie said with a fortifying sniff. "I just found out someone I knew passed away."

"Oh my God," the woman said. "No wonder you're crying. Can I get you some water? Anything?"

Melanie shook her head and the stewardess reluctantly returned to the front of the plane for takeoff. Once in the air, Melanie kept her face to the window, trying to distance herself from reality.

That's the thing about reality.

You can't wish it away.

There is no rewind.

No game reset.

It's the result of choices made, and I keep choosing poorly.

But I can do better.

I will do better.

"I'm sorry, but you look familiar. Do I know you?"

Melanie opened her eyes and looked over two empty seats to a blonde woman across the aisle. Although she seemed pleasant enough, Melanie didn't recognize her. "No."

"You're not the Takedown Cowgirl, are you?" the woman asked.

In confusion, Melanie shook her head. "Who?"

The woman tapped the man next to her. "Doesn't she look like the woman in the video that's all over the news? The one who everyone thought was shooting a scene for a movie, but she was really getting mugged?"

Melanie closed her eyes. *Please. No.*

She opened her eyes, but they were still staring at her.

"She does," the man answered and gave Melanie a thumbs-up. "You kicked some serious ass that day. Kudos."

A teenage girl in the seat behind them stood up. "Who is she?"

The blonde woman said, "I think it's the Takedown Cowgirl. Seriously."

"Oh my God, I have to see."

The lanky girl squeezed over the person in the aisle seat and made her way to sit one seat away from Melanie. "It *is* you! You are my fucking hero. No one will believe I met you. I need a selfie with you." Without waiting for permission, she turned away and leaned back, including Melanie in the background of a picture she took with her phone.

"I can't wait to land and send this," the girl said. She turned back and looked Melanie over with a critical eye. "Did he dump you? That hot guy who kissed you on the video? Is that why you're crying? My mom says you staged the whole thing, but my friends and I don't think you did. Did you?"

The girl appeared to be about fourteen. Melanie prayed for strength and calm. "Look at the expression on my face. Do you think I'm in the mood to talk to anyone?"

"No, you look pissed. But what are you gonna do? Knock me down? Hog-tie me?" The girl laughed. "Because that would be fucking awesome. It would go viral. Just make sure someone tapes it."

"Kara, get back to your seat," a stern female voice said.

"In a minute."

"No, you're about to lose your cell phone if you don't leave that lady alone."

"Fine." The girl flounced back to her seat.

Melanie let out a breath of relief when the seat beside her was once again filled, this time with a thin woman with gray hair cut in curls that framed her face. Her Texan drawl was a welcome sound even if her presence wasn't. "Please excuse my granddaughter— her mother spoils her rotten. That's why she's coming to live with me for a while. Someone has to rein her in. Time mucking stalls should turn her around."

"I am not going to touch equine feces. Not in this lifetime," her granddaughter called back.

The older woman chuckled. "Sex-ed classes should stop using dolls and eggs to represent what it's like to parent. They should send everyone home with a teenager who swears and steals money out of their purse. That's real birth control incentive."

Melanie found herself sympathetically smiling. "Sounds like a handful."

The woman shrugged. "She'll be fine. I'll ride it out. Their brains come back—although it takes a while sometimes. And she's a good kid. I just have to help her remember that."

Gripping her hands tightly in her lap, Melanie said, "She's lucky to have you."

The woman studied her face for a moment quietly, then asked, "Where are your parents?"

"In Telson, on the ranch I grew up on," Melanie said sadly. "They did their best to rein *me* in, but I bucked them right off and bolted."

"They good people?"

"Yes," Melanie answered simply.

The woman put her hand on one of Melanie's and patted it. "Maybe you should go see them when you land. You look like you need someone to talk to."

"I can't," Melanie said, her voice thick with emotion. "Things haven't been good between us. I said terrible things to them. And I never apologized. Never."

"Do you have a child?" she asked gently.

Melanie nodded. "Jace. He just started kindergarten."

"What could you forgive him?"

"Anything," Melanie said in a whisper.

"Then go on home to them, sweetie." With that, the woman returned to her seat, leaving Melanie to think about what she'd said.

Charles strode from room to room in his apartment. Melanie had taken all her things with her. No note. No good-bye. Just gone.

He called her hotel, but she hadn't checked back in.

Stomach churning with emotions he didn't want to begin to try to label, he showered and dressed in a suit.

Well isn't that a punch in the stomach . . . The first woman I ask to live with me takes off like I offered her the mumps.

I could have probably worded the invitation better.

But I said she could bring her son.

What more does she want?

He thought back to how she'd looked, blindfolded and tied to his bed. He'd never tied a woman up before and was chastising himself for not researching a little before attempting it. It had been a spontaneous decision and one that he regretted now. He and Melanie had made a sort of pact to escape their normal lives together. He'd wanted to show her that she could trust him in and out of their fantasy time. Had he gone too far?

He called her cell phone, but it rang through to voice mail. He didn't leave a message.

He was angry.

He was sorry.

He couldn't understand how she could leave without at least saying good-bye. He called for his car to be brought around and slammed the door of his apartment as he left. He phoned his assistant to tell her they'd be working through the weekend. He needed to clear his head.

He drove to his office, grinding the gears of his Mercedes-Benz along the way. *I refuse to chase her. I was perfectly happy before I met her. By next week I won't even remember her name.*

Charles walked past June without greeting her and slammed the door to his office. A moment later the phone on his desk rang on her line. He hit the speakerphone button impatiently. "What is it?"

"You told me to hold all of your calls and I have, but there are some that are urgent and one I think you need to know about. I was up all night wondering if I should have called you instead of waiting to see you today."

"I would hope by now you'd have the sense to know if you should have."

There was a long and awkward silence on the line. In a thick voice, she finally answered, "Sorry, Mr. Dery. These calls fell outside of what you normally receive."

Charles paced in front of his desk, running both hands over his face roughly. He wasn't known for being open to topics that weren't work related, but he also wasn't normally an ass to his staff. "June, I'm in a foul mood this morning. Who called?" It was as close to an apology as he had within him, but it proved to be enough.

Sounding more like her normally upbeat self, June said, "Almost every morning news show out there and some cable channels. They'd like to interview you and a woman they are calling the Takedown Cowgirl."

"Has Javits called yet?"

"Your lawyer? Twice yesterday. He said he tried to reach you on your cell, too. He found what you were looking for."

It took Charles a moment to remember that he'd asked his lawyer to hunt down the boy who had mugged Melanie. "I've been busy," Charles growled, then pulled his temper back under control. It wasn't her fault Melanie had left without saying good-bye. Nor was it her fault that this news illustrated how impossible putting Melanie out of his head would be.

"Call Javits. Put him through as soon as you have him on the line."

"Absolutely, Mr. Dery. You should also call Rawlings. He said he expected something from you yesterday."

Shit.

"I'll call him now. Thank you, June."

He'd like to blame Melanie for causing him to drop the ball, but it was his fault. He'd lost focus. He'd chosen to put everything aside for her.

Lesson learned.

He went to sit behind his desk and slumped in his chair. *I've worked too hard for too long to throw it all away on a woman.*

He turned on his computer, quickly finished the proposal he'd promised Rawlings, and sent it to him. He'd give him an hour to look it over, then contact him.

He looked down at his cell phone on his desk with disgust, hating how much he wanted to call Melanie.

I don't need distractions right now.

I need to get my head back in the game.

Chapter Twelve

It was early afternoon when Melanie arrived in a taxi at her parents' house unannounced. She tipped the driver, took her luggage, and walked up the stairs of the home she'd grown up in. It was a large ranch that they'd built onto as her parents had raised their four daughters. It wasn't a home that would impress the people she'd met in New York, but her father had built most of it himself and had paid it off long ago.

So many memories she loved—and some she hated—came flooding back each time she stood on this porch. Her first kiss. Prom photos. Hot summer evenings spent with her sisters drinking lemonade and sharing secrets. It was also where everything had blown up with her parents.

She put the luggage off to one side of the porch, gathered her courage, and stepped inside. Her father had retired when the factory he'd worked at for years relocated southward.

"Mom? Dad?" she called out. "Anyone home?"

The door hadn't been locked, but that wasn't unusual. They lived by different rules out on her parents' farm. The place was never unattended since there was always a ranch hand around. However, security in these parts didn't rely on electronic monitoring devices. Instead, even a home as nice as her parents' had its share of shotguns. People didn't wander onto other people's property uninvited. Period.

Her parents came out of the back of the house, looking unusually disheveled. Her mother was smoothing her salt-and-pepper hair back into her usually perfectly tied knot.

"Mel, we didn't know you were coming today. Is Jace outside?"

Melanie looked back and forth between her parents' flushed faces and decided she didn't want to know what they'd been up to before she got there. "I probably should have called first," she said.

"No, no," her mother protested and straightened the neckline of her dress. She took a second look at her daughter's expression and was suddenly concerned. "Has something happened?"

Everything Melanie regretted came crashing in on her in one tidal wave of emotion. She began to shake as tears she'd held in during the flight and the ride to her parents' house resurfaced. "I don't know what to do, Mom. I've been wrong so many times. I screwed up my life, and now I've taken something away from Jace that he deserved to have. How can I look him in the eye when I'm a horrible mom?"

Her mother looked at her father, then back at her.

Melanie hugged herself and shook her head violently. "You were right when you told me I should be ashamed of myself. I am. I don't know what to do . . . how to be better than I am. I thought I could make things right, but it's too late."

Her mother rushed to her side and led her to a chair, taking a seat beside her. "You stop right there, Melanie. I said many things I regret and that was one of them. Jace is a wonderful boy. You've been a good mother to him. Just tell me what happened. Whatever it is, we'll deal with it—together."

"There's nothing you can do about this one, Mom. It's done."

"Are you pregnant again?" her father asked gruffly.

"I wish it was that," Melanie said without thinking, then regretted the words that wiped all color from her father's face. She dabbed away her tears in frustration and clarified. "I didn't mean that the way it sounded. I'm not pregnant. I don't wish I was pregnant." She buried her face in her hands. "It's just that I could find some good in that mistake."

Her mother put an arm around her shoulders. "We're here for you, Mel. We always have been. Whatever it is, you can tell us."

Melanie raised her eyes to meet her father's. "I never told you about Jace's father because I was too ashamed to tell you the truth."

Neither of her parents moved while they waited for her to explain.

"I met him at college. We didn't even date."

Her father made a sound deep in his chest, but didn't say anything. Her mother's face twisted with compassion, but she also kept her thoughts to herself.

"We were together one time and then we never spoke again." Melanie choked back fresh tears. "He didn't care about me. I told myself he wouldn't care about Jace, either." Melanie wrung her hands nervously in front of her. "I don't know, maybe I was also afraid he could take Jace from me. I know it was wrong, but I didn't think about how it would hurt Jace to not know him. I convinced myself we were better off without Todd."

Softly, her mother said, "But?"

"But Jace started asking about him. He wanted to know why his father didn't care about him."

"Sounds like it's high time you tell Todd about him, then," her father said in the same stern voice he'd used to issue curfews to her when she was younger.

"I tried," Melanie said sadly. "I went to New York because that was the last place that anyone had heard he'd gone. He'd moved there to be closer to his parents." Melanie closed her eyes as memories from her conversation with Todd's parents replayed in her head. "But I was too late. He died last year without ever knowing he had a son." Gathering her courage, Melanie opened her eyes again and faced her father.

Her father said nothing, but his jaw tightened visibly.

Her mother gasped.

Heartfelt questions burst out of Melanie. "What do I tell Jace? How do I not cry and beg him to forgive me the next time he asks about his dad?"

"You—" Her father started to speak in a harsh tone, but her mother cut him off.

"If you're about to say what I think you are, don't. She doesn't need a lecture right now. We waited a long time for her to come home to us. I *will not* lose her again."

Her father crossed the room and sat on the other side of Melanie. There was a sadness in his eyes that she was all too familiar with because it darkened her own soul. He sat forward with his hands between his knees and said, "No one said parenting was easy, Mel. We all do the best we can and all have to face where we fall short. I've never been one to talk matters out. Your mom knows that. It's why she does most of the talking around here."

His wife gave him a tolerant smile. "I know you're leading up to something sweet, but you're taking your time getting there."

Melanie quietly digested what he'd said. *They're doing the best they can, just like me.* Suddenly, they were human to her. Not just people who had raised and disappointed her, but parents struggling to make things right. Their love for each other and understanding of one another was strong, even in the face of this. Her mother wasn't pointing fingers and blaming her father, but she was making her opinion clear. There was a beauty in the conversation despite how difficult it was to have. And their love for her was there—plain as day.

Her father sat up and looked Melanie in the eye. "You've got nothing to be ashamed of, Mel. Jace is a fine boy. You've done a good job of raising him. Maybe he wasn't meant to meet his father. That's a conversation best left for you and God. When Jace asks, you tell him that his father loved him and would have been with him if he could have been. It's not the whole truth, but something he'll understand until he's old enough to hear more."

Within the comfort of her mother's embrace, Melanie dried her eyes. She'd spent much of the past five years telling herself she didn't want to be like her parents, and now she found herself feeling the exact opposite.

Her mother asked, "What about Todd's parents? Do they know they have a grandchild?"

Melanie shook her head. "I didn't tell them. They sounded like they were still mourning."

Her father stood again. "Children aren't supposed to go first. They'll be mourning for the rest of their lives, but you need to tell them. I would want to know."

Melanie's mother nodded in solemn agreement. "Even though he never met Jace, part of Todd lives on in him. Your father's right. You have to tell them."

Melanie stood and held out her arms toward the parent she thought she'd lost forever. "Dad, I'm sorry for all the awful things I said when I moved out."

Her father hugged her to his large chest and didn't say a word. He didn't have to.

Chapter Thirteen

"I don't want to talk to him," the young man snarled as he leapt from his seat in the social worker's small office and confronted Charles, who was still standing.

"Sit down, TJ," the social worker ordered from his seat at a small, file-covered desk in the corner of the room. Charles doubted that the man intimidated many people, even when he raised his voice with authority. He looked more like an accountant, and it was clear the boy before him wouldn't respect anyone less than a bouncer.

"No!" TJ raged. "You here because I said I'd sue you? You and your girlfriend should be scared. You can't tie people up and then put it all over the Internet."

"No one is suing anyone—" the social worker interjected.

"You can't stop me. I have lawyers calling every day. They say that what you did was wrong."

Charles sighed and held his temper. From what he'd learned about Tanner Jacob Moss, he'd had a rough life and had a right to be angry. His father had been a small-time drug dealer who'd died on the streets. His mother had overdosed when he was nine. Even though he'd stayed clean from drugs, he'd spent the years since then bouncing from one foster home to the next while his bad behavior escalated—just recently turning criminal. "You did steal her purse," Charles reminded him blandly.

"Fuck you," the boy said.

"That's enough, TJ. Wait outside the door for me," the social worker said.

"You think I'm going to wait while you two sit in here and talk about me? I'll—"

The social worker stood and shook his head. "You'll wait because you're lucky you're not in juvenile right now, and that's only because no one pressed charges. Your options are shrinking, my friend, as is the list of those willing to take a risk on you. Go find a seat in the next room and don't move. Now go."

After Tanner left the office, Charles looked at the social worker and said, "He's a handful."

The social worker nodded and motioned to the chair the boy had left. "Please, sit."

Charles politely declined. When his lawyer had called and said that he'd located the boy who had taken Melanie's purse, he hadn't expected to want to get involved. Yet here he was, in a part of town he'd never been in, discussing a boy he was sure he had no business asking about.

The social worker picked up a file. "I'm not supposed to share any information with you, but your situation is unique."

Charles rocked back on his heels and decided not to ask. "Is he in a group home now? My lawyer said he was removed from his foster family."

The social worker tapped his pen on the folder. "Why are you here, Mr. Dery?"

Charles shrugged, as yet still unable to answer that question for himself. "I want to do something for him."

With renewed interest, the social worker asked, "Financially?"

Charles raised a hand and motioned for the conversation to slow. "Maybe. I'm not in a position to give him a home. Are there different levels of group homes? One I could help pay for?"

One of the social worker's eyebrows rose. "They aren't like hotels, Mr. Dery."

Impatiently, Charles said, "Well, what does he need? I'll buy him whatever . . . so he won't have to steal to get it."

"TJ stole because he knew it would get him removed from his latest placement. He wasn't getting along with the father."

"Why didn't you move him?" Charles boomed.

"It's not that easy. TJ is almost eighteen and he's built up a reputation for being a tough placement. I didn't have other options. I was hoping they could work it out. That home has been a good fit for some others. But it wasn't for him."

"So that's it? You're done? He goes to a group home and you give up?"

"Mr. Dery, you have no idea how many children I have on my roster, do you? Each and every one of them needs more time and more resources than I have. I lose sleep every time one of them is disappointed by another adult in their life. But I'm one man. I can't save them all. I try, and sometimes I fail, and I have to live with that. But don't question if I care about TJ. I've been watching out for him for almost seven years. How long have you cared about him? How long will you?"

Charles rubbed his chin roughly. "What would you have me do?"

Some of the aggression left the social worker as he sensed the sincerity in the question. "We have a mentoring program. You'd meet somewhere public once a week. Check in on him. Keep after him about his grades, ask him about who he spends his time with . . . be a stable person in his life. That's what he needs. I'm there for him, but I'm paid to be and he knows that. He needs one person who cares about him. Someone he can't drive away by stealing a purse. It doesn't cost anything, but giving him that could be what saves his life. Can you be that person?"

Before Melanie, Charles would have said no. He would have cited a hundred reasons why his schedule didn't allow for additional time commitments.

But he'd watched the still-trending video at least twenty times since she'd left. And each time, he liked his reaction to the boy less. How had he become a man who lacked compassion? Compared to what Tanner had gone through, his tragedy was minor. After his loss, he'd still had parents who loved him and a stable home. Parents who loved him still, even though he hardly ever went home to visit them.

"I can't imagine he'd want me as his mentor."

For the first time since Charles had walked into his office, the social worker smiled. "Not at first. No. But I'll make sure he meets you. Don't expect him to open up immediately. He's had a lot of disappointments in his life and he's learned not to trust anyone. But keep your appointments with him. Be there to listen to him and that will change."

After a quiet moment, Charles nodded. He'd done many things in his life that he regretted, things he'd give anything to be able to go back in time and fix. This could be his chance to set some of it right.

Charles walked out of the office. Tanner wasn't in the seat the social worker had asked him to sit in, but he was down the hallway and was glaring at Charles.

Charles didn't know if he would reach the young man or fail miserably, but he had to try.

For Tanner's sake as well as his own.

Charles was riding back to his office in his limo when his phone rang.

"You're answering your phone again. Is that a good sign or a bad one?" Mason asked with humor.

Charles glared out the window at nothing in particular. "It's been a long week. My latest client was a hard sell, but I finally have him fully on board."

"Most people sound happier announcing shit like that."

"I told you—"

"I know. Long week. So your bad mood has nothing to do with your girlfriend, Melanie?"

"She's not my anything," Charles snapped.

"Ouch. Touchy subject. Did you have a fight? She kick your ass? You don't have to tell me. No, scratch that—you owe me the highlights. Did she want to tie you up all the time so you broke it off? I'm not into that personally, but for a woman that beautiful I'd pretend to be."

"You're so full of shit. And I'm not having this conversation right now," Charles said and was about to hang up, but Mason started talking again.

"You were a lot more fun in college. What did New York do to you?"

"I believe it's called growing up. You might want to try it." Although his words were harsh, he was ribbing more than reprimanding his friend. This was a conversation they'd had so many times before, it had become a running joke between the two of them.

"No, thanks. You're serious enough for both of us. So now that you and Melanie are over, want to head to Vegas with me for a weekend? I have some friends who are gathering out there. It's going to be quite a bash."

Although they were living very different lives, a part of Charles would always appreciate Mason's friendship and offers. "I'll be working through the weekend."

"Are you going to tell me what happened?"

Charles closed his eyes. "I asked her to stay and she left."

"That sucks."

He almost denied it, but one of the reasons he and Mason had remained friends for so long is that they could be real with each other. "Yes, it does."

"Did she say why?"

"No, she left while I was sleeping."

"The old sneak-out-in-the-middle-of-the-night move. I hate that one—unless I'm the one doing it. Did you call her?"

Charles opened his eyes and rubbed one of his temples. "Yes. Three times. She's not taking my calls. I'm done. Asking her and her son to move in with me was ridiculous anyway. What the hell would I do with a five-year-old in my house? I don't want to raise someone else's child. I don't even want my own. I'm glad she left."

Mason was quiet for a moment, then said, "Maybe you should contact your sister and see if she knows anything."

"No. It's over."

"Okay, if you say so."

"I do."

"So, no Vegas?"

"No."

"Call your sister," Mason said and hung up.

Charles shook his head, and rejected the idea right then and there.

He rejected it again later that day when he sat in his office, blindly staring at its closed door, mulling over what Mason had said.

He was not going to call Sarah. He would, however, stop avoiding her attempts to contact him.

The past week had given him time and perspective. He didn't need to explain his side to anyone.

I offered Melanie everything.
She didn't want it.
End of story.

Chapter Fourteen

That night, Melanie had just put Jace down to sleep when there was a knock on her screen door. Sarah stepped inside and closed the door softly behind her when she saw Melanie. "You're still up. Good. I was afraid I'd have to wait until tomorrow to hear what happened."

From anyone else, the statement would have felt like an intrusion, but Sarah had come to her out of love and Melanie was in dire need of some. "Come in. I just put Jace down, so we'll have to talk softly."

Sarah held out a small paper bag. "I brought chocolate."

"How did you know I needed it?" Melanie took the bag gratefully and walked with Sarah to the living room.

"When you picked up Jace without saying anything about your trip, I figured it didn't go well." She plopped down beside Melanie and dug into the bag, pulling out a piece for Melanie and one for herself. "Did you find Todd?"

Melanie unwrapped the chocolate carefully, not meeting Sarah's eyes as she answered, "I did."

"And?" Sarah pushed gently.

"He died over a year ago. An aneurysm while he was running."

Sarah dropped her candy and put an arm around her friend's shoulders. "I'm so sorry. Why didn't you call me when you found out?"

Melanie continued to play with the wrapper on her lap. "I wouldn't have known what to say. It still doesn't feel real."

"Loss can be like that. It hits you in stages."

Melanie met Sarah's eyes. "It's not that kind of loss. It should be, I guess. But I didn't know Todd very long. That sounds awful, doesn't it?"

"No, it sounds honest."

"I wanted to find him for Jace, you know? I'd put off telling Todd about Jace because I always thought there'd be a better time to tell him. I was fooling myself. I should have told him right away."

"You didn't know he would die."

"No, but I knew what the right thing to do was and I didn't do it."

Sarah nodded and said, "Well, this confirms it. You're human. You make mistakes just like the rest of us."

Melanie stood up. "Don't. Don't brush aside what I did."

Sarah joined her. "I'm not, but I don't want to see you beat yourself up over something you can't do anything about." When Melanie didn't say anything, Sarah asked, "What did Charles say when you told him?"

"I didn't."

"Did you tell him why you were there?"

Melanie turned away from Sarah and walked across the room. "Yes."

"But you didn't tell him about finding Todd? I thought the two of you were . . . that you had . . ."

"We were together, but it's over."

"I don't understand."

"It didn't work out. That's it. I don't want to talk about it anymore."

Sarah went to stand in front of Melanie. "So what are you going to do now?"

"Nothing. There's nothing left I can do."

Chewing her bottom lip, Sarah said, "There is always something . . ."

Feeling cornered and raw from the day, Melanie snapped, "I can't handle your eternal optimism right now. It's been a long day. I'm exhausted. Can we just drop this? Please."

With a slight frown, Sarah walked to the door. "David is still at the main house. Do you want me to send him over?"

"I don't want to talk to anyone about anything, okay? Just leave me alone." Melanie's voice rose with agitation.

"Mama?" Jace called from his upstairs bedroom.

With her hand on the screen door, Sarah said earnestly, "I'm sorry, Mel. I didn't mean to come over and upset you."

Melanie called up the stairs to assure Jace that she was fine, then turned to Sarah. "No. I'm sorry. Thank you for coming. I didn't mean to snap at you. I must be overtired. I don't want to think about anything anymore today."

With a nod, Sarah said gently, "It's okay to give yourself a day, Mel, but then you have to pick yourself back up and go on."

"I will," Melanie said just to make her friend feel better.

"See you tomorrow?" Sarah asked hopefully.

"Jace has school, so I'll be up there right after he leaves."

Sarah stepped outside but lingered on the other side of the screen. "It's going to be okay."

Melanie nodded, thanked Sarah again for coming, and closed the door.

The next morning, Melanie was cleaning the breakfast dishes in the kitchen of the main house when her boss, Tony Carlton, walked into the room. She resumed what she was doing. Tony wasn't the type to engage in idle discourse. Although he'd opened up a lot since meeting Sarah, he would never be the chatty type, and Melanie was comfortable with the relationship they'd had for years: cohabitating without much actual interaction.

He surprised her by coming to stand beside her and taking his hat off. "I don't think you should work here anymore, Melanie," he said in his gruff Texan drawl.

Melanie dropped the plate in her hands and it smashed into pieces at her feet. Neither of them moved. "Are you firing me?"

Tony tossed his hat onto the table a few feet away. He leaned back on the counter and took his time choosing his words. "You don't belong here anymore."

Swallowing hard, Melanie walked to the closet, took out a dustpan and broom, and began to clear away the mess she'd made. She had known this day would come. Tony didn't need a housekeeper anymore. He had Sarah now. Had she gone home upset with Melanie last night? If so, that was enough to make a man like Tony ask her to leave. He didn't like any sort of drama on his ranch. "I understand." She dumped the broken glass into the trash and removed her apron.

Tony swore under his breath. "You'll be better off."

Unable to meet his eyes, Melanie said, "Don't dress it up like something it isn't. You want me to leave, so I'll go. But don't try to make it look like you're doing it for me. I'm happy here."

A sad expression crossed Tony's face. "You have to get on with your life. Just as I have."

"Do you want the house back?" Melanie asked. Tony had given her the deed to her home, but that had been when he'd expected her to keep working there. If he did, Melanie wasn't sure what that would mean for her. Although she'd made up with her parents, she didn't feel that she could go back there. No job. No house.

Things definitely have a way of going from bad to worse before they get better.

David walked in and stopped just inside the door. "So this is where everyone is. Anything going on I should know about?"

Tony retrieved his hat. "I was just telling Melanie that she needs to find another job."

David looked back and forth between them. "Why the hell would you say that, Tony?"

Melanie tried not to show how the announcement had shaken her. She shrugged. "He says it's for my own good."

David turned on Tony. "Where is she supposed to go?"

Tony frowned. "I never said she had to move."

Melanie let out a breath of relief.

"But you don't want her working here anymore?"

"She's better than this." He met Melanie's eyes across the room. "You are. You're no housekeeper. You're too smart for that. Go back to school. You went to college once, didn't you?"

Emotion swelled in Melanie. "I couldn't afford it even if I wanted to."

Tony shrugged. "Shoot, we could probably pay your tuition with the sale of one horse."

His generosity floored Melanie. "I couldn't accept . . ."

Tony turned to his ranch manager. "David, you're real good at talking people into things. Tell her that she needs to do this."

"I'd say you're doing a good job of convincing her without me."

"Convincing who to do what?" Sarah asked as she entered the kitchen.

Tony walked over to his fiancée and kissed her lightly on the lips before saying, "Melanie is going back to school."

Sarah smiled up at Tony. "I knew you could talk her into it."

"I can't let you pay for school for me," Melanie protested.

Sarah shared a look with Tony, then said, "This is what you do for family."

"I'm not . . ." Melanie started to say, then stopped herself. Although they weren't related by blood, Sarah was right. These people had become her family. She would have done anything for them, and it was humbling to see they felt the same way about her. Starting over was scary, but it held the hope of a better life for Jace as well as herself. "I'll pay you back every penny."

Tony said, "How about if you settle the bill by cooking for us now and then? Have you tasted Sarah's cooking?"

Sarah made a face and said, "You said it was getting better."

He kissed her upturned nose. "Because I love you."

Melanie shook her head at the pair and smiled for the first time that day. There were many parts of her life that still felt wrong, but this—this was right.

After Tony and David left, Sarah remained in the kitchen and helped Melanie finish cleaning it. "I hope you're not upset that I told Tony about what happened with Todd."

"How could I be upset? Thank you."

"I told you things were going to be okay," Sarah said in her usual optimistic tone.

Melanie reached out and hugged her. "Don't change, Sarah. Don't let anyone ever change you."

A week after returning from New York, Melanie sat in the shade of a tree late one afternoon and watched her son work a horse by riding him around barrels that had been set up in a small field. The large smile on Jace's face told her that he was where he belonged.

While she'd been away, he'd shadowed Tony extensively, or so David had told her, and they'd gotten on better than anyone had expected. Sarah's influence extended into how Tony interacted with everyone on the ranch, and it was a beautiful thing to see.

She'd brought love and laughter into Tony's life and it had spread across the ranch—and had indeed sparked a feeling of family among people who had worked closely but kept their distance from each other for years.

Now Jace shadowed Tony everywhere, asking him a million questions and practicing whatever Tony suggested. It was a challenge to keep him on the ground and cleaned off long enough to get him to school each day. He raced home, did his chores, then hopped back on whichever horse Tony said he could "work" that day.

Even though Tony wasn't what most would consider a warm man, Jace hero-worshipped him. He and David had been Jace's only male role models since he was born. Overcome by emotion, Melanie swallowed hard against the lump in her throat. *The closest thing to a father he'll ever have.*

She jumped when Sarah plopped down in the grass beside her. "So are you ready to meet Jace's grandparents?"

"As much as I'll ever be," Melanie answered. She knew exactly what Sarah was referring to.

She'd called Todd's parents again. The conversation played in her head, as vivid now as if she'd just hung up from talking with them.

"My name is Melanie. I called the other day looking for your son, Todd."

"Yes," his mother had said cautiously. "I remember you."

"I have something I need to tell you."

"Could you hold on please?" The woman had called her husband to her side and put Melanie on speakerphone.

"What does she want?" Todd's father asked.

"I don't know," his mother answered as if Melanie weren't right there listening. "But I want you to hear it." It was as if she knew that what she was about to hear would change all their lives forever.

"Melanie, is that what you said your name was?" the father asked.

"Yes," Melanie had responded slowly. "I . . . um . . ." Melanie stopped and started again. "Your son and I dated for a very short time in college. Right before he graduated. I gave him a—"

"If you're looking for anything you'd like returned, it's all boxed up back at our house. Leave me your number and I'll contact you when we're there again."

In a much softer tone, the mother said, "We don't like to be there much since we lost Todd. Too many memories."

Melanie said softly, "I understand. This isn't about anything I want back."

The father interrupted, "Why don't you just tell us whatever it is you called to say. My wife gets upset when it comes to anything that has to do with Todd. So let's not drag this out."

Melanie took a deep breath and said, "My son, Jace, is your grandson."

"Did she just say . . . ?" Todd's mother asked, her voice rising with emotion.

"Deborah, don't get excited about this. We don't know her. We don't know if she's lying. Todd never mentioned a Melanie."

"We didn't date long."

"But what if she's telling the truth?" the mother said urgently, her voice thick with tears. "Oh my God. We could have a grandchild."

"Do you have any proof that Todd was the father?" the father asked in a firm tone.

Melanie shook her head even though they couldn't see her. "Are you on a cell phone?"

"Yes," the mother replied, sounding confused by her question.

Melanie scrolled through her phone and sent a message to their phone. "I just sent you a photo of Jace."

There was a long pause, then the sound of the mother crying. "He looks just like Todd did at that age."

"We should do a blood test to be sure . . ."

The mother said, "I don't need a test to tell me those are our son's eyes and his smile. That's our grandson."

"When can we see him?" the father asked.

Melanie swayed.

No going back now.

"We live in Texas on a horse ranch. You're welcome to come for a visit."

"Did Todd know about his son?" the father demanded.

"No." Melanie whispered the truth. "I never told him."

The man muted his phone for a second, then came back and said, "We weren't coming back for another month, but we could fly back early. Where are you located?"

"I have a small house in Fort Mavis."

"We'll stay in the nearest town." He'd sounded like he was about to hang up, but the mother took the phone from him.

"Melanie?"

With tears in her eyes, Melanie answered, "Yes?"

"Thank you. Thank you for calling us."

Melanie said, "I'm sorry it took me so long."

"Don't be sorry, Melanie. You just gave me a piece of my son back. You don't know what that means."

Long after the call had ended, Todd's mother's words had haunted Melanie.

Please, this time, let this have been the right thing to do.

Waving to catch her attention, Sarah called Melanie back to the present. "So I spoke to Charlie again today."

Melanie kept her eyes on her son. "How is he?"

"Miserable. I wish you'd let me tell him why you don't want to talk to him." Sarah picked up some grass and tossed it into the air as she spoke. "That is, if you know why. I'm still not sure I understand."

With a sigh, Melanie looked at her friend. "Your brother is a wonderful guy, but we're too different."

"He doesn't like to talk about anything that bothers him. You don't like to talk about anything that bothers you. Yeah, you're so different."

Melanie turned back to watch Jace. "Did he ask about me?"

"No, but that doesn't mean anything. He expects me to gush and tell him everything. Even I can't believe I haven't."

"Well, thank you for that. I'm not ready to talk to him yet."

"Did you sign up for the interior design course?" Sarah asked, deciding to drop a topic that was going nowhere.

Melanie smiled with relief at the change of subject. "Yes, I can't wait to create beautiful spaces again. I even started keeping a notebook again of designs I like." She turned and winked at Sarah. "Unlike your journal, I'm not worried if Jace sees it."

Sarah blushed. Melanie knew she should probably let her friend forget the time Jace had repurposed her notebook, which was filled with Sarah's first attempts at writing erotica, as his coloring book. Luckily, he could only read a few words at the time.

As Sarah continued to turn various shades of embarrassment, Melanie said, "I forgot how much I loved the creative process. I enjoy taking the ordinary and making it beautiful."

Sarah smiled. "Speaking of beautiful, I can't get over how good you look. Tony says he liked you better before because now his ranch hands are having difficulty concentrating on their training sessions. They get all moony eyed when they see you."

Melanie blushed again. "It's just makeup and a few dresses."

"No, it's more than that, Mel. It's a confidence." Sarah stood slowly and brushed off the dirt from her jeans. "I know it's none of my business, but you really should call Charles. He deserves to know why you left."

"Why?" Melanie said angrily. "You said he doesn't even ask after me."

"Exactly."

Melanie sighed. "I want to, but after how I left . . . I don't know what to say except that I'm sorry. Most likely he's already moved on, and I'd only be rehashing something he'd rather not. I don't know what I should do. I can't think about anything else right now besides Jace's grandparents coming here. What if they're horrible people? What if contacting them was a mistake?"

"No one is going to let anything bad happen to Jace. Tony will throw them right off the ranch if they so much as breathe funny at either of you. And with my brother, I can't guarantee what he'll say—especially not after you disappeared without a word—but you should give him a chance. He's hurting just like you are. I don't need all the details of what happened between you two to know that. Love is terrifying sometimes. It requires a leap of faith. And you're right—it may not work out. But ask yourself, What if it could? What if making a phone call this time could change everything?"

With that, Sarah turned and walked back toward the main house.

Melanie thought for a long time about what Sarah had said. She'd been too afraid to contact Todd, and the consequences for that decision were hefty. She was moving forward in so many areas of her life, perhaps this was another she needed to address.

She took out her cell phone and stared down at it in her hand. She swiped it on and scrolled for Charles's number.

Her finger hovered over the "Call" button.

There was the sound of boy and horse disagreeing and then a thud as Jace hit the ground. Melanie pocketed her phone and was behind him in a heartbeat. "Are you okay? Does anything hurt?"

He stood up and brushed himself off. "Mama, I just fell."

There was a small scrape on his cheek. "You cut yourself."

He touched it, wiped the blood on his finger, looked at it, and said, "A little blood never stopped a real cowboy."

Melanie shook her head and pulled him into her arms. "No, but his mother did. Help me put that horse away for tonight. It's time for dinner."

"You're choking me, Mama."

She released him. Jace straightened his small, proud body and settled his hat low on his head, the way she'd seen Tony do a hundred times. She wanted to keep him little forever, but Sarah was right. He was growing up fast.

Life is going to change with or without my help.

Maybe it's time to stop being so afraid of it.

As they walked back across the huge field that led to their house, she said quietly, "Jace, remember when you were asking about your father?"

Jace looked up at her hopefully. "Is he coming here? Is he coming to see me?"

Melanie stopped walking, bent, and took her son's hands in hers. "No, honey. He can't. He's up in heaven."

Disappointment darkened hers son's expression as he tried to understand. "With Sandy?" Jace asked, connecting death with the only experience he had with it—the dog he'd grown up with and lost a year ago.

"Yes, he's with him."

"I'll pray for him just like you taught me to for Sandy," he said quietly, and Melanie's heart clenched painfully in her chest.

Melanie hugged her son to her. "You do that." She released him and stood, afraid that if they stayed on this topic too long, he'd see her cry. "But your father's parents are alive and they want to come see you. Would you like that?"

"Will they bring me presents?" he asked.

Melanie sniffed, smiled, took him by the hand, and started walking toward their house again. "I'm sure they will."

"Will they bring me my own TV?" he asked, once again sounding hopeful.

"No, because you're still too young to have one in your room," Melanie said with finality. He'd been asking for his own television ever since he started kindergarten and one of his friends told him that he had his own.

"I bet they'd bring me a puppy if I asked for one," Jace said.

Melanie sighed. "Didn't we talk about why getting a puppy is not a good idea right now? I'll be taking classes. You're in school. What would we do with a puppy?"

Jace looked up at her with enormous, soulful eyes and said, "He'd sleep with me. I'd take good care of him. I'd train him to wait for me on the porch like Sandy used to."

Melanie appealed to the sky for support but none came. She gazed back down at her son's pleading expression and partially caved. "Well, maybe we can start looking."

With a whoop of joy, Jace jumped. "Kenny said his dad said we could have one of their puppies for free because they're too old to sell. His dog is super smart, Mama. Can we go see them right now? Can we?"

"Tomorrow, Jace. We don't have anything for a puppy. We'd have to go shopping in town for supplies."

"We can go when I get home. I can't wait to tell Kenny you said yes."

"I didn't—" Melanie started to say, then stopped herself. *I'll just count myself lucky that all he asked for was a puppy. Good thing he doesn't know that I would have said yes to almost anything today.*

Inside the house, Jace followed her to the kitchen instead of running off to his toys as he usually did. "Do they like puppies?"

"Who, honey?" Melanie asked as she opened the refrigerator and took out a bowl of salad.

"My grandparents."

Melanie closed the refrigerator and lowered herself to her knees in front of her son. "I have a feeling they will love whatever you love."

"Will I have to hug them?"

"Only if you want to."

"Do they ride horses?"

"I don't know."

"Grandpa is a good rider. He races me even though Grandma tells him not to."

Melanie smiled, wondering what her father would think of that claim to fame. "Well, when you meet your other grandparents, you can ask them if they've been around horses."

"I might love them even if they say no."

Melanie stood and ruffled her son's hair. "That sounds like a good idea. Now go wash your hands and help me set the table."

"But I—"

"You heard me." Her son went off to wash his hands.

Once he was out of the room, she sat back against the counter. Jace now knew about his father and his grandparents. It certainly wouldn't be the last conversation they had about either topic, but it had gone better than she'd dared hope it would.

Minus the puppy.

But I'm only human.

The more Melanie faced the past, the stronger she felt.

What would Charles say if I called him and told him that I miss him?

Would he rush here to see me?

Or would he politely explain that he's already moved on?

"Mama, don't be mad . . . but I dropped a towel in the toilet," Jace called from the downstairs bathroom.

Melanie rushed down the stairs. She looked into the empty basin. "Where is it?"

Jace turned red and shrugged. "It went away when I flushed. Now the water is coming up instead of going down."

Shaking her head, Melanie dialed David's phone number. He merely chuckled when she told him the situation and said he'd be right over.

What would Charles have said if I'd called him for assistance? She couldn't imagine him fishing in the toilet for an elusive towel. He didn't know the first thing about kids.

Nor did I, before Jace.

She thought about how she'd almost called Charles earlier and decided she was glad that she hadn't.

Is this really what New York's most eligible bachelor is craving? A ready-made family? This crazy life? Me?

Chapter Fifteen

A few weeks later, Melanie stood with her son on the porch of their house. She'd changed her outfit twice already and was tempted to change it again. She'd started the day defiantly in jeans, then switched into a simple cotton dress she'd hoped would make a better impression.

They aren't coming to see me.

Jace was in his usual jeans and plaid shirt, with boots and a cowboy hat. He was a miniature of the men he'd known and was proud of it.

Melanie looked at her watch, reminding herself to breathe, and saw that it was three minutes past the hour the Joneses had said they would arrive.

Please be reasonably sane.

Don't be the type to say things that Jace is too young to understand.

Don't rush him.

Don't dismiss him.

Just love him and be someone he can love.

Please.

"You think they're coming, Mama?" Jace asked, squinting as he looked down the long dirt driveway.

They'd better be. "Of course they are."

Jace took out a piece of construction paper he'd folded up and stuffed into his pocket. It was wrinkled and torn, but he smoothed it out on the railing. "I made them a card. Want to see it?"

Melanie looked over her son's shoulder and felt her chest swell. Sometimes he was such the independent little man. "I would love to."

On the front there was a drawing of two stick figures, one tall and one short. "That's me and you."

Melanie cleared her throat and said, "I love my third eye."

Jace smiled. "That's a freckle. I like freckles on girls."

Melanie nodded solemnly. Jace pointed to a cloud he'd drawn and colored with a white crayon. "That's where my dad is. You can't see him because he's in heaven. And you can't see Sandy because Sandy is with him."

"It's beautiful."

He opened the card. He had drawn four stick figures on the inside. "That's you, me, and my new grandparents. I didn't give them faces because I don't know what they look like yet."

"That makes perfect sense."

He pointed to the cloud. "The cloud is smiling because my dad is happy to see his parents. And I'm smiling because I am, too." He folded the card up again and stuffed it back into his pocket. "Do you think they'll like it?"

Melanie ruffled her son's hair. "They'll love it."

"If they come. Lyle says his dad doesn't always come when he says he will. He's too busy. Maybe my grandparents are too busy today."

"They'll be here," Melanie assured him. *God, please let them be on their way.* She took out her phone and considered calling them, but they were only ten minutes late. Ten of the longest minutes of her life late.

A black sedan turned up the driveway, and Jace ran down the front steps, then stopped. He looked back at his mother, unsure if he should return to her side or run to the car. Tibby, their new pup, bounded around the side of the house covered with mud from the backyard.

"Tibby!" Melanie called and rushed down the steps.

Tibby was running circles around Jace. Beyond them an older couple was getting out of the dark vehicle. The man was tall and average in build, dressed in tan khakis and a light blue button-down shirt. He had Jace's eyes and a dignified mop of salt-and-pepper hair. His wife was dressed in a cream-colored skirt and blouse, with her straight brown hair perfectly tied back from her face in a loose bun. She could have graced a style magazine cover.

Melanie made a grab for the dog's collar, but he dropped playfully onto his elbows, then darted away to chase a bird in the grass. Torn between chasing Tibby and greeting the older couple, Melanie forgot to worry about either when she looked down at her son. He was suddenly all eyes and shy. He stepped back from his grandparents and clung to Melanie, burying his face in her stomach, and his hat fell to the ground behind him.

Todd's parents walked over and Mr. Jones held out his hand. "Thank you for inviting us, Melanie."

Mrs. Jones bent down to Jace's level and said, "You must be Jace. We came a long way to meet you."

Jace lifted his head and looked at her shyly. "Mama said you came from Greece."

The older woman smiled at her grandson and nodded. "We did. We have a house there, but when we heard about you we wanted to come see you."

His grandfather picked up Jace's hat and brushed it off. "You might want this."

"Thank you, sir." Jace took the hat, crushing it between him and his mother when he turned away again.

Melanie placed her hand on her son's head and smiled at her guests. "You two must be parched. Why don't you come inside and we'll get you a lemonade?"

"That would be very nice," Jace's grandfather said.

Melanie turned and started to lead the way toward the house when Tibby flew around the corner of the house again and beelined it for Jace's grandparents as if they had just that second arrived. He barked at them happily, then jumped up and left two large mud footprints on Jace's grandmother's cream-colored skirt.

Melanie gasped and rushed forward, this time catching the dog before he could skirt away. "I'm so sorry," she apologized.

Jace froze and his eyes doubled in size as he waited for her reaction. Part of Melanie wanted to scoop him up and protect him, but she knew she needed to give their relationship a chance.

After trying unsuccessfully to wipe the paw prints off, Jace's grandmother looked across to her husband and said, "Do you remember the puppy you bought Todd? The one I told you I didn't want?"

Her husband smiled at the memory. "The one who loved to dig up your flowers?"

"And then jump all over me. I used to get so upset." Tears welled from her eyes. "I miss that stupid dog."

Her husband walked over and hugged her. "I do, too."

Jace studied the couple carefully. "You like dogs?"

His grandmother bent down again and looked him straight in the eye. "I love them."

"My dad had a dog?"

His grandfather joined the conversation with a smile. "He did."

Jace dug in his pocket for the card he'd made. He pulled it out and smoothed it on his leg, then showed it to his grandmother. Melanie couldn't hear everything he said, but her heart swelled with love for the couple when she saw Jace's grandfather straighten and blink quickly. His eyes shone with emotion when he looked over Jace's head and mouthed, "Thank you."

The regret she'd clung to for so long was replaced by a burst of hope.

I could love these people.

And so could my son.

We're going to be okay.

Chapter Sixteen

Charles picked up the magazine June had placed on his desk that morning and flipped it open to the page she'd marked with a folded paper that sported a round smiley face. He'd made the list, "The Fifty Most Influential People in Manhattan," and his bank account mirrored that accomplishment. Landing the Rawlings account had breached an invisible ceiling between him and those with real money to invest.

Which will make me even richer.

He threw the magazine in the trash beside his desk. Instead of hurting his business, his Internet video had brought him a level of celebrity that people in his line of work typically didn't experience. People wanted to know the story of how he'd met his equally famous "cowgirl." Perhaps because neither of them had stepped forward with an interview, the press had run with their own versions and the story resurfaced now and then. There was even a trending YouTube fruit sitcom loosely based on them in which Melanie was played by a feisty apple and he by a bitter grapefruit.

And the initial video that should have faded into obscurity was now part of the Unleashed, Unchained tour. The rock band rereleased the song they'd paired with the video as a single and was donating part of the funds raised to youth centers in New York City. Charles had negotiated for a portion of the profit to be awarded to Tanner and had tried to set up an account fund for him, but because he was a ward of the state, doing so had proved to be tricky. For the time being, Charles was putting Tanner's share aside, to fund to him when he aged out of family services.

Charles's phone line lit up. June said, "It's Mr. Thorne, sir. Are you available for his call?"

"Put him through." Once he heard his friend click on, he said, "I'm surprised you didn't ring my cell."

"I like to see how flustered your secretary gets when she knows it's me. Is that wrong?" Mason asked.

"Yes." *But not surprising.* Charles looked up at the ceiling and reflected on how patient his secretary had been with him over the past few months. Throwing himself into work had meant her time at the office had also increased, and he wasn't positive he'd always been nice to her during the push. Maybe a raise for her was appropriate. "Next time you come to my office, bring her flowers. I don't want to lose her. Not too many flowers. I also don't want you to sleep with her because—let me repeat myself—I don't want to lose her."

"One sorry-your-boss-is-an-asshole-but-please-don't-think-this-is-a-come-on bouquet coming right up. Sounds interesting. I like a challenge. Back to why I called. You did it. You hit the top fifty. What's the mood like in your office? Champagne? Streamers?" He lowered his voice. "Strippers?"

Charles sighed. "Yes, it's a party with wall-to-wall naked women. I ordered five but they sent fifty. I'm giving them out as party favors."

"I'll be right over," Mason joked back. Then, more seriously, he asked, "You realize this is a good thing, right? You can sound happy about it."

Charles stood and stretched, putting Mason on speakerphone. "I am happy about it," he said defensively.

"Did you call your parents?" Mason asked.

"No."

"Did you call your sister?"

"Not yet."

"Should I fly in and drag your ass out tonight?"

"No, I have a college fair I need to go to."

"For that kid? You still see him every week?"

"Yeah, it's important to him." Then he admitted, "Important to me." Charles paced in front of his desk. "In some ways I've helped him. In others, I've made it harder for him. He's a bright kid, just angry. He doesn't belong in a group home. No kid does, really. But I see real potential in him. He'd do better if he stopped sabotaging himself."

"You're not considering adopting this kid, are you? I don't want to be the bearer of unwelcome reality here, but he might think he won the lottery with you. You'll adopt him, then he'll kill you in your sleep. It happens all the time."

"Really? All the time?"

"If you don't think so, you don't watch the same documentaries I do. Scary shit."

"I'm not adopting anyone. Besides, he's almost an adult."

"You say that, but I haven't believed a word you've said in months. I don't know what happened to you. Oh wait, I do. *Melanie.*"

"This has nothing to do with her."

"Right, and the sun doesn't rise in the East."

"I haven't spoken to her in three months."

"Because you're stubborn. Not because you don't want to."

There was the crux of lying to a good friend—it never worked. "I called her several times when she left. What was I supposed to do, fly out there? Drag her back here? Beg her to forgive me for something I didn't do?"

"Man, you *are* in a bad place. Two of your three suggestions sound reasonable. The other one might land you in prison."

"For all I know, she found Jace's father and is now living with him."

"But you won't know that unless you go see her."

"If I go to Texas, I'm not leaving without her."

Mason groaned. "That does not sound like a man who has moved on. How about toning it down just a tad and asking her out on a date?"

"I don't want to date her, Mason." He slapped both hands down on the table as he finally vocalized the feelings he'd been holding in. "I want her here with me. I'll marry her if that's what it takes. It doesn't matter anymore that she has a kid. I don't care."

Before Charles had a chance to hang up, Mason said quickly, "One last piece of advice? Work on your delivery. I hear everyone down there has a shotgun. I'd miss you."

In Tony's living room, with Jace at her side, Melanie shyly held up the letter documenting how well she'd done her first semester back in college. She wasn't used to having attention focused on her, but Sarah had organized the dinner in her honor and had asked her to show off her grades.

Not much about the past few months had been easy, but she had forged through and come out the other side. She'd taken a job at a convenience store in town that offered her flexible shift hours so she could be home when Jace wasn't in school. She was slowly paying Tony back for the initial investment in her education. And although she was tired, she felt better about herself than she had in a very long time.

She was also incredibly grateful to everyone seated around the table. Each had contributed in some way to her being able to juggle her classes and Jace successfully. Sarah and Tony kept him occupied for an hour each evening with "chores" around the ranch, which Jace exchanged for riding lessons. David was working with him to write his name in a legible way. During the week, the evenings had flown by with Jace's reading log, the occasional ride, and bath time. The full days didn't end for Melanie when Jace went to bed. Those quiet hours at night were when she studied. She had completed just one semester, but added to the credits she already had, she only needed one more.

Melanie's father said, "Don't see what all the fuss is about. We always knew you could do whatever you set your mind to. Now, just get your sisters in college and I'll be happy."

Her sister Bunny shrugged off their father's comment. "Dad, as soon as I'm eighteen, I'm moving to LA. I want to model. You don't need college for that."

"Even a model needs to know enough about money to hold on to it," Melanie's father argued. "You'll be enrolling in a college or you won't be going anywhere."

"Don't waste your breath," Melanie's sister Natalie said. "She's as hardheaded as Melanie."

Melanie's eyebrows rose in surprise.

"Something I take as a compliment," Bunny said to Melanie. "You've always done what you wanted to do and no one could tell you any different."

Humility followed shock at her sister's praise. She looked around the room at those who had gathered in her honor that night. None of them were new to her life. She thought about how desperately alone she'd felt when she really never had been. Her mother had tried countless times to tell her that over the years, but she'd never heard her. *Hardheaded? Yeah, I guess you could call me that.*

Too hardheaded to return any of Charles's phone calls. I should have. He deserved better than how I left. Even though he didn't make the offer I needed to hear, he offered what he could. And he was honest. More than I was with him.

She wished she hadn't left without telling Charles about Todd. She wanted to believe that, given the same circumstances now, she would have woken him up that last morning in New York and not run away like a coward.

I'd like to think that.

Just like I tell myself that if he calls me again, I'll answer and apologize. It's not his fault I'm an emotional train wreck.

Melanie looked across the table at her mother and said, "If I could go back in time, there are a great many things I'd do differently. And I'd definitely tell myself to listen to Mom and Dad more. The older I get, the wiser I realize they are."

Her mother smiled. "Can I get a hallelujah?"

Chuckles broke out around the table. Even her father smiled, then in a serious tone he said, "We're proud of you, Melanie. Now all you need to do is find yourself a good man."

The table went suddenly silent.

Melanie's face heated while some looked on with sympathy and others with amusement. "Dad—" she started to protest.

Her mother said, "Steve, do we have to talk about this tonight? We're here to celebrate. Melanie will find someone when she's ready to."

"I'm sorry," he said without sounding sorry. "There are plenty of men around here interested, but I can't recall the last date she had."

Melanie's sister Katie asked, "What happened to not wanting any of us to date until we're thirty?"

The father looked at his youngest sternly. "It's still true for the rest of you, but Jace needs a daddy. Melanie's not getting any younger. What's she waiting for?"

The front door of Tony's house opened and closed with a bang. One of the newer ranch hands came in and said, "One of those long, fancy limousines just pulled into the driveway. I thought you should know."

David asked, "Is it Jace's grandparents again?"

Melanie shook her head. "No, they said they'd come back around Christmas."

Sarah stood and clapped in excitement. "It must be Charlie."

Melanie went pale. "Charles?" she asked weakly.

Jace went to stand protectively beside his mother. "Is that the man who punched Tony?"

Katie ran to the window and said, "He looks even better in person than he does in the video."

"Who is Charles?" Melanie's father asked gruffly.

Her mother laid her hand on his and said softly, "I have a feeling we're about to find out."

Melanie took her son's hand. "He's not usually like that, Jace. He was very angry that day because he was worried about his sister. He's Sarah's brother."

"That's the only reason he survived hitting me," Tony said, pushing back from the table and standing up. "What's he doing here?"

David stood, too. "I thought you got along with him now, Tony."

"I did, until Melanie went to New York."

Melanie stood angrily and glared at Sarah. "What did you tell Tony about me and Charles?"

Sarah blushed and sank into her chair. "Not everything," she said defensively.

Melanie's father rose from his chair. "What the hell happened in New York?"

Her mother put a hand on his arm to caution him. "Why don't we let the kids sort this out?" When he didn't budge, she turned to her daughters. "Could you girls take Jace in the kitchen for some ice cream?"

Bunny and Natalie agreed to do so, but Jace refused to release his mother's hand. "Mama?" he said, trying to figure out what was going on.

Despite the wildly churning emotions within her, Melanie forced herself to smile down at her son. "Go, Jace. Be good and listen to your aunts and have that ice cream."

"In my day, we didn't bribe children . . ." Melanie's father said, though he stopped when his wife elbowed him. Melanie sent him a silent plea and was surprised when he added, ". . . with ice cream alone. I hope you've got some cake back there as well."

"Do you? Do you have cake?" Jace asked, shrugging off his mother's hand and joining his aunts. "Mom doesn't let me eat dessert except for on Sunday. Is today Sunday?"

"Today is an exception," Melanie assured her son.

"I love ecleptons!" Jace exclaimed happily and trotted off to the kitchen.

Looking up to see Charles in the doorway of the dining room, Melanie didn't have time to do more than smooth a hand over her loose hair and lament her choice of jeans and a T-shirt that evening.

"Sorry to interrupt your dinner," Charles said. Nothing in his expression hinted that he was sorry. His face was carefully devoid of expression. "Melanie, we need to talk."

"Now?" Melanie squeaked, then closed her eyes at her inane question.

"Now," Charles said, softening his command with, "if you'll all excuse us."

Melanie froze, wanting to go with him, but she held back because of all she was afraid he would say. Was it his pride that had brought him there—to demand an explanation and that apology she knew she owed him? Or was it something more?

Sarah crossed the room and hugged her brother. After a brief exchange, Charles turned his focus back to Melanie and waited.

In the silence, Melanie's father's voice rang out clear. "If he's here to court my daughter, why the hell did he come dressed like he's going to a funeral?"

Chapter Seventeen

Frustration replaced whatever anticipation Charles had felt about seeing Melanie again. She was even more beautiful than he remembered. She wore her long hair loose down her back and was dressed in casual jeans and a T-shirt, just as she had been the first time they'd met. But today she looked entirely different. There was a confidence in her that hadn't been there before.

It made him want her more, and he hadn't thought that was possible.

So far, their reunion wasn't living up to how he'd imagined it. Foolishly, he'd imagined her running to him, wrapping her arms around his neck, and kissing him with as much need as had been building within him the past few months. He had fantasized about how he would carry her off to the nearest bed and enjoy her physical demonstration of how sorry she was before claiming her, again and again, as his.

Clearly, his prediction of how this day would go needed to be adjusted.

Tony Carlton, his sister's fiancé, stepped between him and Melanie and drawled slowly, "We didn't expect you today." His tone implied, "or want you."

Sarah gave Tony a look of reprimand over her shoulder and hugged Charles. "But you're always welcome."

Tony made a noncommittal grunt behind her. "Depends on why he's here."

Charles stepped back from his sister, removed his sunglasses, and put them in the breast pocket of his suit jacket, meeting Tony's glare with one of his own. "I don't have to explain myself to you."

Melanie's father went to stand beside Tony. "Just who the hell does this city slicker think he is?"

Charles looked past her father to the other young men in the room. He addressed his question to Melanie. "Are any of them the Todd you told me about?"

Melanie shook her head but with an expression of sadness that confused him. Was Todd still part of her life? Had she found him, been with him again? A dark jealousy gripped his heart and squeezed even as he hated seeing her unhappy.

He had a hundred questions he wanted to ask Melanie, but none of them in front of the present audience.

A small male voice rang out, "Are you going to fight again? Mama tells me to use my words and not my hands when I get angry."

Charles looked down into the serious and critical eyes of Melanie's young son, Jace. He forced himself to relax. "Your mother is a very smart woman."

Jace studied the expressions of the three men as he shoveled a piece of cake into his mouth. "What does court mean?"

Charles shook his head in confusion. "Court?"

Jace patiently explained, "Grandpa said you were here to court my mom. What does that mean?"

Charles looked across the room at Melanie. She had covered her face with both hands in mortification, but as her son spoke she parted her hands enough to watch the exchange. "It means I want to marry your mother."

Melanie gasped and sat down in a chair. Her three sisters chattered in the background.

Sarah joined Tony and slid beneath his arm, hugging him tightly. "Don't laugh at him—you were just as bad."

Tony shrugged unapologetically and returned her hug.

"Is anyone going to tell me who this guy is?" Melanie's father's growled.

Melanie stood and walked across the room toward Charles. "Charles, these are my parents and sisters—Bunny, Natalie, and Katie. You've met David. Lucas, Sawyer, Austin, Gunner, and Travis are ranch hands. They've been here as long as I have." She turned to her father. "Dad, this is Charles. He's Sarah's brother."

"How do *you* know him?" her father asked.

Jace pulled on the sleeve of Charles's suit until he looked down. "Do you ride horses?"

"No," Charles said absently. Every inch of him was humming with anticipation again now that Melanie was headed his way. He didn't care that the general welcome had been less than warm. All he cared about was seeing Melanie again and convincing her to leave with him.

"Do you fish?"

Charles thought about his brother and the lake he'd drowned in and shook his head. "No."

"Why are you all dressed up for church if it's not Sunday?"

Melanie stood just behind her son, and Charles lost the ability to concentrate on anything but her. "It's just a suit. I live in suits."

Jace glanced over his shoulder at his mother and said, "I don't like him. Let's go home." He took Melanie by the hand.

Melanie gazed down at her son for a moment, and a knife of uncertainty twisted in Charles's gut. When she looked up there was yearning and a good-bye in her eyes. Todd or no Todd, it didn't matter. *She's walking away from me. Again.*

If Jace weren't holding her hand, I'd never let her out the door, but what can I do?

"Melanie . . ." Charles said gruffly.

"I'm sorry you came all this way. I should have called you back." She stepped away from everyone, still holding her son's hand. "I can't talk right now, and there is really nothing left to say except that I'm sorry about how I left everything. That was wrong. I'm taking Jace home now. Sarah, thank you for tonight. I wish . . ." She let her words trail away and walked to the door. She paused before shaking her head and leaving with Jace.

Charles stood where she'd left him and cursed himself for being so wrapped up in Melanie that he'd failed to connect with her son. *What the hell do I know about talking to a kid? What did I think, just because I've spent time with Tanner that I can do this?*

Jace saw me for what I am—a poor choice for a father for him. I tell myself I've changed, put the past behind me, but even a five-year-old knows how full of shit I am.

Fuck.

The ranch manager, David, came to stand beside him. "The character of a man is seldom revealed when things go well."

Charles didn't look away from the door Melanie had left through. *That's all I need right now, the Texan version of a fortune cookie.*

Behind him, Melanie's father said, "Looks like you have your answer, son."

"I'm not going anywhere," Charles said with finality. "Not without Melanie."

"I'm definitely moving to the city," one of Melanie's sisters said from across the room, fanning her face.

Sarah nudged Tony. "Do something."

Tony asked, "What the hell am I supposed to . . ." He looked down into Sarah's eyes and then addressed Charles again. "Do you want to learn how to ride, Charlie?"

Charles knew Tony was being sarcastic, but he also knew that he'd never been as sure of anything as he was about being with Melanie. It didn't make sense. It didn't have to.

It simply was.

"If that's what it takes," he said, challenging Tony to withdraw the offer.

Melanie's mother walked over and stood directly in front of Charles. She raised her chin as she studied him critically. He held her gaze, unblinking. "Why do you want my daughter?"

Charles answered honestly. "Because she's all I can think about."

The older woman nodded her approval. "Then you take those riding lessons, Charles, and don't let Tony give you any grief about them. But know that you can't win my daughter's heart unless you win her son's first."

Her husband said, "I can't believe you're encouraging him."

She smiled softly up at her disapproving husband. "My father tried to run you off with an old shotgun, but you kept coming back and you became as close as two coats of paint. Charles, you just worry about making our daughter and our grandson happy. That's all we care about."

"So you don't care that he might steal them both away to God knows where he came from?"

"New York," Charles said calmly. "I live in New York."

Melanie's mother asked, "Are you planning to ask her to move to the city with you after you marry her? Is that where you want to raise your children?"

"I . . . I . . ." Charles wasn't a man who normally struggled for words, but her questions rocked him. "I hadn't thought much past . . ." He blushed and continued, ". . . seeing her again."

She reached up and gave him a sympathetic pat on the arm as if he were Jace's age. Then she walked over to her husband and wrapped her arms around him, ignoring the sour expression on his face. She went up on her tiptoes and kissed her husband's cheek. "I would have followed you to the ends of the earth if you'd asked me—and I wouldn't have regretted one moment of that journey . . . no matter what my father said."

A blush spread up the older man's face. "Why is it that after forty years, I still can't say no when you give me that look?"

"Oh, gross," one of Melanie's sisters said from across the room.

Charles choked on an unexpected chuckle.

David made a similar sound and said, "Why don't we have some coffee and dessert?" Everyone began to return to the table. "Do you have a place to stay, Charles?"

"I'm sure I can find a place in town," Charles said smoothly.

Sarah left Tony's side to hug her brother again. "I'm so proud of you, Charlie."

"Because I've lost my mind?"

She whispered up to him, "No, because you found your heart."

Melanie fought to calm down as she gave Jace a bath, read him his nightly stack of books, then tucked him into his bed with a kiss. She'd have the rest of the night to overthink what Charles had said about wanting to marry her.

She was walking out of her son's room when he said, "Mama?"

She turned back to look at him but couldn't see his expression in the dim glow of his nightlight. "Yes, baby?"

"Are you mad at me because I didn't like that man?"

Melanie let out a shaky breath. "No, honey. It's good to be honest about how you feel."

"Do you like him?"

"I do," Melanie said softly. "I really do."

Jace picked up a teddy bear and hugged it to his little chest. "Are you going to marry him?"

Melanie walked back over and sat beside her son on his bed, pushing a wayward lock out of his eyes. "I don't think so, Jace."

"Because he's always so angry?"

Melanie smiled down at her son. "He's not always like that. He's actually a really nice man once you get to know him."

"Lyle's mom deported his father and married a new man. Now Lyle has two dads."

"I think you mean *divorced*."

"Nope. Lyle said his mom caught his dad cheating and threw all his stuff out the window of his house. He said she deported him."

Whatever Lyle had called it, Melanie was sad that children went through those situations at all. It saddened her that her child had a word for it. She wanted to protect him from the harshness of the world, but the older he became the more she saw how impossible that would be. His world reached beyond the ranch and that was how it was meant to be.

His innocence twisted through Melanie's chest. "I'm sorry that happened to your friend."

Jace nodded solemnly, wise beyond his young years. "If you marry someone, will he be my dad?"

"If you want him to be."

"What if he didn't like me?"

Melanie swallowed hard as emotions clogged her throat. "I would never marry a man who didn't love you as much as I do."

"Does your friend like kids?"

Melanie rubbed her son's arm reassuringly. "I don't think he's been around them enough to know if he does or doesn't."

"He doesn't ride horses."

"No, but he hasn't been around them, either."

"He doesn't fish. I don't know anyone who doesn't fish."

Melanie chuckled. "He lives in a big city, Jace. I'm sure he hasn't had many chances to."

"I could teach him," Jace offered graciously.

Melanie ruffled her son's hair. "You would do that?" She imagined Charles sitting with Jace on the rocks near their favorite fishing spot. *What would he do if handed a bucket of worms? Probably hightail it right back to New York.*

"I'm really good at it. David says so."

"You certainly are."

"Maybe your friend would smile more if he fished. David says every man should know how to bait his own hook."

"Then if I see Charles again, I'll ask him if he wants to take a fishing lesson from you. Now go to sleep. You have school tomorrow." She tucked the blankets tighter around her son's sides, then stood and walked back to the door.

"Mama?" Jace said in the darkness.

"Go to sleep."

"Don't marry a man who doesn't know how to fish."

Melanie blinked back tears. "I won't, baby. Now. Close your eyes and think about something happy."

"Like kittens? Lyle's cat just had kittens."

"We are not getting a kitten. You have a dog. That's all I can handle."

"I'll just dream about them. About how happy I would be if I had a kitten."

"Good night, Jace. I love you."

"Love you, too, Mama."

Just outside Jace's door, Melanie gave in to the emotions of the day. She leaned against the wall. Now that Jace was in bed, she didn't need to pretend to be strong anymore. She covered her face with both hands and took a shaky breath.

Charles is here.

He came for me.

Said he wanted to marry me.

And I walked away from him.

She pushed herself off the wall and walked down the hall to her bedroom. On autopilot, she changed into her nightgown and brushed her teeth. *What else could I have done? Jace was there along with my parents. It wasn't the time or the place for the conversation we need to have.*

She padded back to her bedroom and picked up her phone. *No one is here now.*

She scrolled to his number on her contact list and hesitated. *He's probably on his way back to New York by now, wondering why he thought it would work between us. And he's right.* She thought about how she'd let fear stop her in the past and pressed his number.

I don't want to move to the city.

He's not moving here—no matter what he said about wanting to marry me. There is nothing for him way out here.

No, it would never work between us. He barely spoke to Jace. No matter how much I want to be with him, Jace needs to come first. On the ranch he may not have a father, but he has people who care about him.

But, God, I want to hear Charles's voice one more time.

I swear, I'll stay strong this time. I'll apologize and let him go. Just let me hear him say my name in that husky I-want-you-now tone—one last time.

He picked up on the first ring. "Melanie."

Melanie closed her eyes. His voice was deep and tempting, and exactly the way she remembered when he said her name. "Charles, I hope it's not too late to call you."

"It's only eight thirty," he said in a tone that was warmly teasing.

"Of course. I wasn't thinking . . ." Melanie sat on the edge of her bed and smacked her forehead. *Focus on why you called.* "I owe you an explanation. About New York . . ."

"Are you coming to me or am I coming to you?" he asked and his voice sent shivers of desire through her.

"You're still in Texas?" Melanie asked, her heart beating wildly in her chest.

"Did you think I wouldn't be?"

"I didn't know," Melanie admitted softly and flopped back into the comfort of her bed.

"I said I want to marry you."

Melanie closed her eyes and asked the question that had been plaguing her all night. "Why? Why do you want to marry me?"

Charles was quiet for a moment, as if the question had taken him by surprise. It bothered Melanie that his response wasn't a quick and emphatic "I love you."

Would I have believed him if it had been?

As his silence dragged on, Melanie began to regret that she'd asked the question. Finally, he said, "When I'm not with you, all I can think about is being with you again. We're good together, Melanie. So good I can't think straight when we're apart."

Images of their time together flooded her mind, wetting her panties as her body remembered the pleasure he'd brought her. "Sex is not a good reason to get married."

"Then don't marry me. Live with me. I don't care."

And there you have it, the depth of his feelings and how little the sanctity of marriage means to him. Melanie shook her head. "I care, Charles. I'm not moving my son in with a man I'm not married to and I'm not marrying someone I barely know."

"I'd say we know each other quite intimately."

"Outside of bed, Charles. How well do you know me? Really? Do you know my favorite flower? How I like my coffee? If I sing in the shower?"

"I'd know all that if you lived with me."

"Where? In New York? What about Jace?"

"I said he can move in, also."

"How accommodating of you."

"What do you want me to say?"

"Try to see this from my point of view. What we do affects more than just our lives. He's never had a father. I won't bring men in and out of his life."

"There won't be other men in your life," Charles said definitively. "Marry me."

"No, Charles."

"Does Jace go to school tomorrow?"

"Yes, but I have to work."

"Call in sick," Charles said. "I need you. Spend the day with me."

There were oh-so-many reasons why Melanie knew she should say no, but they didn't matter.

She wanted to be with Charles as much as he wanted to be with her. Even if it was one last time. Even if it didn't make sense to say yes.

"I don't know. If you come here, someone will see your limo," Melanie said, not ready to face the questions that his presence at her house would bring from all directions.

Including myself. Why am I even considering this? Didn't I just say we're a bad idea?

"Nothing will stop me from seeing you tomorrow. The how and where are your choice."

Melanie said, hedging, "I hate to miss any days at work. I'm still new there."

"You're not going to work tomorrow."

"But I—"

"I've wasted months telling myself I could forget you. I know we don't make sense. I know every reason we shouldn't see each other tomorrow, but I don't care about any of them. I need to see you again. I need to know what happened. Why did you leave without saying anything?"

"If I go with you tomorrow—"

"*When*," he corrected.

"I'd have to be back to meet Jace after school. He gets off the bus at three."

"What time does the bus pick him up?"

"Eight o'clock."

"Then I'll be there at 8:05."

"Okay," Melanie whispered.

Charles was quiet for a moment, then he said, "Melanie?"

"Yes?"

"I'm not leaving Texas without you."

The line went dead and Melanie dropped the phone next to her on the bed. Charles was a man who didn't pretty things up. He meant what he said.

He wants me—as much as I want him.

But is that enough?

Chapter Eighteen

Charles entered a small bar across the street from the hotel he'd found in town. He needed a stiff drink or he'd never get to sleep. The interior was dimly lit, with patrons scattered around the room at high tables. Charles took a seat at the counter and ordered a glass of the bar's most expensive scotch. He downed it as a shot.

"Your car break down?" the bartender asked, leaning against the bar in front of him.

Charles shook his head.

"You chasing some serial killer or something?"

"I'm sorry?" Charles asked impatiently, seeking numbness, not conversation.

"I'm trying to figure out if you're FBI or some rich guy passing through."

"Do I have to tell you anything to get a second round?"

"Nope. It's none of my business."

"Exactly."

"It's just that we don't get many rich folk around here. We have Carlton out there on his ranch and a few oil families. Maybe there was a spill and you're the lawyer they sent to cover the story up?"

"I'm not a lawyer," Charles said and accepted the second drink. He downed that one and let out a hiss at the welcome burn of the alcohol down his throat.

Charles felt a shoulder bump. A large man sat down next to him and put a hand on his shoulder. "Well, what do we have here? Looks like one of those big-city types."

Charles's head snapped in the direction of the slurred voice. "Get your hand off me."

"Not while you're sitting in my favorite seat. You need to move."

Charles estimated the man to be in his midtwenties, probably an ex-football player by the size of him and how he instinctively used his shoulders to clear his way. Although Charles had a few years on him, he wasn't intimidated. Charles had kept his body toned and in fighting condition through Tai Chi and running. Clearly, the man behind him had done neither.

The bartender said, "Seth, don't go starting any trouble tonight. You're still paying me for the mirror you and your friends broke last month. Don't make me call the sheriff."

The man lifted his hand to give Charles a shove. "No trouble because he'll move."

Charles clenched his fist on the bar. "If that hand touches me I will shove it down your throat."

The bartender stepped away.

"Try it," Seth said, puffing up into a fighting stance.

Here I was thinking shit like this only happened in movies. Where is the small-town welcome everyone talks about?

Seth took a swing at him, but Charles evaded it easily. Time and experience had taught Charles that not every fight was worth the energy. What would be the gain of pummeling this man to a pulp? None that fit his objective for being in Fort Mavis.

Seth was obviously drunk and his antics well known. Charles stood. "I don't want to fight you. Go sober up somewhere."

Another man about the same size, dressed in jeans and a red plaid shirt, walked over and said, "Seth, what's going on?"

"This guy thinks he's better than us."

The man took a position of support beside Seth. "Is that so?"

Charles faced the other man head-on. "I am here for a drink, that's all."

"We don't like foreigners coming in here and starting shit."

"New York is hardly another country." Although it was beginning to feel like it was another planet. The irony in Charles's tone enraged both men.

"I don't like the way you talk," Seth said.

"That's not my problem," Charles said dismissively.

"Seth, I called the sheriff. Jimmy, take him home and dry him out. Neither one of you needs more trouble," the bartender said.

"You gonna hide behind the sheriff, city boy?" Seth snarled.

Charles didn't say anything, just held his ground and stared them down. He used the time to study his opponents and calculate the best counter to whatever they might pull. He hadn't amassed his fortune by reacting to any situation without strategy and skill. He wasn't looking for a fight, but if one came to him, he would sure as hell win it.

"We should take this outside," Jimmy said. "Mom said she wouldn't bail me out again."

Charles looked from one to the other and almost smiled. *Mom? Bail out again?* His use-what-your-opponent-is-afraid-to-lose-against-him strategy was less effective when dealing with Tweedledee and Tweedledumber.

It also changed Charles's evaluation of how potentially dangerous the two men were. *People with nothing to lose fight differently. They don't honor rules. They don't fear consequences.*

At least one of them is afraid of his mother. That might prove useful.

Tony Carlton walked in and the bar fell silent. Charles half expected to see him sporting a gun belt like in some old western. Tony pushed back his hat, scanned the room, and nodded to Charles when he saw him. He walked straight into the mix confidently and flashed his teeth in mockery of a smile. "Charlie, I see you're making friends."

"Impossible not to in such a friendly town," Charles said with the same sarcasm.

"You know this guy, Carlton?" Seth asked angrily.

"Yes."

"I knew there was a reason I didn't like him."

Note to self, do not use Tony as a character reference in Fort Mavis.

Tony took his hat off and laid it on the bar. "Sounds like you've been drinking too much again, Seth. Go on home."

"I'm not afraid of you," Seth said.

"You should be," Tony said in a low and deadly tone. "Charlie here is my fiancée's brother. A wise man would leave him alone."

"Oh, I'll leave him alone, all right." Seth turned and stepped like he was going to leave, but he picked up a chair and swung it in the direction of Tony's back.

Charles used the man's momentum against him. With a swing of a leg, he knocked him off balance and sent him to the floor. The man beside him swung a fist at Charles, but he blocked it and gave him a slammer of a punch to his nose, sending the man to his knees with a bloody nose.

Seth was back on his feet and furious. He swung at Charles and missed. Charles followed with a punch to his stomach that sent him back to the floor. Looking down at the two fallen men, Charles remembered one of his martial arts instructors consistently labeling his responses as too aggressive, advocating, instead, a defense that involved little or no physical contact.

Yeah, I never mastered that.

Just then, the sheriff entered the bar and flipped on the lights. He looked at the two men on the ground and at Tony. "I thought you were done fighting with the locals."

Tony shrugged, "Don't look at me. I didn't touch either of them. Sarah sent me to see how her brother was settling in."

The bartender said, "Just as I told you on the phone, Dean, Seth and Jimmy need an escort home."

Seth whined, "We're not the ones causing trouble, Dean."

Dean took Seth by the arm. "Right. I've heard that before. You'll be sleeping in a cell tonight, Seth, while I sort this out. Then we'll see if anyone is pressing charges."

He took the other man by the arm. "You, too, Jim?"

The man with the bloody nose was suddenly contrite rather than aggressive. "You don't have to tell my mom about this, do you, Dean? I didn't touch him. Look at him. Not a mark on him. He's some sort of city ninja."

Charles shook his head. "No, just a whole lot more sober."

Looking reluctantly impressed, Tony said, "You've got a good punch to you."

Charles looked down at his swollen knuckles. "I can't remember the last time I hit someone." Then he smiled at Tony. "Oh, wait, I can."

Tony narrowed his eyes, cocked his head to one side, then barked out a laugh. "I've never liked you, Charlie, but you're growing on me."

Dean nodded at Charles. "So you're Sarah's brother. Welcome to Fort Mavis."

"You've got quite a town, here, Sheriff."

"Don't let these two frame your opinion. They're not half bad when they haven't been drinking. They won't bother you again. Do you want to press charges?"

Charles thought about what Melanie had said about Tanner and shook his head. He didn't know what had brought Seth and Jim to where they were, but he doubted an arrest would help either of their situations. "No."

After the sheriff left with the two men, Charles sat back down at the bar. The bartender placed a fresh drink in front of him. "It's from Wyatt over there. He says thanks for the show. We don't get much excitement round here."

Charles turned and raised his glass to the little old man a few tables away. Tony sat on a barstool beside him.

The bartender continued, "He also wanted me to tell you he has a daughter. She's pretty, too. Makes a mean barbecue."

Tony said, "He's marrying Melanie."

"Oh," the bartender replied, then smiled. "Congratulations." He turned to the rest of the crowd, pointed at Charles, and said loudly, "He's marrying Melanie."

The patrons gave a round of applause and well wishes. Once it died down, Charles spoke in a tone just loud enough for Tony to hear. "She hasn't agreed to that yet."

Tony accepted a beer from the bartender and said, "Then maybe it's time to ditch the suit."

"I didn't intend to stay long."

"You thought she'd pack up and follow you?"

"Something like that."

Tony took a sip of his beer. "You've got a lot to learn about country women—especially those with children." He looked him over critically. "Lesson one: show her you're serious." He placed his hat back on his head and tipped it at Charles.

"I am not wearing a hat."

"Do as you please. Just trying to be helpful. It'll be over 110 degrees tomorrow in the shade. You'll look ridiculous in that getup."

Charles shrugged. "Not much I can do about that. This town doesn't have anything open twenty-four hours."

Tony looked over his shoulder and called out to a man across the bar. "Hey, Jeb. You think you could open your store long enough to get this guy into some jeans and boots? He wants to surprise Melanie."

"That is so romantic," one of the women in the room said.

"Anything for Melanie," a tall man with a beer belly and easy smile said. "What do you say I finish this beer and meet you over there?"

Tony turned back to Charles. "Problem solved."

"Are you screwing with me?" Charles asked, eyes narrowing.

"You're the one who said you wanted to marry her. You told her parents you'd learn to ride. Can't do that in a suit. Or maybe you were just saying what you thought we wanted to hear. That wouldn't be a good idea," Tony said, his voice laced with steel.

"I never say anything I don't mean."

"Then finish that drink, because it's time to cowboy up."

Charles stood just outside a changing stall and studied himself in the mirror. The heels on the leather boots felt unnatural, but he'd grown up in jeans and T-shirts. As the son of a construction company owner, his attire had been functional for most of his early life. It had only been when he'd left his small town behind for college that he'd also turned his back on that side of himself.

These cowboys think I was born and raised in the city. They have no idea. His father had named his company Dery and Son when Charles was born, and for Charles that had meant working on construction sites for as long as he could remember. He'd grown up with calluses that would have impressed any country boy. The Dery family believed in good, honest hard work being the only way to make a living.

Funny how easy it is to reject even honorable ideals when they are voiced by your parents.

Although his father had publicly celebrated his son's admission to Stanford, Charles knew it meant his dad had to let go of his dream of one day handing his company over to him. It was the first step in Charles's plan to move away—the start of the life he felt he was destined for. They'd never fought about it because his family didn't fight. They avoided the unpleasant. It was how his parents dealt with Sarah getting a horse even after they told her not to. It was also how they'd dealt with their youngest son, Phil's, drowning at their lake house.

The casual attire brought Charles a flashback to a simpler version of himself. *Is this who I would have been had my brother lived—Rhode Island's work-boots version of this? Would I have stayed and taken over my father's business?*

Would I have been happier?

"When you're done admiring yourself over there, you might want to pay Jeb. He has time for two more beers before his wife comes looking for him," Tony said dryly.

Charles turned and met Tony's eyes. "I'm ready." Even though he wasn't sure if he actually was. He placed his folded suit and shoes in a large bag, then grabbed a few more pairs of jeans along with a variety of casual shirts. Tony silently watched Charles purchase them.

Jeb placed a tan hat on top of the clothing. Charles started to protest, but the man grinned and said, "It's on me. A gift for Melanie."

Charles reluctantly put it on and thanked him. Tony shook his head. Charles adjusted it more forward. Tony shook his head again and tugged the brim of his own hat to demonstrate how to wear it low. Charles pulled the brim lower. Tony nodded in approval.

As they were leaving, Jeb said, "Don't forget to invite me to the wedding."

Charles nearly tripped down the landing and Tony chuckled.

"You seeing Melanie tomorrow?" Tony asked in a suddenly serious tone.

Tempted to tell him it was none of his business, Charles answered, "Yes."

"You know she comes as a package deal. You don't get her without her son."

Temper rising, Charles said, "I never said I wanted to."

"You sure as hell looked like you didn't give him much thought when you met him."

Faced with a truth he couldn't deny, Charles glared at the man who had voiced it. "I'll do better the next time I see him." He shook his head as he gained control of his temper.

"I'll meet you at my barn after dinner."

"For?"

"Jace is exercising one of my horses for me. Might be a good idea for you to come over and see it."

Charles watched Tony cautiously. "Why are you being so nice all of a sudden?"

Tony pushed back his hat an inch and gave him a steady stare. "Sarah says Melanie loves you. I didn't always appreciate the people around me, but Melanie has been on my ranch long enough that she's like family. I won't be the reason you fuck it up with her."

"You say that like you know I'm going to."

Tony shrugged and tugged the brim of his hat down again. He walked off and left Charles on the sidewalk, reflecting on the little he *had* said.

Melanie had a life in Fort Mavis. She had friends and family. It wouldn't be easy to convince her to leave all that behind for him.

And is it right to?

Her son needs a father, not someone who doesn't even know how to talk to him. Can I be that man?

He frowned as he walked back into his hotel.

Life had been much easier before he'd rediscovered his conscience.

Chapter Nineteen

Melanie opened the door of her house the next morning and then stood there, gaping at the sight of Charles in jeans, a snug tan T-shirt, and cowboy boots.

She didn't know if the outfit was his idea of a joke, but there was nothing funny about it. He looked good. Better than he should. The light material of the T-shirt accentuated his muscular chest. He removed his hat as he walked past her into her kitchen.

He hung his hat on the back of one of the chairs as she continued to stare at him wordlessly. He was gorgeous in his suit and tie, but dressed in more casual clothing he had a rugged look she wouldn't have thought would seem to fit him as well as it did. "You look . . ."

"Ridiculous?"

"No, amazing."

Charles smiled and traced her chin with his thumb, raising her face to his. He took a long, deep breath. "Why did you leave without saying good-bye? Why didn't you answer any of my calls?"

Breaking free of him, Melanie turned away and hugged her arms around her middle. "I went to New York to find Jace's father."

"I know."

His easy acceptance of her statement angered her. She didn't know if she was strong enough to give him the explanation he awaited. *But he said he wants to marry me. He said he wants to know me. It's time, then, to show him the real me.* "He passed away last year. I was too late."

Charles pulled her backward and enveloped her in his embrace. "I'm sorry to hear that."

Melanie pushed at his arms angrily but he didn't release her. "Don't be sorry for me. It's Jace who will never have a father. It's Jace I cheated because I was too afraid to do the right thing and tell his father about him."

"You had your reasons."

"That's the thing—they weren't good ones. I was angry with Todd, angry at the world, and I let how I felt rob something precious from Jace. I won't do that again. I won't take him away from everything he loves just because I want to be with you. I've hated myself for so long. Honestly, I'd rather be alone than feel like that again."

Charles watched her quietly. They were different in many ways, but in their core they were more alike than either wanted to admit.

He said softly, "Come here."

She walked slowly over to him. He buried his hand deep in the curls at the nape of her neck and said, "I've thought about you every night since we were together."

"I've done the same. I started to call you a thousand times."

"I thought you left me because of something I did. I thought I went too far our last night together."

She looked up at him from beneath her long lashes and admitted, "No, I never thought I could like that, but every moment was . . . amazing." Her cheeks warmed at her admission.

He pulled her to him, his arousal nudging against her stomach. He bent his head and claimed her mouth. "I love you in dresses," he murmured and ran a hand beneath the loose hem of her dress and up the outsides of her thighs. He lifted her with one arm while removing her panties. "Barefoot and bare-assed. I've pictured you like this a hundred times since you left me. I think about you each night until I ache."

Her hands instinctively sought his belt. "I know exactly what you mean." She undid the top of his jeans and slid them and his boxers down his legs. He slipped out of them and his shoes, his thick cock already fully erect.

He stepped back and removed his shirt.

She pulled her dress over her head and stood before him breathing as heavily as he was.

He advanced again, walking her backward until she felt the cold of the Formica counter on her ass. Her lips parted in anticipation of his next kiss.

Her nipples puckered, eager for his caress.

Her pussy quivered as she wondered where he would start.

Melanie thought about how much pleasure she'd found in letting him take charge and decided it could be equally fun to try it herself. "Are you hot?"

He gave her a raw and sexual smile with just enough curl to it that she knew he knew her game.

"I am," Charles said softly.

Melanie stepped away for a moment and took out a tray of ice from the freezer, then laid it beside her on the counter. She put a small ice cube in her mouth.

It instantly started to melt. She moved it around with her tongue, playing with it and absorbing the almost painful cold it delivered. He closed his mouth over hers, his tongue dancing with hers and the ice. Heat and cold. Skin and ice. The intensity of the sensation was unlike any she'd felt before. He buried his hands in her hair and held her there, thrusting his tongue deeper into her mouth, taking the cold of the ice into his. The only cool in her mouth was then from his tongue and she couldn't get enough of it.

She dug her hands into his neck and held him as tightly as he was holding her. His rigid cock jerked against the inside of her thigh and she opened her legs wider to him, wet and ready. Yes, she knew all about aching for someone. She'd awoken too many nights, still frustrated, after dreaming of being with him like this and not reaching climax in her dreams. Nothing she could do with her own hand rivaled how being with him felt.

She lifted her head and reached for another piece of ice. This time she trailed it down one side of his face and across his neck. Her mouth followed the wet path, her hot breath warming his skin between her touches. "Tell me what you want. Tell me everything," she whispered into his ear.

"Take me in your mouth. Bite me, lick me, do anything you want, just don't stop."

He shuddered with pleasure as she ran the ice cube lower, tracing one side of his cock, which she then took deep within her mouth to warm it. He gripped the edge of the counter. Just as he was beginning to tighten for climax, he eased her off him and reached for his own piece of ice.

He trailed it along her collarbone and down the side of one of her breasts. He circled her puckered nipple with it, then laved the nipple with his tongue between gentle nips.

Ever so slowly, he moved the dwindling ice down her bare stomach. She arched backward and cold droplets fell on her shaven mound. He kissed a path between her breasts and down her stomach. Melanie held her breath.

Very lightly, he traced the inside of each thigh. Melanie closed her eyes and shivered from the sensation. In anticipation of his kiss, her clit was pulsing and her inner muscles were clenching and releasing.

He traced down the inside of her calves, his hot breath following, but he withheld the pleasure of his tongue. Her skin came alive wherever he trailed the ice, and she swore as her senses overloaded.

"Your turn. What do you want?" he growled. "Tell me."

Melanie opened her eyes and looked down at him, hating that he was so fully in control, loving that he was so fully in control. "I want you to lick my clit. Shove those fingers inside me. Take me between your teeth and tease me like you do. Bury that thick tongue inside me while I imagine it's your cock. Fuck me with your mouth."

"Gladly," he said and popped what was left of the ice cube into his mouth. He parted her lower lips with one hand and held the ice between his teeth, holding it to her clit while he pumped his cold fingers in and out of her.

He brought the ice deeper into his mouth and nipped at her clit, running his chilled tongue back and forth over it as she'd asked him to. The combination of his hot lips and the unexpected temperature of his tongue made what was already amazing new and unbelievably erotic.

She crested and came with a cry, loving how he twisted his fingers within her, prolonging her orgasm and sucking hotly on her while she shuddered against his mouth.

He sheathed himself in a condom and lifted her so she was pressed against the refrigerator. He entered her with one thrust; white heat almost blinded Melanie. She wrapped her legs around his waist, nipped his shoulder wildly, and spread herself for him in abandon. This was no longer a game or a challenge. This was animal mating that had them both grunting and slick with sweat.

She came again with a loud cry. He joined her, swearing as he did and knocking the ice tray over as he shifted to sit her on the counter.

When they came back to earth together, the only sound in the room was the two of them breathing heavily. He lowered her slowly to her feet, nuzzling her neck as he did.

Still proudly naked, he disposed of his condom, then walked over and pulled her into his arms, looping his hands behind the small of her back. He absently pushed her hair off one of her shoulders and bent to kiss the shoulder he'd exposed. "What do you want to do today?"

Melanie sighed contently in his embrace. "Besides this?"

He chuckled. "It's up to you. We don't have to leave the kitchen."

Melanie thought about it for a moment, then asked, "Would you like to see where I live?"

He buried his face in her hair. "I'd love to see whatever you want to show me."

"Then get dressed, cowboy." Melanie winked at him and threw his shirt at him. She picked up her dress off the floor and slipped it back over her head.

Moments later, they were outside with Jace's dog barking and running circles around them. Melanie tried to catch him, but the pup darted and widened his circle. She rolled her eyes. "That's Tibby. I don't know why I agreed to him."

Charles bent and offered his hand to the dog. Tibby sniffed it, then rubbed himself against Charles's leg while Charles pet him affectionately. "Every boy should have a dog."

Melanie watched the exchange with genuine surprise. "I wouldn't have pegged you for someone who likes animals."

Charles met her eyes over the dog. "There is a lot you don't know about me."

Melanie motioned for him to follow her. "I'm beginning to see that."

He straightened and began to walk beside her. "What did I interrupt last night? Were you celebrating something?"

"I'm back in school. I'll have my degree finished in one more semester."

"That's fantastic. You must be happy about that."

"I am."

"You'll want to stay here to finish your classes." He seemed to be mulling how that would affect his plans. His plans. Even after what they had shared back in her kitchen, Melanie knew that nothing had changed. Sex had never been their issue. She stopped and turned toward him.

"I'm not leaving Texas, Charles. I'm not moving to the city and you can't convince me you want to stay here. Look around. You'd be bored sick in a day. You don't want kids and I have one. We're all wrong for each other."

"I'm not going back to New York without you."

"You say that, Charles, and maybe you even believe it. But I'm getting more and more comfortable with facing reality head-on. If we had met before Todd, maybe we would have found a way to be together. But my life with Jace is here. And I can't regret that because I can't imagine, for one moment, not having him in my life."

"I know I didn't handle meeting Jace well."

She waved a hand in the air desperately. "You don't have to explain. I know about your brother drowning. I understand why being around Jace is difficult for you."

His jaw tightened visibly. "So that's it. You want me to just walk away and end this?"

"My son needs a father—someone who can love him as much as I do. Tell me, can you be that man?" She issued her last question as a challenge.

"Clearly, you've already determined that I couldn't be."

Melanie held out a hand toward him, then let it drop to her side. "I didn't mean—"

"Didn't you?" he asked, settling his hat on his head with force. "I don't know much about love or how any of this is supposed to work, but I'm here and I'm trying. When you're willing to say the same—call me. I'll be in town until tomorrow. After that, I'm heading back."

He strode to his rental car. Before entering it, he took off his hat and threw it on the dirt driveway.

Chapter Twenty

Long after Charles had left, Melanie walked down the driveway and picked up the hat he'd discarded. She brushed it off, then hugged it to her stomach.

Why is it that every time I feel like I'm doing the right thing, it turns out so wrong?

She knew that he'd lost his brother and blamed himself for it. As soon as she'd voiced the question, she'd seen the memory of that day in his eyes and regret had ripped through her. *I didn't mean it the way he took it. I was looking for reassurance—for him to say that of course he would love my son.*

Not to imply that he couldn't.

Melanie returned to the steps of her house and sat down, laying the hat beside her. She spoke aloud as if Charles were there to hear her. "I don't want to feel bad about myself anymore. I don't want to make you feel badly about who you are. I never meant to do that. I'm so tired of being wrong." She looked down at his hat. "I'm sorry."

"Mama, who are you talking to?" Jace bounded up the steps. The bus driver waved to Melanie from the end of the driveway before pulling away.

Melanie forced a smile. "Myself, I guess."

"Guess what?" Jace asked as he plopped down beside her.

"What?"

"Miss Jeanine said it's Friday and Friday is my favorite day. You know why?"

"Why?"

"No school Saturday and no school Sunday."

"I thought you liked school."

Jace shrugged. "I like recess." He thought about it more and said, "And lunch."

Melanie almost began a lecture, then stopped herself when she realized that the advice she was about to give sounded an awful lot like something her father would say. She wanted to be more like her parents, but perhaps not down to every detail. She winked at her son. "I believe those were my favorite subjects, too."

Jace smiled up at her. "Math is fun, too, because sometimes the teacher lets us eat what we count. Brian ate his M&M'S before he counted them and Miss Jeanine made him count crayons the next time. He didn't care. He ate the crayons."

"Does Miss Jeanine know that?"

Jace shrugged. "His teeth were green."

Looks like I'll be calling someone's teacher. "You don't eat the crayons, do you?"

"Not at school. Those are dirty."

"Don't eat them anywhere. Crayons aren't good for you."

"David said they are not topic, so it's okay to eat them."

"You mean *nontoxic,* and that doesn't mean they are good for you. You're going to make yourself sick if you keep eating them."

She shook a finger sternly at him, even though she thought his stubborn expression was hilarious. "If I catch you so much as nibbling on one, I'm throwing them all away, understood?"

"Yes, ma'am."

"And I'll talk to David. He needs to explain to you what he meant by saying they were okay to eat."

Jace shrugged. "Am I in trouble?"

Melanie sighed. "No. Not unless you've been eating the laundry, too. Why can't I find half your socks?"

A wide grin spread across Jace's face. "That's Tibby. He eats them, then he poops them outside. It's really gross."

I do not need that image in my head.

In response to his mother's silence, Jace added, "Maybe you should have David talk to him, too."

Melanie looked down at her son and couldn't keep a straight face when he continued to grin up at her. "Maybe I will," she said and tickled him.

He rolled on the stair next to her, howling with laughter, then sat up and hugged her. Melanie hugged him back. She'd made so many mistakes in her life, but she never had and never would consider Jace one of them.

She wasn't sure what to do about Charles, but something he'd said echoed in her thoughts: "I don't know much about love or how any of this is supposed to work, but I'm here and I'm trying."

Which just about sums up my parenting style.

"Which horse are you riding at Tony's tonight?"

"Red Dusk."

"Then we'd better go get our chores done and get on over there."

They stood and walked into the house together. Tibby whined a greeting at Jace and ran circles around him. As soon as they entered the kitchen, Melanie spotted the empty ice tray still on the counter beside the refrigerator. She hastily tossed it into the sink, quickly checking the room for any other evidence.

Forget about this morning.

Forget about him.

Some things aren't meant to be.

Charles stood beside his sister while one of Carlton's ranch hands chose a horse for him. He'd almost made it back to his hotel room before he'd turned around and headed back. Giving up was not in his character.

Evaluate the obstacle. Study it. Destroy it.

In this particular case, the obstacle was Melanie's belief that he didn't care about her son. He could understand how she'd come to that conclusion, and once he acknowledged that to himself, he wasn't angry anymore.

He was determined.

Sarah hopped in excitement beside him. Barely shoulder height to him, his irrepressible sister beamed a smile up at him. She'd been trying to get him on a horse ever since she bought her own. "You're really going to do this?"

"I'm getting on a horse, not jumping off a building. I'm sure I'll be fine."

"You might even like it."

Charles sighed. "Doubtful. I don't understand the lure. Motorcycles go faster and handle better. Cars provide better protection from the elements. People rode horses in the past because they had to. There wasn't an alternative. I can't think of a sane reason why anyone would need to be on one anymore."

"For the same reason people create art—the sheer pleasure of it. It's all about the experience. Riding them isn't like driving a vehicle. Cars don't care about you. They don't have good days or bad days."

"I'd say that's a good thing."

"Really? Isn't life without a challenge boring? Riding a horse is like starting a relationship. You have to listen to each other and build trust. Don't be disappointed if your first ride isn't the best. Relationships don't happen in a day."

One thing his sister had never been was subtle. "Why do I feel that this is leading into a lecture I don't want to hear?"

She stuffed her hands into the front pockets of her jeans and swayed back and forth. "I saw your car at Melanie's house today."

Charles watched a ranch hand saddle and bridle what looked like a tame enough horse. He wasn't ready to discuss his relationship, or lack of one, with anyone yet. *Drop it.*

"And since she's not here with you now, I was concerned that—"

"Sarah—"

"I know you don't want to talk about it," she said but continued anyway. "I just want you to be happy. Melanie is a lot like you. She has a tough exterior, but beneath that she's also a big softie."

Melanie fit that description, but it wasn't how Charles saw himself. Raising one brow, Charles looked down at his sister. "That's how you see me?"

Sarah grinned. "Yep. I'm on to you now. I used to think you only called and used that dictator tone because you thought you were smarter than me. It always drove me nuts. But I've realized that it's the only way you know how to express that you love me. You locked everything up inside, Charlie. Just like I did. I know how hard it is to let go of the past, but you have to. It's time. It doesn't have to control you anymore. Texas freed me. I found myself here. I'm finally happy. I want that for you."

"I'm happy."

"Are you?"

Charles didn't want to lie twice. "I will be once I get back to New York."

"With or without Melanie?"

"With. She and Jace are coming back with me."

Sarah chewed her lip. "It's not going to be easy, Charlie. They love it here. Do you have to make them choose?"

"My life is in New York."

"Your life is wherever you find happiness, Charlie. I've never seen you fail at anything. If you want to be here, even part-time, you can be. There is always a way if you want something badly enough."

A compromise. Such a simple solution he'd failed to consider. He realized that it didn't have to be all or nothing as he'd laid it out for Melanie. He'd succeeded at less likely scenarios. He would find a way to make this one work. In an uncharacteristically affectionate move, Charles hugged his sister and was rewarded with a bone-crushing hug in return. Behind her, he saw the ranch hand trying to contain his amusement while waiting with horse in hand.

Charles stepped away from his sister. "Bring on the stallion."

The young man with the horse drawled, "He's gelded and he's twenty-seven. My grandma could ride him and she uses a walker."

Nothing was going to diminish the euphoria Charles felt now that he had a solution he could implement. Not even a young cowboy who was clearly amused by the idea of Charles attempting anything equine related. Luckily, Charles didn't waste much energy on what most people thought of him. He looked the aged horse in the eye and joked, "I believe we've both been insulted."

Tony spoke behind him. "I didn't think you'd show up."

With one hand patting the horse's neck, Charles turned to his future brother-in-law. "How could I miss the chance to try your finest steed?"

Tony tipped his head down, but Charles saw the smile he hadn't concealed in time. "I considered something livelier, but this is your first lesson and Sarah would miss you if you got yourself killed."

"Just tell me how to ride the damn thing," Charles said.

Tony gave Charles basic instructions on how to mount and how to hold the reins. He led him through simple cues to get the horse to move and stop. Then he said, "Most important thing to remember is that every part of your body is communicating something to the horse. Today you're on one that's smart enough to ignore most of the bullshit that comes out of you. Another horse might get nervous right along with you, just for tensing up your legs. Keep your hands light and your legs lighter. He knows what to do. You're the one learning."

Charles bit back the first retort that came in his head. He figured Tony was trying to get a rise out of him, but the day ahead was too important. It wasn't about learning to ride and they both knew it. It was just as Sarah had said. If he wanted Melanie, he would have to find a way to fit into her world just as he was asking her to fit into his.

Riding this horse was about building relationships. If Sarah could find something good on that ranch, then Charles was determined to, also.

Tony stood on the inside of the paddock, but off to one side. Charles had the feeling that although he was leaning back against the railing, Tony would intervene quickly if the ride took a bad turn. It made Charles see him in a new light.

Jace trotted up beside him on a much younger horse. "You do ride," he said quietly.

"If by riding you mean that I haven't fallen off yet, then yes," Charles said with some self-deprecating humor.

Charles searched the perimeter of the large fenced riding ring. There she was, the woman he'd tried to forget and now was willing to do anything to win.

Even ride a damn horse.

As if she could read his thoughts, Melanie smiled and Charles nearly walked his horse into the fence. In all the world, there was not a more beautiful woman.

Jace kept pace beside him and looked him over critically. "First time?"

In love? Yes.

Charles gripped the horn of the saddle tighter as the realization of what he'd just admitted to himself sank in. *I'm in love with Melanie.*

He looked at the young boy on the horse beside him—really looked at him for the first time. He had the same serious expression in his eyes that Melanie often did. The same measured stare. Although the boy was small, he rode with confidence.

"On a horse?" Charles asked, then answered before waiting for Jace to respond. "How can you tell?"

"You're holding on to the horn. Everybody does that when they start. I did it when I was four, but now I'm five. Five-year-olds don't need to hold on."

Charles let his hand drop from the saddle horn. He hadn't realized he'd been clinging to the saddle. "It's a lot to learn. Did Tony teach you to ride?"

Jace scratched the hair on the back of his neck as he considered the question. "I don't know. I think I was born riding. But Tony shows me how to do it better. Is he teaching you?"

Charles glanced across the ring at the man who was still watching him silently while leaning back against the railing. He'd said nothing since Charles had walked off on the horse, and he didn't look as if he was preparing to say much more. "You could say that."

"You're lucky. People come here all the time asking Tony to teach them stuff and he doesn't say yes much. He doesn't like many people."

"Really?" Charles asked and hid a smile. "I wouldn't have guessed that."

Jace's chest puffed up with pride. "I'm good with horses, just like he is." He demonstrated a few moves on his horse, then fell into step beside Charles again.

Charles wasn't just being polite when he complimented Jace. The boy rode with a skill Charles doubted he'd acquire no matter how many hours he forced himself into a saddle. Jace could stop his horse without using the reins and turn him the same way. It was something to admire, and Charles finally understood why trotting a horse through Central Park would not be enough for Jace.

"Mama said it's okay if you don't know how to fish. She said you don't have a place to do it in the city." His next words stole Charles's heart. "I could teach you, if you'd like."

Charles cleared his throat. "I'd like that. I used to fish when I was your age."

"You did?" Jace asked in surprise.

"I didn't always live in the city," Charles said. Memories of his youth came wafting back, but for once they didn't sadden him. "When I was your age, my parents had a lake house and we went there every weekend."

"In Rhode Island?"

"Yes, I'm surprised you know that."

"Sarah told me that's where you're from. She said it's a small place. I want to see it someday. Is everything there tiny?"

Charles chuckled. "No, the state is small, but everything in it is regular size."

"Oh," Jace said in obvious disappointment. "Are your parents in heaven?"

With a jolt of surprise, Charles shook his head. "No, why would you ask that?"

Jace shrugged his small shoulders. "Sarah told my mom that you don't see your parents anymore. My dad is in heaven and so is Sandy. Sandy was my dog, but he died."

"My parents still live in Rhode Island," Charles said awkwardly. Talking to a five-year-old was a whole new experience for Charles and one he wasn't sure how to navigate. He chose what he hoped was a safe subject. "I had a dog when I was your age. His name was Moose."

The boy nodded, then said, "Is he in heaven now?"

"Yes."

"I bet there are a lot of dogs in heaven."

"I bet you're right."

"I hope my dad likes dogs."

The simplicity of the boy's love for a father he'd never met touched Charles deeply. He understood loss and remembered too clearly how he'd struggled to make sense of his own—even though he'd been much older when he'd experienced it. "I'm sure he does."

They rode halfway around the ring before Jace spoke again. "I shouldn't have said I don't like you. Mama was sad I said it."

With emotion clogging his throat, Charles said, "It's okay. You don't know me yet. I hope you give me a chance to change that opinion."

"David told Tony you're the type that takes getting used to."

"He did?" Charles asked wryly. He'd have to remember to watch what he said since Jace was mentally recording it all.

"Yep, and David knows everything. He's not as good with horses as Tony is, but no one is. Tony speaks horse."

A mix of feelings welled within Charles as he listened to Jace talk about the men he idolized. He was glad that, although Jace would never meet his father, he had grown up with strong male role models. The conversation also made Charles miss his own father in a way he had never allowed himself to. He remembered believing his father was just as infallible as Jace thought David and Tony were.

Charles realized he was now about the age his parents had been when Phil died. He'd always looked at the tragedy in terms of what it had done to him and Sarah, but he never really considered how his father and mother must have felt.

They'd never said anything, so he assumed they didn't feel anything, either. But had the past tied them up as it had Charles?

Memories of stilted conversations with them over the years came back in a rush.

He thought of the last time he'd seen them in person. Sarah had expressed a need to see photographs of Phil, and Charles had traveled back to Rhode Island to retrieve them. He'd briefly outlined why he wanted them. His father had gone into the basement. Charles and his mother hadn't exchanged a single word until his father returned with a large box of photo albums.

Albums he'd later looked through with Sarah. At the time, he'd resented how the pictures had brought that chapter of his life vividly back to him.

He was beginning to think he should be grateful to Sarah for forcing him to remember. Sarah didn't live by anyone else's rules. She didn't care if a topic made someone uncomfortable. She plowed through life with an unyielding optimism and openness that Charles was only now beginning to admire.

Sarah understands love. I hope I can one day claim the same.

"You like my mom a lot?" Jace asked while they approached Melanie, who was leaning against the outside of the fencing.

She must have heard, because her eyes snapped to Charles.

Charles answered Jace, but in a volume he knew would carry to Melanie. "Yes, I do."

"You should tell her you know how to fish."

More than a little amused at how Jace saw the world, Charles asked, "You think it's that easy?"

Jace shrugged. "Worth a try."

Charles shook his head and chuckled in concession. *What would Mason think if he could see me now? He'd say I've lost my fucking mind.*

Charles met Melanie's eyes the next time they approached where she stood. "Melanie, want to go fishing tomorrow? You, me, and Jace?"

She nodded, put a shaking hand up to her mouth, and her eyes suddenly shone with tears.

As he and Jace rode out of earshot, Charles said, "Hey, from now on I know who to come to for dating advice."

Jace's eyes rounded. "What is dating?"

Charles chuckled again. "You'll have to ask your mother that one."

Temporarily satisfied with that answer, Jace moved on to ask him other questions. He wanted to know if he had a car and why he always wore sunglasses.

It occurred to Charles, as they made their way around the ring for the twentieth or so time, that riding involved much more than staying on a horse. Just like the ranch was about more than people simply training them. This was a way of life. It was uncomplicated and honest and offered him something money had not brought him—a second chance.

Sarah's words came back to him: "Nothing is impossible if you want it badly enough." He looked across at Melanie and then down at her son.

I do want this.

Charles was dismounting from his horse onto surprisingly shaky legs when his phone rang. He didn't want to answer it. Melanie was sending her son into the house with Sarah for a snack, and that gave Charles the perfect opportunity to speak to her privately. He pulled her far enough away from the others that their conversation wouldn't be overheard.

He kissed her briefly when she joined him, showing restraint only out of respect for the number of eyes still watching them. She smiled up at him shyly. "I'm glad you didn't leave."

"I—" The ring of his cell phone interrupted his admission that he could never leave her. He let the call ring through. But it rang again. And again.

In frustration, he took it out of his pocket and was prepared to silence it when he saw the number. It was Tanner's social worker. "I have to take this," he said and half turned away.

Although he'd had his cell phone number since day one, the social worker had never used it. Adrenaline kicked in as Charles imagined all the possible scenarios in which he would. "What is it?"

"Did you see TJ on Thursday?"

"No, I'm out of town this week. I told him I'd see him next week."

"He left the group home last night. The staff told me he took all his things with him."

"To go where? Why didn't anyone stop him?"

"He turned eighteen yesterday. He has the right to go anywhere he wants to now."

Thursday was his birthday? Shit. "Where would he go?"

"I was hoping you'd know. He ran with a tough crowd when he was with his foster parents. I hope he's not headed back there."

"I don't understand. We had a plan for him. His college would have been paid for. He knew that. Why would he run?"

"My guess is he's afraid to believe you. He doesn't want to give you a chance to disappoint him."

Charles looked down at his watch and let out a string of profanity. "I can be back in the city in five hours. Give me any information you have about where you think he'd go. I'll find him."

The conversation he'd planned to have with Melanie fell to the wayside. "I have to fly to New York tonight," he said curtly as he pocketed his phone.

Disappointment was clear in her eyes. "When will you be back?"

"I don't know," he said as he sketched out a strategy for fixing the situation. How long did it take to find a kid who didn't want to be found? And then what the hell happened once he was found? Take him back to the group home? Get him an apartment of his own? Tell him you'd like to help him more but you're too busy getting laid down in Texas?

"Are you going to tell Jace?" Melanie asked, putting her hands on her slim hips in a show of displeasure.

"Tell him what?" It was difficult to focus on anything but how he'd screwed up.

Melanie narrowed her eyes and spoke slowly, distinctly, expressing her anger through the clipped tone she used. "That you won't take him fishing tomorrow. He thought you were serious."

"I was," Charles said and ran a hand roughly over his chin. *Shit, Jace. Who am I trying to fool? If I can't handle being a mentor, how the hell do I think I can be a father?* Years of frustration with a guilt he'd never been able to shed surged within him, giving his voice a cold, hard edge. "Listen, you were right. I don't belong here. I don't know what the hell I was thinking." He turned away and started walking to his car.

Melanie called out his name, but he didn't stop.

She stepped in front of him and blocked his path, her hair whipping wildly in a sudden breeze. "What happened, Charlie?"

Everything I told myself wouldn't. I fucked up again. Charles took a purposeful step around her, but she moved with him. "I remembered why I chose the life I did. You're a wise woman, Melanie. You saw me for who I am. Jace needs a father he can depend on and clearly that is not me. Now step aside because I'm leaving."

Instead of doing as he said, Melanie put a hand firmly in the middle of his chest. "Not until you tell me who just called you."

"It doesn't matter," Charles said with disgust. The details are irrelevant when the pattern remains unbroken. *I just hope I find Tanner before I have another reason to hate myself.*

She didn't back down. "It matters to me. You came out here because you said we belong together. You asked me to trust you, but I wasn't ready to. I haven't always shown the best judgment when it comes to relationships, and I was afraid to be wrong again." She raised her other hand and placed that on his chest as well, then threw his own words back at him: "I don't know much about love or how any of this is supposed to work, but I'm here and I'm try- ing." A fire lit in her eyes. "And if you try to leave without telling me the real reason, I will show you why they call me the Takedown Cowgirl."

Charles had never seen anything more beautiful or determined than his sexy cowgirl preparing to hog-tie him if he tried to skirt around her again. It pulled him back from the past enough for him to clear his head. He took one of her hands in his and raised it to his lips. He wasn't comfortable revealing his weaknesses to anyone, but Melanie wasn't just anyone. She deserved the truth. "It was a call from Family Services in New York. Tanner ran away yesterday."

"Who?"

"The boy who mugged you."

"Why would they call you?"

"I've been mentoring him."

"You never said anything about it."

"It's not like I did it well. Look what happened. I came here the week of his birthday. He doesn't trust people easily, and I just lived up to the worst of what he expected from me. He took off and no one knows where he is."

"And you're going back to find him?" she asked, even though they both knew she knew the answer to that question. She wasn't asking out of curiosity—she needed to confirm what she believed.

"Yes. Although I don't know what I'll do after that. He doesn't need a mentor who doesn't even know his birthday."

There it was, the ugliness inside him, laid out for Melanie to see. She kept asking if Charles would be a good father to her son—perhaps she should consider this her answer. Perhaps they both should.

Remarkably, she didn't look away in disappointment. She stood there, blocking his way, with an expression on her face he'd never seen. He wasn't sure what it meant, but it sent his stomach into crazy summersaults.

"You made a mistake, Charles. You're human. We all do the best we can and sometimes it's not good enough. But that doesn't mean Tanner doesn't need you." She squeezed his hand in hers. "I need you. Jace needs you. Don't walk away from any of us, even if we tell you to, because none of us mean it."

Charles pulled Melanie into his arms and shuddered as her words washed over him, releasing his prison of guilt and doubt. He took her mouth in his with a crushing kiss, one in which all his pent-up emotions poured out. She met that kiss with a fervor of her own. When he finally raised his head, both of them were shaking from the intensity of their feelings.

Melanie raised a hand to his cheek and said, "Go find Tanner. We'll be here when you get back."

He kissed her forehead. "You really are a sweet woman, Melanie . . . when you're not threatening to hit me with a frying pan."

Melanie chuckled in his embrace. "I meant that, too."

Charles smiled. "That's what made it sexy." He pulled her close to him so his hard-on nudged the soft curve of her stomach. "I love the way you take me down."

Melanie blushed. "The way you say that makes it sound naughty. You just wait until you get back. I'll take you down.

I'll . . ." She whispered some suggestions in his ear that sent his blood rushing to his cock and all coherent thought out of his head.

"Saying that to me when there's nothing we can do about it is torture." He kissed her. "But don't let that ever stop you." He kissed her again. "I'll be back as soon as I can be."

Sarah piped in from near them. "You're leaving, Charlie?"

"I have to." He wasn't going to say why at first, but Melanie prompted him to with a nod. "I've been working with an at-risk kid who thinks no one cares about him. He turned eighteen and took off, but he has nowhere to go. Nowhere good, anyway. I have to find him."

Sarah looked back and forth between Charles and Melanie. "Do you both want to go?" she asked. "We can watch Jace again."

Melanie met Charles's eyes and smiled gently. "No, I can wait for Charles to come back because I know he will."

Charles nodded.

"Where are you going?" David asked in a disapproving tone. Tony stood at his side, looking even less pleased with Charles.

Sarah restated the situation quickly. David nodded slowly, then said, "I know people in New York. One of my marine buddies is a cop in Brooklyn. He could help."

Tony added, "I'll call Dean. He's not just the sheriff, he's also my brother. He'll want to come with us."

"You're all coming with me?" Charles asked, genuinely surprised.

Tony hooked a thumb in the loop of his jeans. "We're family. That's what families do."

Charles didn't have time to question Tony's change of heart. "Okay. Then we leave in thirty minutes. I have a private plane at the Telson airport." He looked past the group to the porch, where Jace stood, and said, "But first I have to do something."

He met Jace at the bottom of the steps. "I won't be here tomorrow. I have to go back to New York. That means we'll have to postpone the fishing."

"Post bone?"

"Do it another day. I have something really important I have to do, but I'm coming back."

Jace looked him over slowly. "When?"

"As soon as I can," Charles promised. "Then you and I and your mother will spend a whole day together. Fishing or doing whatever you want."

Jace looked across the driveway at his mother. "I saw you kiss my mom. Are you two going to be doing that a lot?"

Charles hid a laugh in a cough. "I hope so."

"Lyle's mom and his new dad do that all the time, too. They're having a baby now. Are you going to have a baby with my mom?"

Charles swayed a bit in the face of a question he hadn't thought much about yet. "I—we—"

"It's okay if you do, but I want a brother. I don't like girls much."

"I'll keep that in mind," Charles said and was relieved when Melanie joined them.

Chapter Twenty-One

Once aboard his private plane, Charles started organizing his resources in New York. He called Tanner's social worker and recorded every shred of information he was willing to give about where he'd come from and where he might go. He called his security team and a private investigator. If the boy was still in New York, one of them would find him. He instructed his secretary to forward all calls directly to his phone.

When he finally set his phone aside, he realized he'd been a one-man show for three curious cowboys. They were sprawled in the surrounding cream-colored leather seats as confidently as if they'd been born to such luxury. It would take more than money and fancy vehicles to impress this group. They were assessing him by what he was doing rather than what he owned, and Charles realized that he respected them for it.

He looked around at the sleek interior of the aircraft. It used to be important to him. He'd needed to show himself that he'd made it.

But he no longer gave a damn about any of it. Making a life with Melanie might mean moving part of his business to Texas, but he was ready for the change.

His future brother-in-law laid his Stetson on his knee. "Nothing yet?"

Charles shook his head.

Dean said, "We'll find him. People have patterns of behavior. They go to places they know, especially if they don't have the financial resources to support a real run."

With one hand fisted on his jeans-clad leg in frustration, Charles said, "I don't get it. I don't understand why he left. I set up a trust fund for him with the monies earned from the Unleashed, Unchained video. No, I didn't hand it over to him, but it was his. All he had to do was enroll in any college and everything would have been paid for. He knew that. I couldn't adopt him, but I would have found him a place to live. I could have helped him, especially now that he's of an age that he can make those decisions for himself. Why would he run?"

David rubbed a hand over his chin thoughtfully and said, "When you grow up with nothing, it's hard to believe anything good could last. He probably figured he'd cut you out of his life before you disappointed him."

"I missed one fucking birthday."

Tony leaned back in his chair and watched Charles for a long moment, then said, "And this is the kid who mugged Melanie?"

Charles pinched the bridge of his nose as his head began to pound. "The one and only."

David said, "He's been working with him, trying to turn him around."

Letting out an audible sigh, Tony lamented, "You're making it impossible to dislike you."

Charles met Tony's eyes and decided to lighten the mood with some humor. "I'm sure I'll compensate in other ways."

"I'll still kill you if you hurt Melanie," Tony said with enough steel in his voice that Charles didn't doubt he was serious.

Dean piped in, "What did I tell you about death threats, Tony?"

Tony returned his hat to his head, this time placing it so it partially covered his face. "Never in front of the sheriff." He settled himself back, looking like he was going to nap. "Charlie, we live by a code in Texas. Shoot. Shovel. Shut up. Just remember that."

David nodded in Tony's direction. "He's a miserable bastard, but he's here and he won't go home until you find Tanner. That's how I judge a man. There's a saying in the horse world: you can't ride pretty. Often the most important things about a horse or person are not outwardly, instantly apparent. But if you watch both real close, they'll show you what they're made of."

Charles grew uncomfortable beneath the sustained scrutiny. "If you watch me much longer, you'll see a man who has failed at everything except making money."

"Until now," David said simply, leaned back in his seat, and decided to follow Tony's lead. He closed his eyes and covered his eyes with his hat.

Charles looked across the small aisle at the only other passenger still awake. Dean shrugged and said, "I'm just here to make sure none of y'all get arrested."

"That's not something I normally worry about."

Dean smiled knowingly. "Well, welcome to the family."

Sarah handed Melanie another cup of coffee and joined her at her kitchen table. "He'll be back, Mel."

"I know," Melanie answered and took a sip absently. "He doesn't say anything he doesn't mean."

With a smile, Sarah joked, "You got my brother on a horse."

Shaking her head, Melanie corrected her. "Not me, Jace." The wonder of that realization washed over her again so she repeated it. "He did it for Jace."

"Yes, he did." Sarah sniffed and Melanie realized her normally happy friend was close to tears.

Melanie reached across the table and took her hand in hers. "I'm sorry. Is watching Charles with Jace bringing back memories? I've been so self-absorbed lately. I didn't even think how this could be affecting you . . ."

Sarah smiled even as a tear ran down her cheek. "You are the answer to every prayer I ever voiced for my brother. You don't know what you and Jace have done for him. Done for me. You've given me back the brother I thought I'd lost forever."

Melanie wiped away her own tears impatiently. "Stop it, Sarah. Now you've got me crying. I didn't do anything." Her face reddened as an image of the last time she and Charles had been in her kitchen flashed in her mind. "Well, nothing I could tell anyone about."

That returned the smile to Sarah's face. "I told my parents about you. They want to come down and meet you."

"Oh boy," Melanie groaned. "I wonder what Charles thought of that."

"He barely talks to them. I'm sure he doesn't even know I called. I hope that being with you will help him with that, too. He and my father used to be close. Charlie was a mini Dad. Then after Phil passed, it all just fell apart. *We* fell apart. I thought it was something that was irreversible, like losing Phil. But I see now that it doesn't have to be. They said they'd come when Charlie invites them. Last year I would have said that meant never, but now I'm hopeful. Charlie's going to make that call. I know he will. And when my parents meet you, they're going to love you as much as I do."

Swallowing hard, Melanie asked, "They won't wonder why he chose someone like me?"

Sarah straightened and was suddenly uncharacteristically angry. "*Someone like you?* How can they not love you? You raised a wonderful son. You've been a good friend to their daughter. And now, you've made Charlie happier than anyone ever dared hope we'd see him again. You need to stop looking at yourself through the lens of everything you've done wrong and see everything you've done right."

Melanie stood up, walked around the table, and hugged Sarah. "I'm so glad I never poisoned you," she teased and they shared a long laugh.

Melanie's heart stopped when her phone rang long after she'd put Jace to bed that night. "Did you find him?"

"Not yet," Charles said tiredly.

"I'm so sorry," Melanie said and went to sit at her kitchen table while she talked to him. "Are the guys still with you?"

In a droll tone, Charles said, "Oh, they're here. They're camping out in my living room. I offered to put them up in a hotel, but they said it's not necessary."

Unable to suppress her amusement, Melanie chuckled. "That's real nice of you to open up your home like that to them. I bet they appreciate it."

"Hard to say," Charles said dryly. There was the sound of him moving around and settling himself down on his bed. "How are you doing?"

"Missing you," Melanie said honestly.

"Me too," he said without hesitation. "We'll make this work, Melanie. I don't know how yet, but we will."

"I believe you," she said and found that she did—with every fiber of her being. She saw now that they'd needed their time apart.

She wasn't ready for him when they'd first met. She needed to learn to trust herself before she could trust anyone else.

"How is Jace?"

"Wondering why all the other men got to go to the big city while he was left behind. His nose was a little out of joint when he realized who had left with you."

"I'd like to show him New York. There are parts of it he'd enjoy."

"I would love that."

After a pause, Charles asked, "What if I don't find Tanner? I have people looking everywhere for him and we don't have a single lead. No one will admit they've seen him. The only explanation is that he doesn't want to be found." The depth of the pain of that admission was evident in his ragged voice. "I don't know what else to do, Mel. I'm not used to this feeling. I know where he came from and I get sick thinking about him returning to it. I thought I had saved him, but what if I didn't do enough? What if I failed him?"

Melanie's heart broke for him and that was the moment she knew she was utterly, irreversibly in love with Charles Dery. "I feel that way all the time with Jace. It's called parenting."

Charles barked a short laugh. "Are you saying it doesn't get better than this?"

"Yep, that's what I'm saying. But it's worth it. I wouldn't trade a moment of it for something easier."

"If I find him—"

"*When,*" Melanie corrected him.

"*When* I find him, I want to take him somewhere he can have a fresh start. Do you think a kid who grew up on the streets of New York City could find *redemption* on a ranch in Texas?"

"I did," Melanie said softly. "I'll let you in on a little secret. Don't ask Tony if you should bring him, just introduce him to David."

"He's a tough kid, Mel. I'll understand if you wouldn't feel safe with him around."

Melanie smiled down at the phone. "You're forgetting that I've already kicked his ass once."

"Jace—"

"You don't have to worry about Jace, Charles. Tanner won't be coddled, but he will be loved. There's no better place to learn your manners than here. We'll have him saying 'Yes, ma'am' and 'Yes, sir' in one shake of a polecat's tail."

Charles chuckled. "Are you putting on your Texan for me? You don't talk that way."

Chuckling along with him, Melanie admitted, "You caught me. But it sounded good, didn't it?"

"Not as good as some other things I've heard you say."

"Such as?"

"The way you say my name when you come . . . somewhere between a whisper and a cry . . . I'm getting hard just thinking about it."

"Charles—"

"Yes?" he asked shamelessly, fully enjoying himself.

Melanie settled back in her chair and closed her eyes. "Keep talking."

Chapter Twenty-Two

It was day three of looking for Tanner; Charles was more and more determined to find him. After scouring every hospital and morgue, he had shed his suit and joined his Texan posse on the streets. The PI he'd hired had come back with a couple of leads, but nothing that panned out. Charles and his posse had walked what felt like every street in New York and the surrounding boroughs. They'd entered neighborhoods Charles had previously never even driven through and questioned everyone from the homeless to mothers in the park. Young men, old men, clerks at convenience stores. No one admitted seeing Tanner.

He was there, though. Charles could sense it. He knew when he asked one of the previous foster brothers, and the boy refused to look him in the eye when he answered, that he was close.

Along the way, Charles saw a side of the city he'd never known existed. The neighborhoods he'd once dismissed, upon closer acquaintance, revealed communities as complex as they were in need. He met a volunteer at one of the shelters he'd supported. She was handing out backpacks of books and cheap toys, and explained that often the children had nothing but the clothes they were wearing.

His search for Tanner put a face on what he'd always distanced himself from. In the past he would have felt ashamed, but his journey was inspiring him to get more involved. He would never again be cavalier about which cause he donated to. It wasn't about being invited to all the right fund-raisers, it was about this—the people those charities helped. When he went home that night, he gave a sizeable donation to the charity he knew supported the volunteer he'd met. He wanted to make sure those children kept getting those backpacks.

Where would this revelation take him? He wasn't sure, but he knew he'd never be the same.

It was late in the evening when Charles let himself into his penthouse, and he wasn't surprised to see Tony, David, and Dean sitting on his white furniture eating from take-out containers. But his eyebrows shot up into his hairline when he saw Mason, tie loosened, jacket thrown on the seat behind him, eating right along with them and looking like he'd known them for years.

Mason nodded at Charles in greeting and motioned toward the other men with his fork. "I love your new friends. Where were they when I was studying for that role in *Lone on a Mountain*? I could listen to them talk all day."

"That feeling is not reciprocated," Tony drawled.

Mason smiled and mimicked Tony's accent. "See, even when he's insulting me it sounds cool. Reciprocated. You have to say it real deep, like you just finished smoking a cigar and downing a whiskey."

Tony stood. "A person's friends say a lot about who they are."

"Hard to believe he's a senator," Dean said, watching Mason flip back his long bangs and dig into his bag of chips.

Mason shrugged and smiled at Charles. "My advisers say I should throw my hat in the next presidential election."

"God, no," Charles said with a laugh and sat down on one of the empty chairs.

"That's what I said," Mason laughed. "Have you seen how fast presidents age? It's all stress. I'm fine with what I'm doing. Besides, no one is electing me as I am and I'd make a porn long before I'd put myself through the stodgy makeover they say I need."

David coughed, choking on a chip.

Dean tossed back his head and laughed.

Charles laughed along with Dean while directing his next comment at Tony. "I see your point, and yet I turn to him frequently for advice—so judge me as you will."

Between bites, Mason opened a beer. "On a serious note, did you hear anything?"

Charles shook his head sadly. "No. Nothing. I've started paying people for tips, but they aren't giving me anything that pans out. Wherever Tanner is, he doesn't want me to find him."

"You've only been looking a couple of days," Mason said. "He'll turn up. I had a cat once that went missing. I thought he was gone for sure. He waited until I bought a kitten before he showed back up."

David raised a brow as if he were studying a unique specimen he found fascinating. "You have cats?"

Mason shrugged. "Sure. They're clean. They're easy. I've been told that having them is proof of my sensitive side. Women love that."

"Tanner isn't a cat, Mason. He's a scared kid," Charles said.

"Touchy, touchy," Mason chided his friend. "Technically, he's not a kid, either. He's eighteen. If he wants to throw away his life, that's his choice."

Charles stood angrily. "If you're not here to help, why are you here?"

Mason put down his beer and stood, too. "This man-child you're looking for, make sure you know what you're doing. And why you're doing it. Do you honestly care about him or are you trying to prove something to yourself?" He looked around. "And your new friends."

"You think I give a damn what they think about me? What you think of me? I'm going to find this kid and I'm going to do my best to get him off the streets."

Mason nodded and sat back down. "Okay. Good. What do you need me to do?"

Charles released his tension in a long sigh. "I'm going door-to-door right now. Do you have any better suggestions?"

Mason took out his phone and sent a quick text. "Let me see what my people can do. None of them are local, but they might know someone you don't. I can't guarantee it'll work, but it's worth a shot."

Charles checked his phone. "It's getting late. Melanie is probably waiting for my call. I should—"

"According to these fine gentlemen, you're engaged and didn't call to tell me."

"She hasn't technically accepted," Charles said, not comfortable with the direction the conversation was going in or how rapt their silent audience was.

"How did you ask her?"

Charles shrugged and grimaced. "I told her."

Mason slapped a hand on his knee. "Hold it right there. You went all the way down there to see the woman you've been moping over for months and all you did was tell her you two were getting married? Did you give her a ring?"

Charles shook his head. "It wasn't like that."

With a groan, Mason looked around the room. "Am I the only one who sees a problem here? Do I have to explain women to all of you?"

Dean nodded in agreement. "I have to agree with Mason. Women like to tell each other about how they were proposed to. What is Melanie going to say?"

Charles struggled to defend himself. "I—we—shit . . ."

Tony's smile held a hint of a smirk. "All that money and you didn't even get her a ring?"

"Oh," Charles said sarcastically, "like you probably did any better."

Tony glared at Charles.

Charles glared back.

Mason stood and said, "Don't worry. I have the perfect idea."

David sat forward in his chair. "I'm intrigued and that doesn't happen often. If he says something I agree with, I'm going to have to rethink my entire impression of him."

With a huge smile, Mason said, "It happens all the time. People don't think someone as attractive as I am could also be brilliant. But I am."

He walked over and gave Charles a pat on the back. "You are going to thank me for this. It's genius."

Melanie rolled over in her bed and smiled when her phone rang. She knew it was Charles before even checking caller ID. They used their phones to video chat every night and talked for hours. Although she couldn't wait to be back in his arms, there was something intimate and special about conversations that happened outside of their physical attraction to each other. They'd been lovers first, but they were building a real friendship—and what Melanie had thought was love was deepening with each talk.

"Did I wake you?" he asked in a low voice.

"No, I was waiting to hear from you."

She loved his deep, sexy laugh. "Can we get a babysitter for the first night I come back? Make that two nights."

Melanie blushed. "Jace does go to school."

"For what, six hours? That might be enough time."

With a chuckle, Melanie said, "If either of us wants to be able to walk the next day, I'd say that's plenty."

"I'm sorry this is taking so long. I thought I'd have found Tanner by now."

"Of course I want you here, but this is good, too. In a different way."

"I know what you mean. I can't remember the last time I was on the phone for more than five minutes if it wasn't a business call."

"I've never been much of a chatterer myself."

"I wait all day to hear your voice, though, so maybe you should consider becoming one."

Melanie smiled into her pillow. "I can't stop smiling whenever I think about you. Jace keeps looking at me funny. He's never seen me like this."

"David has been telling me about a pond in the valley. You and I should take Jace fishing there when I get back. We can pack a lunch—make a day of it."

"He would love that."

"Would you?"

"More than I can express in words."

"Good, because I've been thinking a lot about what you said about parenting."

"Yes?" Melanie held her breath.

"I understand now why you couldn't come back to New York with me."

"And?" Melanie said just above a whisper. Her heart started beating double time in her chest.

"I was thinking of only my needs when I wanted to uproot you and Jace. I see that now."

"What are you saying?"

"You were wrong when you said I'd be bored in Texas. When I'm there, I can be myself. Not someone trying to forget the past. Not someone clawing my way to the top. Just me. Just Charlie."

Melanie wished they weren't separated by so many miles, because she wanted to throw herself in his arms just then. "So which one should I call you? Charles or Charlie?"

"Whichever one you like better . . ." he said in his deep, bedroom voice.

Melanie rolled onto her side. "I like Charlie and that's the man I want my son to know." She lowered her voice to what she hoped was sexy level. "But Charles is really good in bed."

Charles groaned. "You're killing me. How am I going to sleep now?"

Melanie tossed her hair over one shoulder and chuckled. She felt young, alive, and beautiful. Both Charles and Charlie had given her that gift.

Chapter Twenty-Three

Charles sprinted out of the elevator in his office building and down the hall. As soon as June had told him someone was waiting for him in her office, he'd known.

Well, he'd hoped.

He slowed his approach as he entered the outer lobby. He caught a glimpse of Tanner before the boy saw him. He was sitting in one of the chairs, dressed in a dirty sweatshirt and jeans, hunched over defensively.

Charles nodded toward June as he entered the room, and she stepped out into the hall.

Tanner stood when he saw him and glowered at the floor. "I heard you were looking for me."

Taking a deep breath, Charles said simply, "I was."

"I told everyone you were trying to get money from me because of the video, but that I didn't have any . . . only you wouldn't believe me."

"Is that why so many of them threatened to kill me?"

Tanner looked to the side, still not meeting Charles's eyes. "Probably."

Charles paced in front of the door, then stopped. "Sorry about your birthday. I didn't realize it was Thursday."

"No big deal."

"Yes, it was. I should have been there." They stood for a moment in awkward silence. "Where did you go, Tanner?"

"I lived on the streets for a few years. I have friends. People who would kill for me if I asked them to."

Charles sat back against June's desk. "And probably ask you to do the same."

Tanner half turned away. "Yes. Especially when everyone has seen me get my ass kicked by a girl. They wanted me to prove myself."

"That's a dangerous lifestyle to choose, Tanner. And one you don't have to live."

His eyes glittering with anger, the young man confronted Charles. "I'm eighteen. I'm no one's problem anymore. You don't have to pretend you give a damn what happens to me."

Charles met his eyes and said calmly. "I wasn't pretending. If you want a fresh start, I'll help you make one."

"What are you going to do, just give me your fucking money? No one does that. No one gives anyone something for nothing. What do you want from me?"

"I'm not giving you anything. You'll have to earn your way, just as the rest of us did. What I'll give you is a place you can do it honestly and with people who will care about you."

"I'm not joining some fucking cult."

"First, easy on the profanity. People judge you by how you speak."

"I don't give a fuck what anyone thinks of me."

Charles sighed. "Second, the place I'm talking about is not a cult. It's a ranch in Texas. The man who runs it is world famous for training horses."

"I'm not a fucking horse. What the hell would I do on a ranch in fucking Texas?"

"I guess you'd have to go there to find out, wouldn't you?"

When Tanner didn't say anything, Charles said, "You have enough money in a fund to pay for a place to live and any college you want to go to. But I'm not releasing that money to you directly. Don't go to Texas. Enroll in school and you'll even get a small allowance."

"If it's my money, why the hell do you get to tell me what I can do with it?"

"Because you were mugging a woman in the video? Does that ring a bell? You're lucky you're not in jail for it. And because I have more lawyers than you have friends, so there is no way in hell you'll get a dime unless I see you turning your life around."

"What do you get out of this?" Tanner asked with narrowed eyes.

"A second chance," Charles said honestly.

Tanner studied Charles's expression for a long time, then said, "I could use one of those. I don't want to go back to the streets."

"Then your choice is college or Texas."

"Fucking Texas I guess."

"I'm sorry, I didn't hear you right."

A decision had to be made, and Charles knew that Tanner was just as aware of it as he was. The angry, defiant child TJ had been would have to step aside if Tanner was going to become the man he was meant to be. But no one could make that happen—except Tanner.

After another long pause, Tanner repeated his answer, less the profanity. "Texas. I wouldn't mind seeing how they train horses."

Charles felt he needed to prepare Tanner, give him a chance to choose college. "They'll expect you to work as hard as they do. There are chores and some of them are not pleasant. I don't get the lure of shoveling horse manure, but they all seem willing enough to do it."

"So why would you send me there?"

"Because I have never met a more caring group of people. Half of them have spent the last week scouring New York City for you. You treat them well, and you might find yourself part of a family."

Tanner looked down. "It's too late for that."

Charles walked over and patted his shoulder. "It's not too late. Not for you. Not yet. You can turn your life around, but you have to want to."

Tanner's eyebrows furrowed together and he studied Charles again. "When did you get so fucking sentimental?"

Charles smiled and shrugged. "I fell in love."

"Fuck."

Charles narrowed his eyes at him.

"I mean *shit*."

When Charles continued to stare him down, Tanner corrected himself again.

"I mean *holy macaroni with meatballs*."

Charles shook his head and laughed.

Tanner smiled tentatively as if not trusting it to last. "I don't know why you're doing this, but thank you."

As they walked out of the office together, Charles stopped and said, "Just one thing."

Tanner stopped in his tracks, instantly tense and defensive.

No matter how glad Charles was to have found Tanner, something needed to be said. "There is only one deal breaker to everything I said today."

Tanner crammed his hands into the pockets of his jeans and waited.

"Don't mess with Melanie or her son, Jace. Do that and you'll wish I'd left you on the streets."

Even though Charles had issued a threat, it wasn't one that appeared to upset Tanner. In fact, it was one he seemed to understand. "Yes, sir."

Charles smiled.

Take that, all you cowboys—this Wall Street investor got the first "Yes, sir." Stick that in your Stetsons.

That night, after he'd hung up with Melanie, Charles called his parents' home. His father answered the phone after several rings.

"Hello?"

"Dad."

"Charlie?"

"Yes, it's me."

"It's midnight."

Shit. "Sorry, Dad. I can call back."

"No," his father said, sounding like he was sitting up in his bed. Charles heard his mother in the background, asking who had called. "It's Charlie."

"Did something happen?" his mother asked at a high pitch. "Is it Sarah?"

"No," Charles said hastily, cursing himself for not checking the time before he called them. "Everyone is fine."

His father calmed his mother down, then asked, "Is there something you need? Are you in some kind of trouble?"

"I'm fine. I told you, nothing is wrong. I've just been thinking . . ."

His father listened quietly.

"I'd like you to come for a visit sometime."

"Down to New York?" his father asked.

"Yes, and I'll be spending a lot of time at the horse ranch where Sarah is. You and Mom would like it there."

"What is he saying?" his mother asked impatiently in the background.

"He wants us to visit him," his father said.

"Is he dying?" his mother asked, sounding on high alert.

"Tell Mom I'm not sick—unless you call being in love an illness. I met a woman I'd like you to meet. Her name is Melanie, and I'm going to marry her as soon I get back there. She has a five-year-old son, Jace. I'd like you to meet him, too."

"He says he wants us to meet his girlfriend," his father said to his mother.

"The woman Sarah told us about?"

"I think so."

"He's never asked us to meet anyone."

"He says he's marrying this one."

"Give me the phone," his mother said, and Charles chuckled as he pictured her taking the phone from his father. "Are you drunk, Charlie?"

"No, Mom."

"Did you really just invite us to visit you?"

Wow, I have been an ass to them. "I did. I miss you."

His mother said, "He said he misses us."

"Well he damn well should. He never calls or comes to see us."

His mother cleared her throat. "Your father said he misses you, too."

No relationship is built in a day, Charles reminded himself, and after over a decade of avoiding his parents, he knew the road back to them would have a few bumps. He wasn't afraid of them anymore, though. He wasn't afraid of anything.

"Tell Dad I love him."

His mother gasped. "Oh my God, Charlie is having a nervous breakdown. We should go see him." She continued on as if

Charles hadn't been able to hear her last comment. "Where are you, Charlie? We'll come tonight."

Charles laughed into his hand. "I'm in New York. I need a little time to finish a project I'm working on, then I'll fly you both to Texas."

"If that's what you want," his mother said, still sounding concerned.

"Mom?"

"Yes?"

"I love you, too."

Instead of sounding shocked this time, his mother answered, "Of course you do. And we love you. There was never a question about either. Now tell me one more time about this Melanie. If you're marrying her, she must be something special."

Charles smiled. "She sure is."

Chapter Twenty-Four

A week later, Stetson firmly planted on his head, Charles was sitting on a rock beside Jace, watching him happily release his latest catch back into the pond. He'd lost count of how many times they'd done it that day. How many worms fit into an old paper coffee cup? Too many in his opinion, but it had given him time to get to know Jace, and that had gone better than he'd dared hope.

A day beside the water with a child. A few months ago, he would have said it was something he'd never be able to enjoy, but being with Melanie had forced him to face his old demons.

He looked out over the water and thought:

Phil, I'm sorry.

Sorry I didn't pay better attention to you that day.

Sorry I didn't understand how dangerous the water was for you.

I'd give anything to go back and not walk away to talk to Mom and Dad.

Anything to have you back with us.

I probably don't deserve the second chance I found here, but I'm taking it.

He looked down at the young boy beside him.

If you can hear me, help me keep Jace safe.

Help me do it right this time.

Charles nearly jumped when Jace put his hand on his arm. "You okay, Charlie?"

"I'm fine. Sorry, my mind wandered."

"That's because you're old."

Charles raised one eyebrow at his young friend and Jace laughed joyfully. Charles found himself laughing along with him. "Old, huh?"

"Yes, sir."

Charles laughed again and ruffled the boy's hair. "I'm not so old that I couldn't beat you in a race to your mother." He looked back at Melanie, who was reading on a blanket in the sun about fifty feet behind them. Charles half stood, giving Jace time to scramble down onto the grass before him. He kept pace with the boy, letting him win by a few steps.

Jace threw himself into his mother's arms for a hug. "Mama, did you see that one?" He held his hands out in front of him. "It was hunormous!"

"Enormous?" Melanie asked with a smile.

"And huge," Jace added with a nod. "I wanted to take it home and put it in the bathtub, but Charlie said he's so big he probably has a family in there waiting for him."

"Charlie is a very smart man." Melanie winked up at Charles and his breath caught in his throat.

A warm feeling spread through him as he sat on the blanket watching Melanie and Jace. She took some toy cars out of a bag and set him up playing in a dirt patch beside them. Tibby came running and started to dig excitedly beside the boy.

Melanie turned so she could watch Jace while leaning back on Charles. Charles moved closer and settled her between his legs, her back on his chest. He tucked her hair to one side and kissed her neck gently. She smiled over her shoulder at him.

"Thank you for today," she said.

"I should thank you—this is the best day I've had in a long time."

Melanie took one of his hands in hers and clasped it against her stomach. "You don't miss your life in New York?"

He rested his chin on her shoulder and said softly, "I have a business to run and employees who depend on me. I'm looking into a satellite office in Dallas, but I'll still need to spend time in New York. And you'll have to come with me sometimes if you really want to help me create the Dery Foundation for the Homeless. I spoke to my lawyer. We're moving forward with it. We'll start in New York and branch out as we grow."

"I do want to be involved with that project. I gave you a lot of grief in the beginning about not caring where your donations went. I was a bit of a hypocrite."

"You?" he teased gently.

"Shut up," she joked back. "I'm serious. I love my life here on the ranch, but I'm done hiding. I want to help you with that foundation, and I'd like to get involved with what's going on in Fort Mavis. You make me feel like I can make a difference."

"You can. You changed my life for the better."

Melanie turned her head and gave him a brief kiss. Lacing her fingers with his, she asked, "Did you tell Tanner about the foundation yet?"

"I did. I told him he needs a degree in business and sociology if he wants to run it someday. David is helping him sign up for one course at the community college in the spring. Hopefully, he follows through."

Melanie let out a content sigh. "David won't let him back out of it. You were right to bring Tanner here. I saw him smile for the first time yesterday. He was brushing down a horse and talking to it. He looks a little scared, but he'll do fine." She rested her other hand on his thigh. "I'm still going to finish my classes. But after that, I'm all yours."

Charles shifted beneath her, letting her feel his arousal against her back. She gave him a peck that broke off painfully quickly. If they had been alone, they'd already be rolling around naked on the blanket, but they weren't and, strangely, that was okay. *We have the rest of our lives together. There is no need to rush.*

"I have something I want you to listen to," he said softly in her ear and dug into the back pocket of his jeans for his cell phone. He tucked a two-carat diamond ring in his hand beneath his phone and scrolled to his music files. A country melody began with the gentle strumming of a guitar and Melanie's heart began to beat wildly in her chest. With the sun shining brightly, Jace playing near them, and Charles's arms around her—Melanie thought this was the closest to heaven a living person could get.

A male vocalist with a deep, gravelly voice filled the quiet afternoon air with words that took Melanie's breath away.

Top of my game
Top of the world
Yeah that was me
'Til you took me down

My Takedown Cowgirl
Strong and brave
Wild and free
I need her and she needs me

I wasted time

Wasted my life
Looking back at what I couldn't change
But now I see
Here in front of me
My chance to finally get it right

My Takedown Cowgirl
Strong and brave
Wild and free
I love her and she loves me

So take this ring
Take this leap
Nothing matters without you beside me
At the top of my game
At the top of the world
Loving how you take me down
Again and again

My Takedown Cowgirl
Strong and brave
Wild and free
Marry me
Marry me

As the song came to an end, Charles called Jace over. "Jace, I want to marry your mother more than I've ever wanted anything in my entire life. Do I have your permission?"

Jace stood up, walked over to them, and wiped his muddy hands on his jeans. "Why is she crying?"

Melanie sat back and pulled her son to her side. "Because I'm so happy."

Jace looked back and forth between them. "You'll take care of my mom?"

Charles nodded solemnly.

"And me?"

"Yes."

Melanie's heart was bursting with pride as her son weighed the decision like a man. "What would I call you?"

Charles answered easily, "Whatever you want to."

"Will you be my dad?"

"If you let me."

"Can I have a kitten?"

Charles wisely looked at Melanie first and Melanie shook her head. "No," he said.

Jace gave them both another critical once-over, then smiled. "Okay. Now can I go play?"

Alone again with Charles, Melanie returned to how she'd sat in the beginning with her back against his and her eyes on Jace. She fought back a fresh wave of happy tears.

"Did you write that song?"

"No, I told the songwriter how I felt about you and he put it to music."

"Will you play it again?" she asked.

He started it over. "We'll also listen to it tonight when we're alone," he promised and nuzzled her neck.

Melanie blushed and shivered with desire at the thought. As the lyrics filled the air again, she asked, "Is that the lead singer of Unchained?"

"Yes. I figured he owed me a favor."

"They aren't even a country band. How did you get him to do it?"

Charles kissed her neck. "I can be very persuasive when I want to be."

Laughing joyfully at him, she asked, "Did you bribe him or threaten him?"

"Doesn't matter as long as you like it," he said vaguely. "It can stay private between you and me, or they can add it to their tour and you can hear it played on the radio. Your choice."

"Is there anything you can't do?" Melanie asked in amazement.

"Yes," he said and raised her hand to his lips to kiss it. "Live without you." Charles held out a ring in front of Melanie. "I love you. I never thought I could love anyone, but you changed that. I can't imagine my life without you. Say yes, Melanie."

Melanie turned on her knees with tears running down her face. Everything she felt, everything she'd hoped he felt, was there in that song. "Yes. Yes. A million times—yes."

He slid the ring on her finger, then called Jace over.

Melanie relaxed in his arms and let the words of the song wash over her again.

But now I see
Here in front of me
My chance to finally get it right

And this time we will. Both of us. Together.

A few days later, David made a long-distance phone call. "Looks like your idea worked. Melanie has played that song so much, it's stuck in my head, and Charles is walking around grinning like he sang it himself. You were right."

Mason let out a deep laugh. "I don't know why people doubt me."

David had always been of the mind that if a person couldn't say anything nice, they should say nothing at all—so he held his tongue. "Where do you want me to send the money?"

"From the bet? Keep it. It wasn't fair anyway. I'm gifted when it comes to knowing how to please a woman."

"Apparently so," David said dryly.

"Call me if you ever need any advice about the ladies."

"Never going to happen," David said in amusement.

"That's what they all say," Mason volleyed back with a self-assured chuckle. "Want to bet on it?"

Also in the Lone Star Burn series by Ruth Cardello

If you loved Melanie and Charles, read on to see how Tony and Sarah met in *Taken, Not Spurred*.

Taken, Not Spurred

No real adventure ever started by waiting patiently on a doorstep.

Still, Sarah Dery hesitated before reaching for the handle on the screen door of her friend's immense white farmhouse. The shelter of the wraparound porch did little to alleviate the heat of the midday Texas sun, but was that a good enough excuse to enter? *What if no one is home?* Since there was no cell phone service, there wasn't much else she could do unless she was willing to wait in her SUV.

Wiping one suddenly cold hand across a jean-clad leg, Sarah straightened her shoulders and opened the door decisively. She hadn't survived the three-day drive from Rhode Island only to pass out from heat exhaustion on the porch because Lucy was late.

"Hello?" she called out. "Anyone home?" No answer.

The interior of the house was similar to the mammoth horse barn she'd searched a few minutes ago: well maintained but lacking any personal touches. She was surprised that her friend lived like this, but perhaps when you worked all day on a ranch, decorating wasn't a priority.

Sarah assessed the living room. It looked and smelled clean—the best compliment she could give it. The few pieces of wooden furniture, decorated with outdated, plain blue cushions, had probably never given a person a moment of comfort. She returned to the foyer and appreciated the beauty of the room's woodwork, even as she noted that the walls lacked photos and artwork.

The house reminded her of the mansions in her hometown, built by wealthy factory owners who had long since left the area, along with their businesses. Although this house showed no obvious signs of disrepair, it felt cold. Empty. *Can a house be sad?*

She wandered through the downstairs rooms and marveled at the absence of electronics—no television, not even a radio. Lucy had hinted that her life in Texas wasn't happy, but this was Sarah's first glimpse of how truly barren her life down here was.

No wonder she invited me.

Although she hadn't seen her old roommate since college, they'd kept in touch via email and the occasional uneventful video chat. Until Lucy had asked, "How's your writing going?"

What writing?

"I've been busy," Sarah had said lamely.

"Didn't you say that you'd taken the job at your parents' company so you'd have time to write?"

Yes.

Apparently, time was not the issue.

Can you be a writer if you don't write? Like a musician who never picks up an instrument? Who are you when the person you are in your heart doesn't match the life you're living?

I always wanted to be a writer—tell stories that would sweep readers away on a journey of laughter, tears, and growth. I dreamed of discovering myself through the characters I crafted.

So why can't I write?

What's stopping me?

God, I need this trip.

Lucy said she was desperate for companionship, and the invitation to spend a summer on a working Texas cattle ranch had been too tempting to pass up. Taking a deep breath, Sarah announced to the empty house, "I'll admit, so far this isn't living up to how exciting I thought Texas would be, but it'll work out." *Maybe I watched too much* Dallas, *but I'm not ready to give up on my fantasy just yet.*

She could almost hear her brother's telltale sigh, which was often followed by a lengthy lecture. Charles Dery was a successful Wall Street investor and a self-appointed dictator when it came to his little sister. Moving to New York rather than staying and working for their family's construction company hadn't stopped him from getting involved as soon as she'd announced she was taking a leave of absence from her office job at Dery and Son—a company that should have been named *Dery and Reluctantly Employed Daughter.*

"Mom and Dad called me," her brother had said. "They're upset. There is no way you're quitting your job to travel cross-country alone."

"Yes, I am, Charlie."

"Why the hell are you doing this?" he'd stormed.

"I need this," Sarah had fired back, knowing that a deeper conversation wasn't possible between them. *I need this.*

Before it's too late.

Maybe it already is.

Twenty-five.

What is it about a milestone birthday that makes a person reassess her life? She'd graduated from the University of Rhode Island with a bachelor's degree in English, but she could easily have gotten a degree in basket weaving for all she'd done with it since.

Lucy's question had haunted her, especially during her last birthday party when the forest of candles on her cake had hit Sarah like a flaming dose of reality. *How did I lose myself?*

She wished there had been one grand event she could blame, but the truth was discontent had arrived much less dramatically than that—more like a flower wilting in the sun until the life she thought she was meant for was nothing more than a pile of dried-out, brittle regret.

Charlie said I should think of how this is affecting others and not be so selfish. Easy for him to say from New York.

I tried to be the one who stayed behind to make everything okay, but the price was too high. Be good. Follow the rules. Avoid all unpleasant topics. I can't do it anymore. I can't be the perfect daughter in the perfect family. I'm an adventurer. A pioneer. Texans hadn't stayed where the Mayflower dropped their parents. They'd boldly left for parts unknown.

Like I did.

Life in Rhode Island wasn't awful. Her office position at her parents' company paid enough for her to live in her own apartment and afford Scooter, the horse she rode four nights a week at an exclusive equestrian facility.

I didn't have anything to complain about.

Or anything to look forward to.

Until Lucy called.

"Hello . . . anybody here?" The silence was eerie, but this wasn't the movies—nothing extraordinary was going to happen.

Sarah grimaced. Nothing ever did.

Lucy had probably just run to the store for some last-minute supplies. *Isn't that how it always works? You step away for a few minutes and your company arrives.*

A bead of sweat trickled down Sarah's neck. The light cotton shirt she had chosen so carefully that morning was now plastered against her back. Sarah plucked at it while renewing her resolve.

She'd adjust to the heat. Comfort didn't matter. This was about finding herself, finding her voice.

She returned to the living room, plopped on the unforgiving couch, and flung out her arms in victory. *I did it!* The drive may have taken her three days, giving her trailered horse time to rest along the way, but even that part of the journey had been amazing. Each bed-and-breakfast she'd stayed at on her way down had intensified her anticipation. Each time she'd told the other guests where she was going, she'd felt even more alive.

This is what life is about: seeing new places, meeting new people, grabbing life by the balls and squeezing until it coughs up a story worth telling.

I should write that down.

She whipped out the purple spiral notebook she'd purchased specifically for this trip and stopped halfway through recording her thoughts, hesitating before writing a word she normally avoided: *balls.*

I'm twenty-five, not five. Writers are not afraid of words. On the very first page of her notebook, she wrote:

Balls. Balls. Balls.

And smiled with pride. With renewed enthusiasm, she wrote:

Big balls. Hairy balls. Bald balls?

Chewing on the end of her pen thoughtfully, Sarah decided to designate a section of her notebook to research topics. She drew a margin on the right side of the paper. In her finest penmanship she wrote:

Do some men shave their balls?

I should write: What woman my age doesn't know that? But this is not about passing judgment. Positive energy brings positive results. Accepting yourself is the first step toward improvement.

God, I've been reading too many self-help books.

It's time to stop thinking about why I'm not living the life I want and just live it.

Which was why she'd chosen to bring a notebook instead of her laptop. *Real change sometimes requires a clean sweep.* No more wasting time searching the Internet hoping a topic would end her writer's block. No more reading countless articles on how to write. *Just a pen, a notebook, and Texas. If I don't write something this summer, I deserve to work for my parents for the rest of my life.*

Time to color outside the lines.

No more settling for good enough.

Like Doug.

Her recent breakup with the man she'd dated chastely in high school, then slept with through college, had been as unexciting as any of the sex they'd ever had. Not that they'd had sex at all in months. Which should have mattered, but it hadn't. *Because I didn't love him. Just like every other choice I've made up until now, he was safe, the type of man everyone expected me to be with.* Smart, successful, and someone who fit into her parents' social circle. He'd never said a single thing anyone objected to. *Tapioca in a suit. Bland in and out of bed.*

Why was I with him for so long?

The wrong-size shoe doesn't fit just because you want it to.

She slammed her notebook shut and hugged it to her chest. She took another look around the room, then whispered, "The only one who can give me the life I want is me. Right now. Right here."

Returning to her more immediate concerns, Sarah looked down at the damp cotton material of her shirt. Who knew how long Lucy would be gone? *What if she comes home and she's not alone? I can't meet people looking like this.*

Coming to a quick decision, Sarah rushed back to her SUV and hauled her luggage into the foyer. She rummaged for a change of clothes and, taking just her small bag with her, headed off in search of a place where she could freshen up.

The bleached-white downstairs bathroom was as Spartan as the rest of the house, but it revealed a beautiful . . . no, a *heaven-sent* shower. She closed her eyes for a moment and imagined washing off the dirt and sweat under the cool spray.

Would it be so wrong?

Tony considered taking the shotgun from the back of his truck when he saw the vehicle parked in his driveway, but quickly decided to toss this intruder off his land with his bare hands. *Hell, it might even make my day.*

A Rhode Island license plate? Someone had traveled a long way for a good old-fashioned Texas beating.

'Course, there was a slim chance that his ranch manager, David, had invited a buyer to pick up his horse directly from the ranch. *No, David's smarter than that.*

Tony opened the door of his truck with more force than was necessary and took stock of the scene in his driveway. No one he knew would have driven this flashy gray two-horse trailer or matching silver Lexus SUV—both of which looked spanking new.

Upon closer inspection, the trailer looked more like a delivery truck than a pickup. The rear-loading ramp was still down. Clearly, someone had unloaded a horse and led it into the barn.

He checked the barn's interior first. Nothing out of place. The stalls were secure. He scanned the paddocks. All his horses were accounted for.

What the hell? Whoever had driven that trailer had had the gall to put their small horse in one of his paddocks, smack-dab in the middle of his prized quarter horses.

A delicately boned bay horse, Paso Fino by breed. Tony's eyes narrowed. Pampered, by the looks of it. Definitely not used to working. The sparkling painted black hooves and pink halter stopped him in his tracks.

The intruder is a woman. Cursing, Tony strode toward the house, the pace of his footsteps picking up speed as his anger grew.

He considered each of his past female companions, although none were recent. He chose partners with care—experienced women who understood that he had nothing more than a few hours of mutual pleasuring to offer them. He didn't promise them anything, and they were too smart to think they could come to his ranch uninvited and receive anything but a cold escort back to the road. The only people who were welcome on his ranch were the ones who worked there, and even they knew to stay out of his way.

The pink-and-green checkered luggage that greeted him as he entered the house brought a rush of heat up his neck. He heard the downstairs shower running and a female voice mixed with the sound of the spray. Almost positive he must be hallucinating from the heat of the day, he walked toward the bathroom. With a bang he opened the door, stepped inside, and stopped dead when he saw the outline of a small woman dancing behind the fogged glass.

She must not have heard him, because she kept singing—some pop song, he figured. Not a tune he knew. The tone he chose was one that had caused many grown men to cower over the years. "What the hell are you doing in my shower?"

Author's Note

This story was a moving experience for me to write. As the youngest of eleven children, I'm well acquainted with how arguments can cause rifts and the importance of working your way back to each other. I'd like to think that as well as being a romance, the story of Charles and Melanie is also a journey toward family for both of them.

Cowboy up and enjoy this Rhode Island–born Yankee's fantasy of love in Texas.

Acknowledgments

I am so grateful to everyone who was part of the process of creating *Tycoon Takedown*. Thank you to:

My very patient beta readers for reading multiple versions of the same chapters until I felt they were right.

Shannon Godwin, for helping me polish the story.

My Roadies, whose continued kindness and support often bring out my sloppily grateful and sometimes tearful side.

My readers, many of whom have come out to meet me at conferences. Meeting each of you is an incredible experience.

As always, thank you to my husband, Tony, who listens to the story so many times he dreams about the characters. I love you, hon.

And to my family, which supports me in this adventure and is the reason I do what I do every day. Love you!

About the Author

Ruth Cardello was born the youngest of eleven children in a small city in northern Rhode Island. She lived in Boston, Paris, Orlando, and New York before coming full circle and moving back to Rhode Island, where she lives with her husband and three children. Before turning her attention to writing, Ruth was an educator for twenty years, eleven of which she spent as a kindergarten teacher. She is the author of eight previous novels, including *Bedding the Billionaire*, which was a *New York Times* and *USA Today* bestseller. *Tycoon Takedown* follows *Taken, Not Spurred* as the second book in the Lone Star Burn series.

Made in the USA
Charleston, SC
16 May 2015